Sing If You Can't Dance

For everyone who has had to adjust their dreams to changing circumstances: may the life you find instead turn out to be even better.

First published in the UK in 2023
by Faber & Faber Limited
The Bindery, 51 Hatton Garden
London, EC1N 8HN
faber.co.uk

Typeset in Sabon by M Rules
Printed and bound by CPI Group (UK) Ltd, Croydon, CR0 4YY

A CIP record for this book is available from the British Library

ISBN 978–0–571–37380–2

Printed and bound in the UK on FSC® certified paper in line with our continuing commitment to ethical business practices, sustainability and the environment.
For further information see faber.co.uk/environmental-policy

2 4 6 8 10 9 7 5 3 1

Sing If You Can't Dance

ALEXIA CASALE

faber

Before

Breathless anticipation.

Whispers that keep rising until a chorus of voices say, 'Shh!'

Runners bustle around the studio, shepherding competitors on and off set. Technicians glare as they manoeuvre their huge rolling cameras to get the best angle on each group.

The air thrums with urgency and excitement and anxiety.

Nearly our turn, nearly our turn.

Just a few minutes now.

Keep it together. Keep the energy up. Harness it.

Swallow down the swoop of sickness. It's just nerves. So many nerves I almost feel dizzy.

But I'm not, of course. That feeling in my chest is tension. I'm fine. Everything is totally one hundred per cent fine. I am not sick or injured. And I'm certainly not going to do a Pip and start whinging on about fainting just because I'm a teeny-tiny bit nervous.

We're about to record our second-round TV audition for a national dance competition. This is officially the biggest thing to happen to anyone in our whole school in the history of forever. So we're all allowed to be nervous. But, as leader, I'm not going to be the one turning it into a drama. I've got this. Everything is totally, completely, absolutely fine.

After all, we got full points in the first audition, sending us straight through. Now this – today – will determine whether we get onto the live shows.

Just one year ago there was no PopSync. Now look at us, standing on the verge of a future so big and amazing I feel myself sway as if the ground's gone unsteady, sending me jostling into Maddie.

She yelps as my sudden weight tips her into the wall.

'Shh!' a harassed young man screeches as he hurries past with a roll of gaffer tape.

Maddie wraps her arms around me as we giggle into each other's shoulders.

'Ohmigod!' she whispers in my ear. 'Ohmigod, Ven.'

'I know, I know, I know,' I whisper back, so overwhelmed I can't think of a single thing to snark about.

'Ready?' says the smiley assistant floor manager, whose job title seems to translate to 'person in charge on this side of the set'.

And here it is. Our moment.

One second we're walking forwards, then we're on stage and Maddie and I are introducing PopSync. A moment later we're in position and our music is on and this is it, this is it, *this is it*.

I want to remember every second, relish every breath, but I'm puffing for air in that irritating way I've been doing on and off this last month, as if I've somehow been getting less fit from all the rehearsing. And I know it's just nerves, got to block it out, focus, but my muscles are pulling and aching too – have been for weeks . . .

But I can't fail now. Not when we're a minute away from the finish line.

Just focus.

My eyes blur on the lights. I tip off balance mid-spin, reeling then correcting. Did anyone see? I'm at the back for this part so maybe they didn't notice . . .

But now my knee is doing that thing where it feels like it's bending in different directions above and below the joint and I can't seem to get my foot down right and the next spin is wrong too.

I'm mucking it up. I'm mucking everything up.

Don't panic. Just keep going.

Only my knee is stabbing pain up and down my leg and my flick-kick is wrong, there's something wrong, and I really might throw up, oh God I'm actually going to throw up because my leg is wrong, wrong, wrong and I can't breathe and I'm going to throw up in front of all these cameras, on-stage, on the best day of my life.

One of the technicians has obviously realised because they're lowering the studio lights. Thank God for that.

Maybe they'll fade us to dark and let us start again . . .

The whole stage goes black.

Raised voices all around. A hand on my arm.

I need to say something – keep the girls calm till they put the lights on again.

Then someone pulls the floor away.

And I fall and fall and fall.

18(ish) Months Later . . .

Before we start, I'm going to be totally upfront and tell you that I don't care whether you like me or not. That's your problem.

Sure, we all fancy the idea of being the type of person everyone likes. The type of person who never has a bad word to say about anyone – the type of person who never has bad words said about them. But how blah would you have to be to pull that off? Honestly, that sort of person sounds like an idiot to me.

I'm not an idiot. I'm a hedgehog. I've got some nice bits but mostly I've got spikes. And sarcasm, which isn't something hedgehogs are known for, but there you go; metaphors are either clichés or they fall apart the minute you examine them. For instance, I'm pretty sure I'm softer on the outside than on the inside. It's a pity that you're in my head, but I'm not going to nice it up for you.

You can call me Ven. It's short for Venetia (pronounced Ven-ee-sha) but if you call me that you'll regret it.

You're probably wondering why you're here, but I don't care about that either. Stay, go, your choice. I'd stick around out of interest, but then I'm smart and you might be dumb as a rock.

First thing to think about if you're sticking around is my Year 12, spring term, Monday to-do list.

Item 1: get to school as late as possible (without officially being late) in order to avoid the temptation to damage Abigail Moss: winsome purveyor of goodness, light and purest spite. It's delaying the inevitable but the anticipation makes it all worthwhile.

Item 2:

Oh, for God's sake. That's *my* parking spot. Yes, literally: not only does it have the disability symbol on it, but my name to boot. (If you're wondering why I'm driving at sixteen, it's legal in the UK when you've got a serious enough mobility impairment so let's keep our focus on the person actually breaking the law – and the rules of basic decency.) I back up then angle in so I can peek at the woman's dashboard – not a blue badge in sight.

Well then excuse me (or don't) while I make judicious use of the horn.

And the finger.

And the roll-down-the-window-and-shout-obscenities.

And here comes Ms Walker, head of Sixth Form, just as I'm really getting into the swearing.

My life is complete. With detention as the cherry on top.

Item 2: figure out a dastardly plan to make whichever teacher is running detention at least twice as miserable as I am. I'll probably just keep up a steady stream of impolite conversation. That usually does it for most people.

Ms Walker's telling off means the pair of us miss assembly. I'm devastated.

I only get one day's detention (and I'm allowed to choose the day) even before I do the casual-lean-against-the-car-door then the I'm-just-going-to-slowly-slide-down-into-a-heap.

Before The Disaster with PopSync Ms Walker would have told me to stop being a drama queen. Now she immediately ushers me inside and offers to call an ambulance – the standard 'this school is not inviting a lawsuit, we did everything strictly by the book' response. I decline in a show of womanful stoicism. To be fair, I'm not putting it on – but that's not to say I'm not happy to make the most of it.

'I really don't know what else we can do, Ven, to avoid these ... regrettable disturbances over your parking situation. I understand it's very provoking, but as we've now added a named signpost I can't see what other options there are. We *do* send all our parents regular bulletins about parking issues ...'

I zone out. I'm only in trouble because of the number of dimwits who think there's nothing wrong with parking in disabled spots provided they're in a rush and 'it's just for a second'. Because, yeah, with ten of you doing that one after another, of course that won't be a problem. And then there are the ones who think that if they're helping a disabled person run an errand they're entitled to a little 'extra convenience'. Just give me a Licence to Savage and I'll 'extra convenience' them into needing their own disabled parking, then we'll see how they feel about it.

Ms Walker is still mid hand-wringing à la 'it's not our responsibility to ensure you can actually park at school', so I do the 'casual leaning on the wall' thing again and Ms Walker takes the hint. 'Shall I walk with you to class?' she asks.

'Nope, but I'd better go so I can sit down.'

'Just make sure you report for detention when you're able or ... Under the circumstances ...' She rubs at her forehead. I slump a bit more and work on looking pale. 'Let's forget it this one last time. But please don't take this to mean that we're condoning your behaviour.'

I resist the urge to perk up, then slope off to class. I must be pulling one of my most unpleasant faces, and slopping along particularly badly, as it's one of those rare days when people coming the other way actually move for me. Why is it that those in a rush are usually so unwilling to skirt around people in the slow-moving-obviously-mobility-impaired category? Today, I'm both glad and frustrated to be given a wide berth. I would dearly like to gift at least one idiot an 'accidental' smack with my stick.

And, lo, destiny has answered my prayer, for who is leaning in the maths classroom doorway but my favourite person in the world, Abigail Moss. Now, if I can just time this so my stick goes down *plunk*, square on the middle of her foot, without it looking entirely intentional ...

'Venetia, darling, are you all right? You're looking shocking,' she says, all wide-eyed innocence.

My moment for 'accidentally' damaging her is gone. Fate still hates me.

'Get out of the way,' I snap.

Although she is purposefully blocking the door and making a patronising pity-face, she draws back as if I'm the one being nasty for no reason. 'I'm just offering you a hand, Venetia.'

'I'll take your hand when you're happy for me to detach it from the rest of you first,' I gasp, leaning against the wall as frustration and tiredness set the corridor rippling under my feet.

Abigail makes her face go all hurt, though her snake-eyes tell the usual story of delight. Then one of her pack draws her away, making comforting noises, and I manage to slip past. My classmates look away as I head for the first empty seat. It's messy going and I know I am clenching my jaw and my eyes are glazed, but the alternative is a nosedive into the carpet. And if you've seen my school's carpets, you'll understand why this is to be avoided at all costs.

When I get to the chair, I tuck the strap of my bag around the back, brace my hands on the desk and let myself drop, slowly crumpling forwards till I can rest the side of my face against the – *yuck* – slightly sticky surface of the table. Someone comes up, as someone always does, and starts to Fuss at me. I raise a slightly shaking hand and present them with the 'leave me alone' finger.

There is a wash of tutting then the gossip resumes over my head.

When I hear the change in sound that signals the arrival of Mr Singh, I slowly sit myself up and try to drag my hair into some semblance of 'that'll do'. Propping my chin on my hand, I take a stab at gazing soulfully out of the window.

I'm not sure I'm doing it right – I still feel pissed off rather than wistful.

Just past the school wall, a boy is getting out of a car: a tall, slim boy with long black wavy hair. I don't recognise him (and I know I'd have remembered, even if we'd just passed in the corridor), but second week of spring term seems a weird time to join a new school.

The boy raises a hand to run it through his curls then suddenly pulls the hand away and hunches his shoulders forwards, letting his hair fall back over his face. It half makes me want to look closer, and half makes me feel I should look away.

Before I can decide, there's a noise by my shoulder. I look up to find that Mr Singh is not amused by my 'staring soulfully out of the window' efforts.

MONDAY TO-DO LIST

Item 3: find a way to make it Tuesday already.

Lunchtime

(Will this day ever end?)

Maddie spots me the minute I slope into the cafeteria for lunch. 'VEN!' she screams, but her hug is tentative and careful, her eyes more on my stick than on my clothes or shoes, even though I am wearing the most gorgeous pair of brand-new maroon leather ankle-boots, low-slung with a triple set of silver buckles. If I am going to slop about disjointing every two secs, I am definitely going to do it with style.

Maddie doesn't even notice, too busy ordering the rest of PopSync to make room for me. I get that she's literally demonstrating that I still have a place at their table, but it's a Pity Place.

'How's training going?' I ask, because it would be weird if I didn't. There of course follows a wave of noise as they all talk over each other. It's wonderful, everything rushing back – but only for about five seconds.

There is no more dancing for me. There's just the memory of how it felt when my body still did everything I wanted it to. I'm not even an adult yet – I'm not ready to lower my expectations and accept that I can't do all the things I used to. I haven't had enough time. And I know – I *know* – everyone must feel like that when the years start catching up with them, but I've hardly started and there's already so much that's over.

The cafeteria glazes with tears and I can feel the others going silent one by one. A hand comes down on my shoulder, but so gently. Too gently.

'Oh, Ven,' Maddie says.

I run away.

Well, obviously I don't. But I get the hell out of there as fast as I can, and I don't care how messy it is or how stupid I look. If that isn't bad enough, when Maddie tries to follow, the words 'Why do you always make everything worse?' tumble out of my mouth. Then I wrench away, pushing through the doors and out into the corridor.

It's a lie. Or part of a lie. It's not her fault any more than it's mine, but neither of us knows what to do, so, although we don't mean to, we keep tearing strips off each other, trying to hold on when everything is pulling us apart.

We were meant to follow our dance dream together. And though I want to support her – of course I want to support her – it's like lemon juice on a fresh cut.

With all that roaring about in my head, I'm not looking where I'm going. I get about fifteen steps before I walk straight into someone, knocking us both to our knees, my stick clattering to the ground.

I look up, eyes blurred with tears, face probably distorted with grief and fury and the realisation that I've dislocated my hip, and there is The Boy With the Raven Tresses . . . Only I see now why he aborted that gesture to sweep them romantically back when he was getting out of the car. Half his face is spider-webbed with scar tissue.

His eyes are wide and startled, then full of horror and shame. He's wrenching up and away before I have time to blink, my brain too busy going, 'Wow, you are absolutely gorgeous.'

You know the type of beauty I mean – the type that catches your breath, tugs you forwards and, for a white-out second, takes away all capacity for thought. When they say truth is beauty, I think this is what they mean. The boy isn't beautiful because of the scars or in spite of them, he just is.

But obviously he's only beautiful-*looking* because he ups and leaves me sprawled on the floor. And I know I was the one who knocked into him but *HELLO – nothing wrong with YOUR legs*. So although he's utterly gorgeous, unfortunately he's also a ginormous jerk.

My internal grousing is interrupted by someone hefting me to my feet without even asking if I want help. Of course this is not helpful at all and hurts even more than being sprawled on the floor. But custom dictates you acknowledge those who assist you, so I turn with a smile.

If you think I'm about to say thank you, you have clearly not been paying attention.

Ten Minutes Later . . .

TO-DO LIST

Item 4: *eviscerate fellow student. DONE!*

Item 5: *undislocate hip.*

Medically speaking, a dislocation is when you completely separate a bone from its corresponding joint: for example, when the top of your humerus ends up completely outside your shoulder socket. A subluxation is when you displace a bone from its joint without separating it completely. Officially, I don't dislocate very often but here's the thing – if you have to manually put a bone back into its joint because it's so far out it won't go by itself and you don't have any choice but to figure it out because it's so agonising you just can't wait . . . If that happens and someone tells you you've *only* subluxed yourself and it's not *really* a dislocation, you will understand one of the many reasons patients with chronic conditions hate (most) doctors with an exquisite passion.

So, for the record, when I have to ball my fist into my butt-cheek and lever my leg up, round and over so that – insert dull, echoing crunch – my femur resettles itself properly in my hip joint because half of it had fallen out, I am going to be calling it a dislocation.

Also, for the record, you can't do this lying on the floor – at least I can't. I need a chair so I can lower my leg beyond the horizontal: it's the only way to lever such a large bone back into such a stubborn joint. And if I'm in a long, flat corridor, there is *one* option – get back on my feet and walk with my leg half in and half out of my hip to the nearest chair, then fall into it as best I can (lowering myself carefully is not possible). Then I put myself back together.

Fifteen minutes and a lot of painkillers later, I still have to go to class. I slop in, sweaty and miserable, with a mumbled, 'Sorry. Had to undislocate myself.' Because one of the great joys of all this is having to explain things publicly that are nobody's bloody business.

Then I look up and, lo, He of the Raven Locks is scrunched into a chair in the far corner, peering up through his curls. For a moment I forget why he's all 'I'm going to hide behind my hair', because he is so truly drop-dead gorgeous. Then I remember that, duh, people feel shy about scars. And sticks. And slopping and sloping instead of walking. It's not that it's objectively ugly, but it's different and sometimes the way people look at me makes me feel ugly. Sometimes I feel ugly even when no one's looking because my body used to be different and I liked it how it was, not how it is.

And yet I didn't know the boy before the scars and I think he's beautiful. If that's possible, maybe one day a stranger will look at me and think I'm beautiful. No ifs, no buts, no 'in spite of' – no logic or reason at all, just instinctive reaction, the way I see the boy with the black curls. And he may be a jerk, but I should probably tell him what I see because he clearly doesn't think anyone ever will look at him like that. I'd want to know if it were me.

But of course just the thought of saying it out loud makes me shudder. There's quite enough humiliation in my life already, thanks. Now this boy's giving me a headache and we haven't even spoken yet.

And that's before factoring in ninety minutes of English lit with Abigail Moss. Is there no end to the varieties of pain this day is determined to inflict?

Apparently not, because when I let myself in the front door after school, it's to the sound of very bad music belting out of the sound system. It zings straight into my brain, an off beat to the pain already pulsing there.

'Not a chance!' I call, hooking the strap of my bag over the post at the bottom of the stairs so I don't need to bend down to pick it up later.

Heading into the kitchen, I find Dad has the table spread with paperwork. Mum wafts in behind me, shutting the music off.

'Really? No good?' she asks, pulling out the pen pinning her curls back and using it to make a note on the list clipped to the fridge. 'I've been listening for *hours*,' she whines. 'I can't even tell any more – I've got such a headache. And, yes, I know, why didn't

I take a break . . . I just kept thinking the next thing was bound to be decent, but apparently the law of averages doesn't apply in the music industry.' She taps pause on the iPad, then collapses over the kitchen table with a groan. 'O best beloved daughter, please make me a nice cup of tea.'

'The joys of getting showered with music demos. I thought that was a sign of success?' I say as I start fetching down mugs.

'Cheeky.' She reaches out to tug at one of my curls. 'Don't you go parroting my positive thinking back at me when I'm nose-deep in Demo Hell.'

So, my family runs an annual three-day music festival at the start of the summer. And when I say 'family', I don't just mean my parents. Aunt Jinnie, Aunt Sarah, Uncle Geoff and most of the rest of our family (blood and chosen) have now been roped in since it's pretty hard to dodge the call of duty with a motto like 'Putting the Family into Family Festival'. It's been going twelve years now (so all the lifetime I remember) and has finally stopped losing money and started making it. There's a tipping point with these things and we've reached it with strong word of mouth and a growing group of loyal visitors who come every year because Mum has a knack for picking acts who are about to be big and getting them to commit to the festival before they're *too* big for us to afford. The downside is that we listen to a lot of unmitigated shite in the process.

When Mum says, 'Ven, there's one I want to play you a clip of, just to check I'm not missing something', years of experience has me replying, 'You only say that when they're crap but you think they're my generation's version of cool. I'm dealing with enough pain and torment already.'

Only it comes out weird because I need to keep stopping to breathe and the words seem to be going squashy in my mouth and ... *Ah.*

The kitchen has gone dim and distant and I'm losing track of which way is up. I reach out to grab hold of the counter. It's fine. I've got this.

I haven't got this.

There are exciting varieties of fainting you've probably never heard of, just like dislocations versus subluxations. If you're thinking, 'Oh no, not more medical information', I have three words for you.

Get over it.

If you don't want to hear it, think about how much I fancy living it.

The official term is 'syncope', though I always want to call it syncopy to jazz it up – yes, that was a bad, bad music pun. My special brand of syncope is 'vasovagal syncope', which basically means 'fainting caused by blood pressure issues'. My blood pressure has this delightful habit of plunging as if I've just suffered catastrophic blood loss. Unsurprisingly, this renders me unconscious.

I am getting so much practice with passing out that sometimes I can see it coming and lie down before it happens. Other times I manage a controlled fall. And sometimes I wait just a little bit too long in case I'm not actually going to pass out after all, only I am and it's too late to do anything about it. Today, I demonstrate my excellent technique at slowly sliding down the furniture – *sloop, gloop, splat*. A moment later, I'm scrunched down between the chair and the counter, and Mum is patting my shoulder as I breathe nice deep breaths.

'Do you want to crawl to the sofa?' Mum asks.

'What's going on?' Dad calls.

'It's fine!' I croak. 'I'll be up in a minute.'

'I'm making the tea,' Mum says. 'Why don't you go and book yourself into that chronic pain group at the community centre that you promised me you'd try?'

'Blackmailer,' I grumble. Then I heave a sigh. 'Fine. I'll book in. *And* I'll make tea too because I'm that devoted.' It's a bit feeble even to my own ears – and not just because I am absolutely looking for an excuse to 'forget' about the group. If I try to be self-sufficient right now it's likely to end in a second gloop down the furniture. When I get stubborn, I end up doing a *lot* of glooping before conceding defeat.

I can imagine how surprised you are to hear this. But here's the thing: it's important not to *always* give up. Sometimes I keep pushing just to know I'm not quitting. If that's the best I can do, then I'm bloody well going to do it: *sloop, gloop, splat* and all.

Dancing is over but my life isn't.

Everyone says I need a little time to figure out my new goal so I can feel like I'm headed somewhere again, and maybe they're right. But what if the best bit of my life is already over and the rest is making do with what I have left?

The Next Day . . .

TUESDAY TO-DO LIST

Item 1: come up with a new life goal and detailed plan – no probs.

Item 2: don't stare at The Boy with the Raven Tresses.

Item 3: brainwash Abigail Moss through hypnotism/subliminal messages to go queasy at the sight of me so she has to change schools. Won't work: brainwashing requires a brain.

Despite my best efforts at self-control, I spend all of English darting glances at Him. He's so busy hiding behind his hair, he barely looks up, so at least I'm not in danger of being spotted. Just as well since I'm still at it as we pack up at the end of class. He slinks through the crowd and out into the hallway, moving like a fox, all lithe and graceful and . . .

Yes, we've established that I fancy the proverbial underwear off him.

As I slip out into the corridor, I realise that, for once, no one is whispering about me – they're too busy gossiping about him.

'Do you know what happened to his *face*?'

'Is it a burn?'

'Is he an arsonist?' asks Abigail Moss in the fake-concerned way she uses to cover her bullying. 'Do you think he just got out of prison?'

I consider shoving past her, but it would almost certainly hurt me a lot more than her, so I just give her my nastiest glare. She answers it with her usual snake smile. One of these days I'm going to see she has a forked tongue and it is not going to surprise me at *all*.

Imagining it occupies my attention as I slop through the corridors to music, where guilt makes me stop dead in the doorway. Maddie's got her feet up on the seat of her chair, arms wrapped round her knees. Her eyes brighten as she sees me and there's a split second when she starts to smile before it fades into something tentative and uncertain.

I sink down next to her. 'I am a sucky best friend.'

'Sometimes,' she says, dropping her head onto my shoulder.

And that's that. It's not fixed but it'll do for now.

'Today,' says Ms Meade, as she dumps her stuff at the front of the room, sweeping her ombre-dyed hair twists back over her shoulders, 'since it's somehow February already, so we've only got three months till A-level mocks and your first set of coursework deadlines, we will be focusing on your group projects. I hope I don't need to remind you that you need a good recording of your group performing, a critical reflection on that performance, and the sheet music of at least one piece you've written or arranged for your group . . . Hello. Are you my new American student?'

We turn as one.

Guess who is loitering in the doorway? He of the Raven Tresses slinks into the nearest chair and pretends to be busy taking stuff out of his bag.

Ms Meade rolls her eyes at his non-greeting. 'Bottom line is that you all need to pair up to compose an original piece of music, or do an arrangement – a cover, if you will – that puts an original stamp on an existing piece. When your composition or arrangement is ready, you need to rehearse it with Singing Group or the orchestra – unless I've agreed a special exception, like Maddie for PopSync – then include it as part of a recorded group performance so you can write a critical reflection on the whole process.'

Maddie and I both had special dispensation to count PopSync as our group project. It was going to be the most fun any two people ever had doing coursework. Of course, now it's just Maddie and I'm stuck, partnerless, with Singing Group. Talk about adding insult to injury.

Pretty much everyone who can play an instrument has abandoned Singing Group. After last term, I'm seriously considering taking up the triangle. Or even – pause for gasp – the tambourine. But I like to sing. I always have. The thing is, as with dancing, I prefer doing it in a group. Neither my voice nor my dancing is special enough for me to be a soloist, but I'm surprisingly good at blending with other people, both vocally and in terms of movement. And the truth is I like that about myself. I know I'm bossy and pushy and difficult and different – 'one of a kind', as people who're trying to be nice put it – but with singing and dancing I'm good at being part of a group. For once, my talent is blending in, not standing apart. Belonging.

So while it's a bad sign that Singing Group is now into term two and we still sound like a bunch of angry cats yowling along to a mistuned radio, at least we're only in our first year of A-levels. There's still time to bring things around. We just need someone to step up and sort it out – and perhaps The Boy with the Raven Tresses is that person. A newcomer, with a new voice and vision, could be the perfect solution to our problems. Well, assuming that (a) he joins Singing Group, and (b) he decides not to spend the rest of his life hiding behind his curls.

'Now, new student,' Ms Meade says, fixing her most frightening smile on him. 'Hello again.'

'Hi,' he mumbles, which doesn't bode well for his leadership potential, but maybe he just needs to warm up to us.

Ms Meade's smile doesn't waver. He'll have to try much harder than this to get under her skin. It's one of the reasons Ms Meade's far and away my favourite teacher: she takes precisely zero nonsense. Also, she once gave Abigail Moss a full week of detention for 'accidentally' bashing me with her bag in the corridor.

'I speak English, French and even the odd bit of Arabic and Wolof, but *not* Monosyllabic Angst, so it seems my only option is that most dreadful of all teaching techniques . . . the introductions round.' There is a horrified silence. 'If anyone tries to abstain, we will do ice-breaker exercises until you are all crushed and broken inside. So, everyone into a circle, then we'll do names and musical interests. Maddie, you start.'

I tune it out as long as I can. It's easy enough with the orchestra lot, but then we reach the first two members of Singing Group.

'I'm Roksana—'

'And I'm Orla, and we're into hip hop and hip house—'

Who doesn't love people who come in matched pairs of ick?

Me, that's who. Yeah, I know – you're shocked.

'Which, for those of you who've been living under a rock, is a crossover between house and hip hop,' Roksana finishes.

But the pain is not yet over because what do we have next? A variation in three parts.

'Hi, I'm Benjo and we' – he gestures down the line of chairs at the twins, accidentally poking the nearest one in the neck – 'have our own barbershop trio, though we're looking for a fourth to make a full quartet. Last summer we started doing gigs.'

Probably at retirement homes given that their sound is best described as retro snooze-fest. They're the opposite of Roksana and Orla: the boys' melodies are on point, but they have absolutely no style. Roksana and Orla are all about the meaning of the words and doing stuff with rhythm and stresses that's so original you can't help but listen . . . to the fact that they can't hit a note. While it might sound like they'd complement each other perfectly for Singing Group, the result is uniquely excruciating – and this from a person living with chronic pain.

Ms Meade raises an unimpressed eyebrow at the twins when they just look at their feet.

'Fred,' mumbles Twin 1.

'George,' mumbles Twin 2.

Which doesn't help at all, because unless one of them opts to wear blue and the other red from now on – or they never move from their current seats – I still cannot see any way of telling them apart. I've been trying since the beginning of the year and the only thing that cheers me is that everyone, even Ms Meade, seems just as clueless.

'Fred and George Wesley,' Twin 2 adds in a voice of gloom. 'Yes, our mum's a legend. And, yes, we've heard *all* the jokes.'

I'm just about to explore whether the latter is true when Ms Meade butts in.

'Your classmates will doubtless see that as a challenge,' she says drily (and correctly), then turns to the next in line – the new boy.

He darts a look round. 'I'm Ren. I play the piano and sing.'

His accent isn't what I expected. There's a slow velvet note to it, almost – but not quite – a drawl. I feel my cheeks heat as I think about how he'd sound singing, soft and low, with stage-lights reflecting off his black, black curls.

When Ms Meade keeps staring at him rather than turning to the next person, he shifts uncomfortably, tilting his face to uncover the eye on the unscarred side so he can look at her beseechingly.

'And what sort of music do you like, Ren?' she prompts, her tone a friendly threat.

'Classical for piano,' he mumbles. 'Gospel and blues for singing,' he adds quickly when her eyes narrow dangerously.

'I'll keep going with the questions,' Ms Meade warns. 'Let's see if you can give me at least two dozen words on this next one. Ready? So, Ren, where were you living before you came to join our happy little school?'

'America. My dad's in the military, so we move a lot. I mean, we used to move a lot, but we're staying put this time to be near Mum's family, 'cause Dad's the American one. Japanese American.' Ren's eyes flick oddly to the side and I realise he's counting his words. 'Please could I stare silently at the floor now?'

'Fine, fine,' she says and moves on to an orchestra person.

I don't even have to try not to listen. I am too busy staring at Ren, wondering which side of the family the cheekbones are from because by God he has good bones. I mean really, *really* good bones. His face is all angles and shadows, and his eyelashes are every 'boy with long lashes' cliché ever written. Am I allowed to think that? I don't think it's weird – it's certainly not about stereotypes or exoticness or any of that crap. I'm not likening his skin to food or anything. I mean, I figure I can't be too far wrong if I just describe people as people rather than things. Like, you can describe me as short with dark curly hair (call it frizzy at your peril), rather than starting with the stick. It's not a part of me. It's not even how I *look*. It's something I use.

I manage to stop staring at Ren before I'm caught at it when the introduction round reaches me, then have to scramble for something to say because I want to be funny and witty and self-deprecating and I am so mahoosively overthinking this and everyone is staring at me and . . .

'I'm Ven,' I squeak. 'I used to dance but now I sing. Um.' My brain shows me an image of the festival, but of course I can't talk about that. The trouble is my mind is otherwise empty. 'Um,' I say again. 'Er, um . . . huh?' I stare at Ms Meade.

You have brain fog, the voice in my head informs me. *Duh.*

'I have brain fog,' I echo, sounding enough like a zombie that no one makes the standard 'requires a brain' joke.

Instead Ms Meade gives me a slightly concerned look. 'Since you're not usually lost for words—' A snigger washes through the room while I hunch into my seat and wish DEATH AND DISMEMBERMENT on the whole class (with the exception of a certain newcomer, because obviously he gets a 'first week at new school' pass).

'Moving on,' she adds menacingly, as she turns to the next person in line.

For a moment, I let the classroom dissolve into the background while I contemplate the wonderful first impression I've just made on Raven Tresses, all while putting the final nail in the coffin of gaining any sort of respect from the rest of Singing Group.

The brain fog fades just in time for me to hear Ms Meade

decree that everyone has to give up at least two free periods and a lunch-break for Singing Group or orchestra every week for the rest of the school year.

Universe, whatever I did I'm sorry – deeply and truly sorry.

The others look as if they're thinking much the same, only they do it with more pouting.

'Maddie, you can go to the library. Orchestra, you're in the hall. I'll come with you now, then I'll be round to see you, Maddie, then back here in about half an hour to check on Singing Group's progress,' Ms Meade says. 'Ren? You ready to pick your poison?'

His lips quirk into an almost-grin. 'Will I disrupt things if I join Singing Group?' He casts a quick look round at the rest of us.

'They'll manage,' Ms Meade says, then starts chivvying the others out. 'We can always discuss it further next week.'

When she turns away, Ren buries himself in faffing pointlessly with his bag. Rather than (continue) staring at him, I focus on how to get my growing discomfort under control. First, I shuck my boots (tooled black leather, side-zipped but with false lacing up the front to the knee) and plonk my feet on a spare chair, then close my eyes as the pain drops from I-don't-think-I-can't-stand-this-much-longer to merely much-ow-ness.

I let things go with Singing Group in autumn term after the others made it abundantly clear that even my gentlest attempts at steering things in a happier direction would be viewed as evidence I've yet to outgrow my Little Ms Bossy-Boots days. That's the nickname Abigail Moss gifted me in Year 7 when I got elected to the student council and was promptly put in charge of various otas; of course that suited me fine but did rather cement a certain eputation among the rest of the year. I've been trying to turn over a new leaf with Singing Group, but it's just not working.

Something has to be done and it seems it's going to have to be me who does it. Ren is clearly not the leader type, and I am *not* prepared to let this bunch of bozos ruin my plan for a clean sweep of As if not A*s, since our group projects represent half of our coursework grade. If I have to drag the rest of them along on my path to A-level glory, so be it. My stupid body is going to complicate pretty much every career path out there, but excellent exam grades are one way I can still set myself apart and prove that I'm both clever and hardworking.

'The trouble last term was that we didn't have a sound,' I say into the foreboding silence. 'We need to agree on a style.'

'Translation: I'm going to tell you what to do and expect you to hop to it because I'm the bossiest person on the planet,' Roksana sneers from her seat on one of the tables that had been pushed to the back when Ms Meade ordered us to circle up for introductions.

Ren hasn't moved from his place four seats along (not that I'm hyperaware of how close he is or anything), but Benjo and the twins are gathered around the whiteboard at the front (thankfully doodling notes instead of penises). They all pretend not to notice my attempts to start a group conversation.

'Did you hear me saying what style I wanted, Benjo?' I ask loudly, but with a sneer in Roksana's direction, because why shouldn't I when she started it?

Roksana rolls her eyes. 'Dazzle us then.'

I know I'm not everyone's cup of tea because some people are unreasonable morons, but I'll never understand why so many prefer to hate me over letting me make everything better. Suppressing my need to point out this self-evident truth, I take a deep breath and try my version of diplomacy (i.e. the tips Aunt Jinnie gave me when I messaged in a panic last night, begging for *something* that would help me mimic being a 'people person'). 'Why don't we brainstorm something we can all get on board with? Or maybe you'd prefer to fail this portion of our portfolio because instead of working as a group – this being, you know, *group work* – we just keep doing our own thing and hoping it miraculously starts to sound vaguely like music. And don't tell me we're *arranging* in pairs, because we're also *performing* together, as a group.'

'You just want to make us like your little dance posse: same-y, same-y synchronised pop-robots,' Orla says.

'When Singing Group did assembly last term, we didn't even start and finish at the same time. Not to mention the slight issue that none of us was singing in the same key,' I point out.

Orla raises her middle finger. It's not just perfectly manicured but decorated. She and Roksana run a not-remotely-secret and yet officially forbidden nail-styling business in the lunchbreak. Even the teachers use it. I have a grudging respect for the fact that, though their nails are ridiculous – and how do they have so little to do that they manage to keep them that nice all the time? – at least they're profiting from their vanity.

'You want to throw shade about the assembly, don't look at us.' Roksana tosses her hair so elegantly the envy is almost greater than the desire to punch her. 'Benjo *et al.* were droning on like they were competing for Most Boring Throwback Performance. We were just trying to get it over with – for everyone's sake.'

'Aka you were doing your usual "let's speak really, really fast so no one notices we've yet to find a note".' Benjo folds his arms triumphantly, elbowing the twin beside him in the process. The twin just sighs, clearly used to this.

Roksana is the one giving Benjo the finger.

I rub my forehead. 'All this great mutual respect and team-building aside, does anyone have an actual suggestion?'

'Screw you?' Orla says.

Benjo raises a hand. 'Veto. Not into girls.'

'New rule,' I say. 'If you don't have an actual musical suggestion, shut up.'

Roksana's lip curls. 'Who made you queen?'

'We need some structure,' I tell the ceiling. 'We don't have to like each other. We just need to get through this.'

There follows a mutinous silence.

I stab my fingers into my temples, trying to push the headache deeper into my skull so I can think for a minute. Looking around the room, hoping for inspiration, I accidentally catch Ren's visible eye. I'm so busy trying not to get lost in how freaking long his eyelashes are, the words come out before I've even passed them through my brain. 'Ren said he's into gospel and blues . . . How about that?'

They all go worryingly quiet.

'What?' I ask Benjo, since he's sitting closest.

He raises his hands in a shrug. 'I figured you more for "here's a plan" than "let's riff on someone else's suggestion". It's a nice revelation.'

I narrow my eyes at him, waiting for the passive-aggressive follow-up, but he just looks back at me – sincerely. 'Huh,' I say, then manage a nod of acknowledgement by way of an olive branch. 'So what do you all say to *Sister Act* meets *Pitch Perfect* by way of *Glee*? A bit more pop-rock than full-on "let's pretend we're instruments" acapella but nothing appropriation-level in terms of the gospel elements?'

'Fine, but we're not interested in swaying and doo-wop-ing in the background while you stand centre-stage,' Roksana says darkly.

'Actually, Maddie was centre of the PopSync formation because she has the best technique. I just led the group off-stage because that's what *I'm* good at.'

'The boys and I are going places too, you know,' Benjo says pointedly. 'We're getting gigs and everything.'

One of the twins shifts awkwardly. 'We played your cousin's wedding, mate.'

Roksana snorts. 'Props.'

There's a knock at the door and Ms Meade pops her head in. 'How's it all going?'

'Great,' says Orla. 'We're making so much progress.'

The rest of us nod vigorously.

Ms Meade gives us a fond smile. 'All my classes are different, but you lot are special. If you could just pull together half as well with singing as with lying you'd really get somewhere. I've got two words to leave you with by way of motivation. Trust exercises,' she says, then beams when we perform a perfectly synchronised shudder. 'Progress already. I'll leave you to it.'

'Taking over this disaster's the last thing I want,' I say, when the door has clicked shut, 'but someone's got to do something or we're all going to fail. So, could we just see what happens if I get one song to try to make this work?'

They all look at their phones or the floor.

'OK, new deal, you cooperate for one song and if I can't get us all on the same page I shut up and play follow-the-leader, no arguments? All in favour?'

Every hand (except Ren's, as he's apparently too busy trying to get the floor to swallow him whole) promptly reaches for the skies.

Home Is Where the Nagging Is . . .

Item 1: *figure out a plan for Singing Group – ha!*
Item 2: *learn all about gospel music and impress the pants off Ren and set a good example as leader.*
Item 3: *sort all outstanding homework and festival work. (114 days to go!)*

Thankfully, Item 3 at least is achievable since it's literally months away and by that point of June our exams will be over, so 'outstanding homework' will be a moot point, and as for the three-day run-up and three-day onslaught of the festival itself, I'll just have to hope I've figured out a really great plan.

My determination to get my life in order barely survives opening my front door; my loving mother tells me 'You're all flushed' before I've even crossed the threshold. 'Have you told any of the consultants about that? I'll put it on the list to mention at the next appointment.'

Mum lives in hope that if we report every slightly odd thing that happens with my body the doctors will figure out how to fix me. It's a nice thought but if the last eighteen months have taught me anything, it's that the doctors don't really understand what's going on even for standard people with the condition I have, let alone freaks like me who have all the most unusual versions of pretty much everything on the list of possible symptoms. Trust me, when they say 'be unique', they don't mean medically.

Case in point, I yawn and – *shit*.

'What?' asks Mum. She squints at me. 'Your face is wrong.'

I know my face is wrong. If you'd dislocated your jaw, you'd know it too without being told.

Here's another thing I bet you didn't know about dislocations. 'Normal' people dislocate in specific ways, so doctors can fix them easily, whereas people like me dislocate in such unexpected ways no one knows what to do – except tell me to 'have a go' since I can 'feel where the bones need to be'. Yes, seriously. They don't even give me tips. Which is *super* helpful when it's my first time dislocating a particular joint. I've become good at figuring it out though, because once a dislocation is reduced at least the pain is too.

So now I wriggle my jaw as out of place as I can get it because it's always easier to undislocate myself when I do that first. Once my jaw is all listed over to one side, I open my mouth halfway and put my hands against my face, fingertips on my cheekbones and base of the palms on my jaw. Then I slowly but firmly push my face sideways until – *click-crunch* – *ta da!* (Insert flourish on the cymbals.)

And then I say *ow*. Or I think *ow* because it's better not to move my mouth for a while – with the tendons and ligaments stretched after a dislocation, it's really easy for a bone to fall back out again. You do not want to know my personal best for consecutive dislocations.

'Why don't you watch TV for a bit?' Mum suggests.

'I have homework. And coursework. And I need to learn everything there is to know about gospel music. And I need to work on the festival merchandise,' I mumble, carefully holding my jaw in place. 'You *do* know you're meant to be making me get on with my homework, like a responsible adult, right?' Tucking my feet up onto the arm of the sofa, I immediately drop them down again because I am a Good Physio Patient who is not resting her joints at the limit of their extension. 'And I really do need something to take my mind off . . .' I wave a hand at my entire body. 'Could you hand me the blue folder? I've got to figure out which charities the festival's collecting for this year, and Aunt Jinnie'll have my head if I don't sort out the T-shirt numbers for her soon.'

So, bottom line is that I have a job at the festival. And yes, it's my family's festival, but I earnt that job – and I more than earn the money that comes with it. I mean, don't get carried away – it's not that much, but it's mine and I'm proud of that.

I've helped out at the festival since I can remember. When I was old enough to grasp simple instructions, I helped direct people to the right entrances. Then I graduated to selling merchandise with Uncle Geoff. Then to helping Mum and Aunt Sarah in the box office, then to running the box office during the three days of the festival. At which point I started getting paid. By then I was curious about other things, like how Aunt Jinnie figured out what merchandise to order and how much of different items and sizes of clothing, and somewhere along the line I ended up in charge of most of that as well. Which may sound like a lot, but not only am I an organisational genius, I've discovered that distraction is the best pain management method available – and I have a lot of pain to manage. It's a win–win for me, and my family, and all the festival visitors.

Unfortunately, brain fog (which is an actual medical term in case you missed it during the WORLDWIDE PANDEMIC we've just enjoyed) and merch spreadsheets are a really bad mix: it's like trying to think through soup.

Eventually I give up and shuffle into the kitchen. Dad looks up from his paperwork. 'Growl,' I tell him.

He holds out an arm and I slouch over, sinking into the chair next to him and tucking myself against his side. 'That good, huh?' he says, pressing a kiss to my hair.

'I'm grumpy and I hurt and I can't take any more painkillers and I'm grumpy and I can't think to take my mind off it and I'm very, VERY grumpy.'

'Would double-fudge brownie ice cream be medicinal in this situation?'

I wrinkle my nose. 'I've put on enough weight. Making myself even less able to fit into my favourite clothes is going to make me grumpier. And I'm already *very* grumpy.'

'You must be if you won't have ice cream,' Dad says.

'I hate everything.'

'That's nice, darling,' he says, turning back to his papers.

My brain may be non-functional but that doesn't mean it's silent and still. The inside of my head is full of splinters of thought and memory: frustration over my English coursework, misery that there's a PopSync rehearsal this evening, disgust at my loss of muscle tone since I stopped dancing, anger over what a mess Singing Group is . . .

I sigh, pulling over the nearest bit of paperwork, then promptly shoving it away again. 'If you're debating the relative merits of allowing an advertisement in the festival programme for things to pee into when there's no loo around, the answer is so very, very no. Portaloos are disgusting but this is next-level grim.'

Yes, festival organising is *all* the glamour.

And that's before Dad hands me the order form for this year's cleaning products and makes me check it matches what we used last year plus five per cent in case of a repeat of The Great Poo Catastrophe of Year Seven.

Don't ask.

Seriously, you thought the medical stuff was TMI? This is a whole different league.

Caffeine is a wondrous thing (though opiates also have their place when agony is involved) and within the hour I am pleasantly surprised to find my brain capable of thought once more. This means I can finally – *finally* – get on with my coursework. So, of course, my phone almost immediately starts buzzing.

I think about ignoring it, but it's impossible not to peek … Maddie.

My heart sinks. She's meant to be in rehearsal and I don't want to hear about it if I can't be part of it. I know that's selfish, but it's selfish of her too so at least we're even.

I put the phone aside only for a message notification to ping in a second later.

Pick up the phone, Ven.

I groan as it immediately starts ringing again, but this time I hit 'accept'.

'I need a PopSync favour,' Maddie tells me without even saying hello. 'Pip has an Idea.'

'Pip always has Ideas.' I've never been Pip's biggest fan. Not only is she a lot of work, but sometimes she hangs out with Abigail Moss, which is about as big an indictment as you can get. 'Pip's ideas are always, and without exception, Bad Ideas. Sometimes they are Atrocious. One or two have put her in the running for Worst Idea Ever.'

Maddie doesn't laugh. 'I know,' she says wearily, 'but I can't shut her down the way you can without feeling horrible.' A pause. 'That came out wrong.'

'You want people to think you're nice, whereas we both know I'm OK with pissing people off. It's not mean to do that when you're right.'

'But not everyone's as sure they're right as you are, Ven.'

'I'm *not* sure most of the time. I'm just good at telling when other people are wrong. Even eight-girl dance groups need leaders – so lead.'

'What if I'm only cut out to be a follower?' she asks quietly.

'Don't be wet. You've got this.' I try to make my voice encouraging, but we can both hear the 'shut up now' note in it. 'You don't have to be me. Do you – just firmer than usual.'

'Ven, please. We miss you. I miss you. Between school and practice, we hardly see each other. Just come back. You can be the coach – the manager – and boss us all about from the sidelines to your heart's content.'

'Yeah, 'cause the girls are really going to listen to me if I've been sitting on my arse for an hour while you're all dancing.'

'We listened before – even Pip did.'

'Because I was working harder than everyone else, so it was pretty hard to complain when I said we had to go again!' I try to stop it, but my voice is getting louder and louder, the anger building in my chest. Why does she have to keep poking at what she has to know is a raw and open wound? I want to be a good friend and not hate her for still having everything I've lost, but does she have to keep rubbing it in?

'At least come over for pizza with us. We're still your friends even if you don't want to be ours.'

'Don't,' I whisper. 'Just don't.'

'It's not the same without you,' she says.

I hang up on her. Then I turn my phone off so I don't have to see if she messages with an apology. Also to stop myself repeatedly typing then deleting one of my own, or ugly-crying while looking at old pics of PopSync.

I see the pictures anyway, as if my memories have been projected onto the walls. Our first rehearsal. Our first public performance at King's Cross to raise money for charity – £458! Like a slideshow, I see us smiling, laughing, fierce with concentration and joy.

My whole life used to be tied up in dance, whether it was planning and practising or researching dance schools. Now the only way I can bear what's happening is to put all of it behind me, only Maddie won't let me. And I know it's because she's afraid I'll end up leaving her behind too, but I don't know how to make it work when, between Maddie busy with PopSync and me busy dislocating, we barely get a few hours together a week.

At my last hospital appointment, we talked about what I'm finding hard (pretty much everything), what I'm doing to improve things (nothing that's proving effective) and what my goals are . . . and, stupid me, I offhandedly said, 'Obviously it's a stretch at the moment, but the end goal with physio is to see if I can get back to dancing.'

The look on the consultant's face . . . She didn't need to say a word for me to understand everything that no one had told me.

I suppose when a doctor has just ordered you to avoid standing for more than fifteen minutes at a time, no one thinks you also need to be told 'dancing is out for-*e-ver*'. But if you're only sixteen and you're planning a future as a dancer, someone needs to tell you that, not skirt around the words as if they're unsayable.

There's still a hell of a lot I'm good for – more than enough to make myself a happy, fulfilling life. Maybe one day it'll even feel as good as the one I had to give up.

Woeful Wednesday

Item 1: patch stuff up with Maddie.

Item 2: whip Singing Group into order.

Item 3: make some pigs fly – start with Abigail Moss?

Maddie avoids me first thing, so I give up on dealing with Item 1 till lunchtime and focus on – oh joy unbounded – free period in the music room with Singing Group. We get off to an amazing start: everyone, including Ren, ignoring me when I try to talk about our first song. It's no surprise with the others, but I'd hoped Ren, as the new boy, would want to play nice; it's rapidly becoming clear that 'sullen jerk' rather than 'shy and brooding' is his standard setting after all.

In the end, I turn up the volume on my phone and play a video of nails scratching across a blackboard. They all shudder, while Orla wrinkles her nose, looking me up and down with disgust – which is just plain stupid as my new skirt is A-MA-zing thanks to a lucky scoop on eBay on both a simple apple-green skirt and a mystery box of old buttons that I've been slowly (and badly) sewing around the hem while I'm brain-foggy and need something to distract me.

'Right,' I say, before the others can turn back to their phones. 'You all agreed to give me one song, so what's it going to be?'

'Are we seriously going along with this?' Roksana asks the others. 'Your dance group didn't even get to the live shows,' she tells me as if I've missed this fact, 'so maybe it's still big news for you, but it wasn't exactly a historic event.'

'Just wait and see what the girls do this year,' I tell her staunchly.

Roksana shrugs. 'Whatever. It won't be anything to do with your leadership, will it?'

'Thanks *so* much for that kind reminder that, through no fault of my own, I don't get to enjoy the thing I worked so hard to create.'

That shuts them both up. Orla flushes and Roksana shifts uncomfortably. 'OK, sorry, that came out mean,' Roksana says, flashing me a look that says the apology is sincere even if we *are* Enemies. 'But you have the least experience of anyone in Singing Group, bar Ren. It's a bit hard to take.'

'We all agreed, so let's just see what happens,' I say. 'First off, *please* can we stop calling ourselves Singing Group. And, no, I didn't name PopSync – that was all Maddie. Any thoughts?'

Insert dead silence. Crickets chirp. Eternity passes.

After about a century, the door opens and Ms Meade strides in.

We all beam at her and present a perfectly synchronised thumbs up. She rolls her eyes, then turns away to unlock the filing cabinet in the corner, grabbing a handful of files before leaving in a swish of ombre twists.

'We're all going to be very sorry if we don't have some progress to report at our next class,' I point out inarguably. 'Can we at least agree a song to work on?'

'I thought you were picking as part of your trial-run as self-appointed dictator?' Orla says with a sniff.

'Well, I'm going to take a veto on terrible ideas so no one sets me up to fail, but I'm fine with taking suggestions.'

'Huh,' says Orla, sitting back in her chair but, for once, looking at me as if we might one day be able to exchange two consecutive civil sentences.

I do my best to catch Ren's eyes through his hair, but once again he is apparently fascinated by the floor tiles. 'Does anyone have a favourite song or, I don't know, something from their heritage—'

'You think I want you lot mangling a Pakistani hit, as if that's going to make me feel included any more than Orla fancies listening to you destroy an Irish folksong? That's a no from me,' says Roks.

I hold up my hands. 'That's fine, but maybe one of the others feels differently. I wasn't even looking at you,' I add under my breath.

'Benjo,' Twin 1 says, elbowing him.

'That song your dad loves,' Twin 2 adds.

'Dad music? Wonderful.' Roksana heaves an impressively world-weary sigh.

'Look, your dad might have sucky taste, but mine actually knows his stuff,' snaps Benjo.

Roksana gives him such evils even I almost want to back away.

'What song?'

I turn in astonishment when I realise Ren is the one who asked. His one uncovered eye peers at us, before he goes back to his staring competition with the floor.

'It's called "Be Like Him" and it's an acapella mix of South African Zulu and English.'

'I love the idea of that,' I say, 'but is it religious, 'cause I feel like we should avoid that? Also, if there's Zulu in there are you . . . can you help with the pronunciation and stuff?'

Benjo purses his lips but nods. 'My dad's bilingual and he's like the biggest Kirk Franklin fan ever so I've heard that song about a billion times. Anyway, it's religious in intention but the English isn't explicit or anything. Just listen and see.' He promptly drops his phone on his foot, but once he's finally finished swearing he gets the song playing.

Five minutes later, The Singers (yes, that's the absolutely genius name we've settled on) agree for the second time. I'm too tired after the battle over picking a song to object to the name, which can always be changed later. The important thing is that we now have a temporary leader – me – and a song for me to lead on.

Only Lunchtime?

Which brings me back to my Wednesday to-do list, Item 1 . . . but I can't deal with patching things up with Maddie while the whole cafeteria (including Abigail Moss) watches, so I grab a sandwich and head straight back to the music room. Everything hurts by the time I've slopped myself down the ridiculously long corridor, so it takes me a moment to realise that someone is playing the piano. You'd think a given note would sound the same whoever is playing, but it's not true. There's magic in this person's touch.

I sink onto one of the chairs in the corridor, rest my head against the wall, and let the music carry me away. When I feel tears start to gather, I contemplate letting them fall; I don't even know why I'm suddenly so emotional – probably just everything catching up with me. Clenching my fists, I will myself slowly back from the brink.

I'm still feeling scraped raw when there's a noise in front of me. I lurch upright, realising that the music has stopped. But because all fast moves are An Epically Bad Idea nowadays, I end up hunched over in pain.

'Um,' says the person who was playing the piano. 'Um, are you OK?'

'Um, what the hell does it look like?' I grit back.

'Can I get someone for you?'

I'm so intensely miserable, I don't even put two and two together with the fact that precisely one person in our school speaks with a low, American drawl.

'Yeah,' I snap. 'You can get God down here and we'll have a long chat about His choices and walking ten miles in my shoes. Then, since that much walking isn't possible for me any more, we'll be stuck with a potentially cataclysmic paradox that will probably bring about the end of days.'

Mr Eloquent says nothing. To be fair, I probably wouldn't either under the circumstances. I take a deep breath, push my hair back and look up. 'Oh God, it's *you*.'

Ren blinks for a moment, then a wide trouble-incarnate grin spreads across his face. 'Nope. Flattering as it is, it's probably tempting fate to agree that I am truly divine.'

I do not gape at him, OK? Not even for an instant.

OK, maybe for an instant.

And no, it has nothing to do with how incredibly sexy that grin is. Because it's not.

I mean, it is, but while I may faint (a lot), I *never* swoon.

'I don't like you,' I tell him. But then my big, stupid mouth spoils it by saying, 'But you play beautifully.'

Ren looks like he'd be blushing if he were the blushing sort. 'Um,' he says again, then he does this little start, his hand coming up to his face as if suddenly realising his scars are showing.

I want to say something super nice and sensitive that makes him smile. Or something clever that makes him laugh. But I am one hundred per cent out of words. I'd like to put it down to the fact that I'm feeling particularly ropey, but I suspect the hair and the cheekbones and those big dark eyes have at least as much to do with it.

'I didn't figure you for ever being short of words,' he says then, face lighting up with mischief.

I slowly raise my middle finger and give him a look that says quite plainly, 'Who needs words?'

He laughs. 'Fair enough. Are you coming to English? Because I've forgotten how to get there.'

I glance at the clock at the end of the corridor. 'We're going to be late, but if you arrive with me no one will argue. In exchange, you can carry my bag.'

'Sounds fair,' Ren says, stepping forwards.

'No, don't help!'

He wrenches his hand back.

'Trust me, helping is not really helpful for getting me on my feet. I need to do it myself. It's just going to take a while.'

He shrugs, but his smile is gone. 'So I'm good as a pack-mule but no touching?'

I'm in the middle of levering myself out of the chair as I look up at him. I can't figure out from his expression if he's trying to make a joke or if he's sneering at me. 'Pretty much.'

A muscle bulges in his jaw. Wow. Who knew that actually happened? I guess it requires an official 'sculpted jaw' and I didn't realise that boys truly came equipped with those.

We walk to English in near silence, though I know Ren is waiting for me to ask what he thinks is the obvious question. But here's the thing. I'm curious – of course I am – but I also know it's none of my business and my curiosity is the sleazy, voyeuristic, treating-other-people-like-a-freakshow kind. We're all guilty of that sometimes – it's part of being human – but we don't need to indulge it. You wouldn't believe how often random strangers think they have a right to ask what's wrong with me and whether it was a car accident or something. Whatever else I am, I'm not a hypocrite. So I don't ask and I don't ask and I don't ask.

When we get to English, Ren gives me this strange look – surprised and pleased and grateful, angling his head so his hair doesn't cover his scars as much as usual – and I find myself smiling back.

Thursday

(i.e. – way too long till the weekend)

Item 1: identify and undislocate whatever bit of me is stuck in the wrong place.

I woke up this morning unable to turn my head properly. After slathering myself with ibuprofen gel – carefully, so I don't turn my hair gloopy, but only because I hate the feeling, not because I'd rather die than let a certain gorgeous piano-player see me like that – I head off to school, telling myself it will work itself loose during the day. Instead, it's after lunch and every time I try to look to the side, my neck rewards me by shooting pain straight into the centre of my brain. I'm fairly sure that the problem isn't actually my neck, though it keeps going crunch whenever I try to loosen the muscles. The real problem is almost certainly that my shoulder blade is dislocated.

Yes, that's a thing.

If it were the left one, it'd be fine. I've been ace at getting that back in since before anyone would agree that it was actually dislocating and kept insisting I was getting a tendon trapped, because of *course* the solution to that is to wedge your scapula against the top of a chair-back then rotate your arm slowly up, out to the side and backwards until something goes scrunch and slots back into place. I've tried that little trick four times already today, but for some unfathomable reason it never works on the right shoulder blade.

Which is how we arrive at Mr Singh asking if I need to go to the nurse. Why do half the teachers go all pity-gooey-yuck over me and the other half are just 'suck it up, whinger'? Where is the middle ground that they're always preaching about?

I smile my sweetest smile. 'I'll be fine here, thanks, if everyone would just stop staring and get the hell on with their work.'

Abigail Moss tosses her head and whispers, not at all quietly, 'She really cannot get enough attention.'

As everything hurts too much for me to think straight, the wittiest retort that my brain will supply is, *I hate you so much.* What it offers in objective, verifiable and defensible accuracy, it lacks in pretty much everything else, so I ignore her in favour of taking out some pain pills and self-medicating. Then I tune out as much as possible, only realising towards the end of the lesson that every time Mr Singh turns in my direction, Ren puts his hand up to ask him to explain the differences between American and British maths. I hadn't realised there *were* differences – aren't numbers just numbers? – but it turns out that there are plenty. By the third time Ren sticks his hand up, a chorus of groans echoes round the classroom.

I only twig that this is for my benefit when, with the clock-hands crawling miserably forwards and still twenty minutes to go, he leans on his left elbow so that his sleeve brushes my arm and out of the corner of his mouth whispers, 'Don't shoot the messenger, but you look like you need a doctor and I don't think those pills you took are working.'

I turn to glare at him then have to squeeze my eyes shut as pain sparks up into my head and down to my fingertips in one delicious zing of agony. If I were the sicking-up type, I'd walk over to Abigail Moss and make my day. Instead, I am the tougher-than-nails type, so I open my mouth to tell Ren to mind his own business. What I end up saying is, 'I know. But I'm not going.'

'Just thought I'd mention it,' says Ren.

There's something like amusement in his voice, but it's dry and sort of friendly and it makes me smile despite the pain.

'If it's just because of the awful brunette, I'd figure you've got better things to do than show off your stoicism for her.' He quirks an eyebrow. 'I get the whole "I want to murder you" thing as a turn-on, but she doesn't seem your type, given that I suspect her to be mostly brain-dead.'

It jolts a laugh out of me that immediately makes me hunch over, breathing carefully through the pain. Then something weird happens. There's a sort of fluttering on the back of my hand. I open a wary eye. Ren's hand is literally ghosting over mine. I look up at him.

Is he . . .?

No, of course not, Ven. Don't be an idiot. He just feels sorry for you. You're looking pitiful so he's trying to be kind because it turns out he's not a total jerk after all.

'No touching?' Ren whispers when I just sit there blankly, busy with my internal monologue. He pulls a face and I tense, expecting pity, but it's sympathy: real, proper sympathy. 'Isn't there anything else you can take for the pain?'

I give it some serious thought. There is, but then I'll have to go home and I'm not ready to concede defeat yet. I shake my head and hunch some more because his kindness is making my stomach hurt with longing.

Boys do not fancy girls who walk like you and literally fall apart in lessons, I remind myself.

'Don't maim me, OK?' Ren whispers, and lets his hand sink on to mine.

Then we sit staring at our hands until the bell rings.

'Did my touch magically make it all better?' Ren asks.

I can't very well say that it was lovely but also torturous because of how much I wanted it to be more than sympathy, so instead I turn my hand over and grab his wrist. 'Yes,' I gasp dramatically. 'Never leave me.'

Then we grin at each other as I let go and work on standing, only to end up swaying on my feet.

'Is the human-metronome thing a good or bad sign?' Ren asks lightly as he collects our bags.

'Don't catch me,' I tell him, making myself breathe slow and deep. 'Seriously. It'll make everything about a hundred times worse. If I fall, just let me. I know which bits I can afford to land on.'

'OK?' he says, making it into a question. 'Right. Message received. We're going to music class even though you look like you need to go straight to bed by way of a hospital, aren't we?'

I really don't want Ren to watch me trying to walk right now, but at least by the time we get to music I can be confident that any hint of romantic interest will be deader than my dancing dreams.

'We are, indeed, going to music,' I tell him. 'Whoopee!'

Ren sighs. 'We really need to do something about the name. Might as well have just stuck with Singing Group.'

You know that scene in choir and band movies where, with the right leader, everything just slots into place and the group finds their sound/groove/mojo? You'll be astonished to hear it doesn't work like that in real life.

When Ms Meade sends Maddie and the orchestra lot off to use the second half of the lesson for practice in the library and assembly hall, leaving the music room to The Singers, we're all delighted as it means not having to give up our free period after lunch, but it's all downhill from there.

First, we didn't think to actually play a chord to get us in the same key. Then we all went at a different pace. Then there was the issue of everyone trying to put their own spin on the material. Then I lost my temper.

'Maybe we could have a break?' Ren suggests.

Absolutely all of us glare at him. Then we stomp off in different directions in our usual groups – which basically means the others all have someone to complain to and I just sit where I am and pretend I'm not trying to put my hip back in place.

Thankfully, it works first time, unlike the shoulder blade. There is the usual dull, crunching pop and I feel myself grunt as my body goes limp and noodley with relief. Well, apart from the muscles in my shoulder, which are still stiff and tender and angry at me.

'Do I want to know what that noise was or will I vomit?' Ren asks as he sits down two chairs along.

'You'd be the sort to call an ambulance every time you dislocate your hip, I suppose,' I say airily because, although my common sense seems to have deserted me, sarcasm will be with me to the bitter end.

'Yeah, I totally would. Which makes me wonder ... are you all alien or just half and, if so, which side of your family is from Elsewhere?'

'Are you really going to press your luck not knowing the extent of my extra-terrestrial powers?'

'If Abigail Moss is still living, I'm safe.'

'Female solidarity won't save *you*.'

'I'm pretty sure Abigail is more bovine than anything else.'

I raise an eyebrow. 'Most people just see that she's pretty.' Ouch. Didn't mean to let the banter slide so close to the truth.

Ren pulls a face. 'Yeah, but most people are idiots.'

'Oh, I hadn't noticed,' I say, gesturing at the furious huddles in the corners of the room.

'Someone needs to conduct,' Ren says.

'I tried, remember? Roksana kept starting early on purpose.' I narrow my eyes at him for a moment, then let my lips slide into a smile.

'I don't like that look,' he tells me. 'We've only been on a mutual snarking basis for about two and a half hours, but I really don't like that look.'

I swivel in my chair, reach over to the piano and hit a stunning discord. The others wince, but go quiet.

'Ren's going to conduct,' I announce. 'And this time we're all going to stay on key and on time.'

They glare at me. I glare back.

'I've still got' – I squint up at the clock – 'twenty minutes to try to make this song work for us. Until then, what I say goes.'

They all shuffle back into place.

'Shut up, Roksana,' I say, not even looking at her.

'I didn't actually say anything.'

'Shut up anyway. Now, we're going to sing it v-e-r-y slowly, just as notes. No style. No inflection. Just the melody. Ren, a demonstration on the piano?'

'Some boys would go for this type of bossy,' he grumbles as he leans over the keys.

Yeah, you don't fancy me even apart from the walking. Thanks for clarifying.

'Mark us off,' I order.

And suddenly there is a chord hanging in the air and then another. Suddenly there is harmony. Eight whole bars of it. Eight whole bars where everything else vanishes and I'm happy. Purely, totally happy. I close my eyes and listen, feeling where my notes sit amid the music, softening my tone so my voice blends smoothly into the music we're making.

'Ven, if you shut your eyes, there's not much point having a conductor,' Benjo says in the quiet that follows.

I open them and look around. It's not all wide-eyed wonder, *Oh my God, we're instantly like The Best Group Ever.* But there's a shared sense of, *You know, what? That wasn't a disaster.*

'I'm fine with a song or two that have, like, family importance, but I don't want our whole programme to scream tokenism,' Roksana says. 'I want something that means something to me, if that's our theme.'

'I agree,' I tell her, 'but we need to do a bit of musical walking – or crawling – before we make things complicated. So let's do "Be Like Him" again and everyone can start thinking about what type of song they want to arrange for coursework.'

When I next look at the clock, turning my whole body because of the situation with my shoulder blade, we have just five minutes left.

'That was as close to decent as we've ever got,' I tell them pointedly, 'so hands up if you want to carry on like this instead of going back to the way it was.'

The twins and Benjo have a silent conversation, then all reluctantly raise their hands, Ren along with them.

Orla and Roksana heave matching sighs. 'Fine. Democracy rules,' Orla grunts.

'They do say it's the best bad system we've got,' Roksana adds sweetly, giving me a snake-smile nearly worthy of Abigail Moss.

'Are you stalking me, angling for a lift or do you have some weird duckling gene that makes you imprint on people then follow them around?' I ask Ren when I realise he's trailing behind me as I slop towards the car park. I know he's just lonely and I'm probably the closest thing he's got to a friend after all the deep bonding we did today, snarking intermittently at each other and not quite holding hands, but I still feel my pulse pick up and that yearny thing start gnawing away at my stomach.

'I'm observing.'

'I didn't think stalkers copped to it so readily.'

Ren sighs, but moves to saunter alongside me. It's hard to make it look natural to walk next to someone going as slowly as I am, but he does his best. The situation isn't helped by the fact that I'm short (five foot one AND A QUARTER) and he's tall (towering over me by at least half a foot), so glancing across at him involves looking up, which isn't a function my body is currently providing.

'I'm trying to figure out if you're stoic, self-destructive or just blithely incapable of recognising your own limits.' He shakes his head. 'I always thought I was a tough guy. You're making me feel inadequate,' he whines.

I can't help but laugh.

'Seeing you to your car is a start, and if you fancy giving me a lift that's great, but mostly I want to know *you* get home safely because you look like you need a hospital if you don't want to end up in the morgue.'

'This is the weirdest way anyone has ever asked for my number,' I tell him, slipping my phone out of my pocket and holding it out to him, being careful to keep my voice completely blasé. 'I'll drop you off, then message you when I get home if it'll soothe your duckling tendencies. At least on the way to yours I can start explaining the British education system before Mr Singh jumps out the window mid-lesson. I like him and I don't want that on my conscience, even though Maths is only on the ground floor.'

Ren makes a humming noise as he taps in his number, then hands my phone back. I reach for it only to double over, cradling my wrist.

'What-happened-and-is-it-my-fault?' Ren squeaks.

I use my left hand to put my phone away and then, stick dangling from its loop about my wrist, I look him straight in the eye and, wishing my shoulder would be half as cooperative, I pop my fingers back in. One, *crunch*. Two, *scrunch*. The expression on Ren's face says that he is suitably punished for everything he's ever done wrong.

Turning away, I slop on without him.

He gives it a minute then catches up. 'Sick alien powers you've got there with the joint-popping thing.'

'Sick sense of humour,' I fire back, making a vomiting gesture.

'Hey, I'm off my game. You squicked me out. And don't you say that it's your body and it's normal for you. Obviously it is, but you use it like a weapon – and you know it.'

Well, what else am I going to do with it when I'm full of yearning and you're busy being grossed out by everything I do?

I don't say that of course, just give him a superior look and walk on. He laughs, then we carry on bantering away and I think sensible, mature thoughts about how friendship is more important than romance anyway.

Liar.

It is weird driving Ren home, but in a nice way (well, ignoring the agony in my shoulder and neck). Even weirder is learning that he's surprisingly chatty now he's started talking. I mean, maybe it's different one-on-one versus in a whole group of strangers who already know each other, but it's still a nice discovery that he doesn't only speak when made to.

Somehow, it's even weirder driving home alone after I drop him off. And it's weirdest of all when I message ten minutes later to tell him I'm back alive before I even get out of the car. It makes me feel odd and jumpy and anxious and excited and . . . unsettled.

It leaves me with a tricky question to answer: do I dare pair myself up with Ren for the arrangement bit of our coursework, or would it be asking for the worst sort of trouble?

Friday

(Thank all the gods)

My to-do list remains the same – *undislocate shoulder blade* – but the urgency inches up another notch now that I've been in unrelenting pain for more than twenty-four hours and, unsurprisingly, haven't really slept. Nowadays, there is one position I can drift off in: flat on my back, left knee bent out and propped on a pillow, right leg flat and straight. If I don't sleep like that, I either don't sleep or I wake up having dislocated myself. Sometimes I do anyway.

Given that this position is murder on a dislocated shoulder blade, I am thoroughly wretched by the time I drag myself out of bed. I look it too: hollow-eyed with bright red cheeks. When I am feeling at my roughest (short of actually being unconscious) I flush prettily so everyone says how well I look. The flush is actually because my blood-pressure is all wrong and my veins and capillaries are doing Bad Things. And yet it gives me this amazing 'glow'. There really should be a note in my file that says, *Patient should not be blamed for eviscerating persons commenting on her obvious good health when she feels like shit.*

The morning starts with my parents looking at me and their faces falling. I try not to take it to heart.

'Do you want to stay home?' Mum asks.

'No.'

'Should I drive you in?' Dad asks.

I shake my head, instantly wincing as my shoulder says, *OuchOuchOUCHOOOOW* all down my back and up into my skull.

'Yes,' I say in the least grateful voice of any teenager ever. 'Thank you,' I add, in the same voice. It's the thought that counts, right?

'Did you book the chronic pain group?'

I groan, but nod. 'Sunday after next.'

Mum and Dad exchange relieved looks.

'We're proud of you,' Dad says.

'Can you just . . . not until I'm in a slightly less foul mood?'

'Are you getting your period?' Mum asks.

I groan again, and flop forward to press my sweaty forehead to the table. On the one hand, the fact that I am, indeed, about to get my period explains why everything is suddenly so bad. It also means it's going to be worse before it gets better.

'Shall I get your spray?'

Period hormones naturally make women's joints more flexible. If you're already hypermobile that means you start flopping about like a badly jointed puppet. The 'spray' dispenses a blob of clear jelly-like oestrogen that I rub into the outside of my forearms – yes, it's weird with a capital WEIRD – to balance my hormones so I don't come apart at the seams. It's actually hormone-replacement therapy for people who're menopausal – like I need anything else to make me feel like I'm turning into an old person before I've even reached adulthood.

I take some morphine too because, even though it's early to be starting on the hard stuff, I really, really need it. And before you ask, yes, the next thing we do is try (for the second time) every trick we know to get the shoulder to go back in. It refuses to cooperate. Sometimes that happens and the only thing to do is wait out the agony.

Resigned to a day of misery, I contemplate my beloved blue suede boots, but I can't face heels. Instead, I tug on the ratty old trainers I wear to physio, then shuck them for my plain pumps: boring but un-awful. I had the best outfit planned, but there's just no point when I look and feel like death warmed over.

Dad has to help me into the car. I slouch in the passenger seat with my shoes off and my feet up on the dash as I message Ren. *Getting a lift today. You'll have to find your own way home.*

My life is pure sorrow, comes the reply.

I put the phone away, then realise Dad is darting little looks at me. 'What?' I demand.

'You were smiling.'

'I do that, you know.'

'Not on days I have to drive you in. And never like that.'

I frown. 'Like what?'

'Sweetly,' my loving father says. 'You have a beautiful "world domination" smile, and a charming "I always know best" smile, and an inspiring "this plan will work or else" smile, but you don't generally do sweet and shy. They're not really your colours, darling.'

'I just told the new boy to get lost,' I inform him.

My father turns his attention back to the road. 'It's all in the delivery, though, right?'

Since Abigail Moss is having one of her less subtle days (she likes to change up her bullying between overtly nasty and covertly cruel for extra LOLs), she spends the morning perfecting a variety of impressions of my walk, the way I'm hunched around the pain in my shoulder, and the faces I keep pulling, despite my best efforts not to as I trudge from the car to assembly to class. At least there I'm distracted by hyper-awareness of Ren sitting at the next desk.

At lunchtime, my feet take me to the cafeteria. Maddie sees me and for a moment I think she's about to turn away, then she clocks my appearance. Her face falls and, despite everything, she comes running. 'You look like shit,' she tells me, as only a best friend can. 'Actually, you look worse than that. Ven, you need to take something or I'm calling your mum.'

'Not the mother!' I protest, but her face has that mutinous, thin-lipped look that means I'm not fooling her in the slightest.

'Did you sleep?'

'Define sleep,' I say, yawning and leaning sideways to rest my head on her shoulder, even though I don't deserve to.

She sighs, but touches her head to mine. 'What's it to be? Pick your poison.'

'You know my meds basically are poison, right?'

'No, your meds are what dimwits would call an Excellently Good Time. Now, do I have to guilt you about *hanging up on me like a total cow* or will you start behaving sensibly?'

Maddie makes me call my mum, then walks me outside to wait for her, *then* insists on helping me into the car like an invalid (I call her something rude by way of thanks). She waves me off, looking worried. There's something in the slump of her shoulders that makes me feel even more awful than I did before, which I hadn't thought was possible.

I spend the rest of the day on the sofa, channel surfing and failing to make my brain work enough to do homework. When I realise I've read the same page four times and still can't remember a single word, I conclude that, as I've temporarily become a massive air-breathing goldfish as far as retention of information goes, I might as well give up.

My phone chirps and I snatch at the distraction.

Ren: *Do you want to guess what Abigail Moss thinks assonance means?*

I feel my lips tug up in a smile, then make myself stop, then shake my head because what does it matter? It's not like he's flirting with intent. Anyway, I could do with a friend who doesn't remember me from before – who doesn't see all the things I've lost every time he looks at me. Plus Maddie's talent for sarcasm has always been limited. (Thankfully, her appreciation of it isn't.)

Yes, but save it for when I can mock her to her face, I reply. *Did I miss anything?*

I quote: Read the book. No, Abigail, not just the Cliff's Notes. And not the Wikipedia summary. Write an essay.

There a topic for this essay?

I'm trying to maintain an air of mystery.

My finger pauses for a minute as I consider such erudite rejoinders as 'What's the title, jackass?' Then my phone buzzes again.

It's not due till next Thurs so I'll draw out the suspense till tomorrow. Want to do coffee and talk shop? I can come to you . . .

You just want to know where I live, stalker-duckling. Then I add, *Sunday at 11?*

Yes. Feel better.

Working on it.

Work faster.

Why do I have to do everything?

Because you're the bossy, controlling one. You're like an alien rather than magic-powered Hermione.

Best. Compliment. Ever.

Dork.

Nerd.

Ren doesn't reply. I watch my phone. I check the battery levels. I check my reception bars.

I turn it off. I turn it back on. I check it's connected to the Wi-Fi.

I'd carry on but by then I have bigger things to worry about.

Saturday

(not that it helps)

Item 1: FIX SHOULDER NOW!!!!!

By morning, there is no help for it. I need to see a doctor. The doctor wants to send me to A&E with a letter explaining what's happening. He spends the appointment talking to Mum instead of me.

'My body. My appointment. Why's he talking to you when I'm sitting right here?' I say loudly. 'Next time you're not coming in with me, Mum.'

Mum and the doctor exchange looks. I mean, I get that I'm not at my most socially acceptable but, hello, forty-eight hours of sleepless agony will do that to a person.

'I'm starting to suspect that the reason people have to go to medical school for seven years is because it takes that long to turn otherwise intelligent people into blithering idiots,' I say, louder still, as we cross back through reception.

'Ven, you mustn't antagonise people,' Mum tells me as we get into the car. 'I understand you're in pain and the doctor wasn't very . . . um . . .'

'Helpful? Keen on talking to me like a person? Possessed of a functioning brain?'

Mum sighs.

'He hummed when I told him what was wrong, basically said he didn't believe me when I told him how long it had been since the shoulder went out, and spoke primarily to you even before I got belligerent. And why shouldn't a person be belligerent when faced with that sort of behaviour? What he's even *for* since he basically just passed the buck? All I needed was for him to shove my shoulder back in and make it stay put.'

'Well, it's not his area of expertise—'

'Because the hospital staff are going to be soooo much more knowledgeable, aren't they?'

Mum's fingers are white on the steering wheel. 'Maybe we'll be lucky today,' she says brightly.

Yeah, because the universe is practically shouting that I'm going to have a wonderful day.

I hate the urgent care nurse with a deep and abiding passion. It's only been about fifteen seconds, but I have mentally consigned her to at least seven different levels of hell.

The first thing the nurse says, when I am shown into the examination room half an hour after the appointment the GP set up this morning, is, 'Your shoulder isn't dislocated. I can see that from the way you took off your coat.'

I give her a baleful look. 'It's the shoulder *blade*, actually. It's in my notes. And in the doctor's note. To be technical, the scapula has been subluxed for about fifty hours. I have not slept. I have had Oramorph and co-dydramol, and I am over a seven on the pain scale and have been for a while, and I need someone to get my frigging shoulder back in and figure out a way to keep it there before I start screaming.'

The doctor arrives then. I dislike him on sight too, a first impression almost instantly confirmed when he says, 'Well, that shoulder's not dislocated.'

I turn around and show him my shoulder blade.

'Oh,' say the doctor and the nurse as one. 'The right one, is it?'

No, it's the one that *isn't* the wrong shape and *isn't* all swollen up above and below and rigid to the touch.

'Yes, it's all winged out, isn't it?' adds the nurse.

You don't say!

In case you're wondering, 'winged out' is an actual technical term for when you move your shoulder so that the triangular bone at the back juts out from the spine. That's normal. It's not normal for it to get stuck that way. If they can't fix it, then they are going to need to give me so much medication I don't know which way is up because otherwise I am going to lose my mind.

I say something to this effect. It's not entirely coherent.

The nurse looks at the doctor. 'How do you usually put it back?' the doctor asks me.

This is why I hate the doctors at both the emergency clinic and A&E. They. Know. Nothing.

'If I could put it back, I would have done that fifty hours ago. I'm not a doctor' – *hint, hint, HINT* – 'but I figure I need a local anaesthetic or a muscle relaxant or something to stop it being so swollen, then we can try manipulating it back into place.'

'We can't give you a local here, but we can send you to A&E – it's literally next door,' the doctor says, brightening noticeably.

I fix him with the fury of fifty hours of sleepless pain. 'No.'

The doctor's face falls like I've cancelled all holidays for the next six years. It's balm to my soul.

'Let's do the muscle relaxant,' I tell him. 'I'll need a shot direct into the shoulder. A pill won't be targeted enough, given we've already tried heat, massage, ice, ten per cent ibuprofen gel, Salonpas patches, Pernaton gel and ibuprofen pills.'

The doctor and nurse inspect my shoulder. 'We can try that,' says the doctor, 'but since I'm not an expert in this field it'll need to be your decision. I can't say I recommend it. Why don't we send you next door—'

'So you can palm me off on more non-experts who don't know what to do? No, thanks. I'm your problem. So, shall we try the shot?'

The doctor looks at Mum, who nods.

'It sounds like the most sensible step under the circumstances.' She takes my hand, staring at the doctor and the nurse until they leave.

'This a good idea, isn't it?' I ask.

'Our best shot?' Mum says, doing her best to grin.

'Punning at my bedside. Bad form, mother.'

Then the doctor comes back and starts preparing the injection.

'I'm going to have a bad reaction to this,' I warn him.

The doctor just about resists the urge to roll his eyes. I am starting to suspect his med-school specialism was Enhanced Patronising Disdain. 'It's a very common drug. Side effects of any significance are extremely unusual, but if you don't think it's a good idea—'

'Since no medical professional I've seen today has had any useful ideas of their own, we'd better try mine,' I point out.

He gives me the shot then looks at me triumphantly. I can tell he enjoyed the fact that an injection directly into a muscle that's been rigid for fifty hours HURTS.

I take a breath. Then another.

'See? All OK,' says the doctor.

I give him a smug smile. 'My blood pressure is going to crash now.'

Then the room tips upside down and I can't breathe and my heart doesn't like it and I might throw up. Mum orders the doctor about and, together, with a bit of uncoordinated semi-conscious help from me, I end up lying down. One of Mum's hands is in mine. The other strokes my hair. I keep my eyes closed and make myself breathe slowly and shallowly and will my heart to work properly.

Slowly the room stops pretending to be a rollercoaster. I open my eyes.

Mum smiles down at me, though everything about her screams STRESS.

A look about the room reveals the doctor and nurse have scarpered.

'I'm going to put my shoulder back in a minute – it feels like it'll go now – then please could we head home?' I ask.

'Once you're steady on your feet, we can do that,' she says, because my mum is brilliant and there is literally no point staying here.

Sunday

(which is something, I suppose)

I wake up in stages, gradually registering that my limbs seem to weigh a ton and I have a massive medication hangover, though at least I'm home in my own bed rather than a hospital one.

Throwing back my duvet, and shoving aside my now stone-cold hot-water bottle, I sit up carefully. My shoulder and neck are sore but they move. There are no shooting pains when I turn my head to look at the clock on my bedside table. It is indescribably nice not to be in hideous, endless agony.

My phone is buzzing on the dresser. I reach for it, yawning.

Ren: *Are you ignoring me on purpose or accidentally? I'm in a mood so it had better not be on purpose.*

Do I want to know why you're in a mood? Accidental. Was in hospital. Then drugged.

There's a pause.

Are you OK?

Am much better than I was. And then I remember about our

plans. *Here's your chance for my address, stalker-duckling.* I tap it in. *My parents are freaks,* I add.

Whose aren't? See you at 11.

Better be via the front door and not binoculars.

You're taking the stalker thing too far. It's only funny to a point. It affects real people, you know.

Huh. He has a point there. How unfeminist of me. I shall blame the drugs.

I concede that this one time, when I am ill and drugged, you are correct and I am not. If it takes a hospital for you to best me, it doesn't mean you've really won.

We'll schedule a rematch if we both survive coffee and homework still talking.

I don't think we've ever really talked, Ren. It's more a long sequence of insults.

I think I win this battle of wits after all since Ren doesn't reply.

'Mum, Dad, the new American student from my class is coming over to fill me in on what I missed and get some additional tips on the British education system in return. You are prohibited from being embarrassing. We are not dating. We are nearly grown-ups who happen to have different sex organs. It doesn't mean sex is imminent – or going to happen between us ever. We basically snark at each other and insult Abigail Moss in tandem. It's a solid basis for a friendship.'

My parents peer at me from the study, which is currently swamped by paperwork for the festival.

'That was a lot of words to say a friend's coming over,' Dad points out. He exchanges a rude and obnoxious look with Mum.

'Don't be vile,' I tell him.

He spreads his hands in a 'What did I say?' way, but the grin is Dreadfulness personified.

'Shut up. And stop doing' – I wave at his face – '*that* before Ren arrives or I'll lock you in here.'

'That's fine, we're busy,' Mum says, already back to tearing her hair out (literally, by the looks of it: she's grasping it in bunches on either side of her head and pulling) thanks to the particularly awful demo murmuring away in the background.

'I'll lock you in here without caffeine if you don't make Dad behave,' I tell her.

'I need caffeine to deal with your father. I will go on a psychotic killing spree before the hour is out if I don't have coffee and cookies.'

'Why am I always being got at?' my father says, pouting.

'We are punishing you for the patriarchy,' my mother tells him. 'Also for being a swine.'

'Just for teasing our daughter a little?'

'Yesterday you palmed your revolting brother-in-law off on me to discuss bands for the Big Top.'

'Oh,' says my father. 'I did, indeed, involve Geoff unnecessarily. Accusation of porcineness accepted. Remind me why we let him be involved?'

'Because we "put the Family in Family Festival",' Mum and I quote at him.

I leave them to it.

For some reason I get down the nicest mugs and arrange a plate of fancy biscuits and, even more unfathomably, I pick a few flowers from the garden and put them in a little vase. What is wrong with me? The drugs have obviously addled my brain.

Thankfully, the doorbell rings before I have a chance to go even more Domestic Goddess and start baking or something. As I usher Ren down the hall, he freezes and I realise my parents are peeking out of the study door.

'Forget them. I'll caffeinate and feed them shortly, then they'll settle down.'

Ren is hiding behind his hair, but he offers a hand in their direction. 'Hi,' he says.

I have to remind myself that I'd probably be shy too in a new country, on a new continent, meeting the family of my one and only friend at my new school. OK, I wouldn't be shy because I'm me, but you get the picture.

'Don't do that,' I tell him. 'It's weird when you're polite.'

'I can't be rude to you and polite to your parents?'

'No,' I say as my father moves to shake Ren's hand. 'Get back in the study and deal with the fencing quotes,' I order my parents. I do not need them realising how much I fancy Ren. I am not in any way prepared to be teased about it.

My father shakes Ren's hand anyway. 'She's very bossy. You're allowed to disagree. We'll back you up,' he says disloyally.

'That's a lie,' my mother tells Ren, leaning around Dad to shake his hand too. 'I'm only the second bossiest in this house, and Ven's father has always been a pushover.'

'Some things should stay within the family,' Dad says, looking long-suffering.

'Does this mean I'm more or less safe arguing back when I'm here versus at school?' Ren asks.

And I know he's just making nice, but the yearny bit of my stomach is screaming that there's more to it: that this is how boys behave 'meeting the parents'. Why can't they all shut up before I do something stupid like get my hopes up?

'We're going back to the quotes now,' Mum says. 'You promised us coffee and cookies, Daughter.'

'I indicated you'd get them if you behaved.'

'Weren't we nice? Weren't we welcoming and polite and reputable and not at all weird?' Dad asks Ren.

'You have a lovely house,' Ren tells him with a completely straight face.

'I'll get you coffee and the biscuit tin,' I call over my shoulder as I lead Ren to the kitchen, where I make the world's loudest pot of coffee. 'I'm still medicated,' I warn him. 'I'm sure there's a legal loophole for dismembering people when you're medicated.'

'I don't see what I've done that merits the leap to dismemberment,' he says, leaning over the counter to frown at my coffee-making and, urgh, the way the pose stretches his T-shirt against his stomach makes mine turn over and ... *Stop it, Ven!*

'I had to go to the hospital,' I remind him in my blankest tone, even though he's crossing his arms and showing off the lean muscles in his shoulders and ...

Stop it! Think about yesterday. All the fun at the emergency room.

That does the trick.

'I hate the hospital,' I say with not a trace of breathless lust in my voice at all. 'I despise doctors.'

'I'm not a hospital or a doctor.'

No, you're drop dead gorgeous, I think.

'You come bearing essay questions,' I say.

'It's a bit harsh to blame me for that. Can I invoke the "don't shoot the messenger" rule?'

My reply is cut off by a furious rapping at the back door. I scoot around the counter to find Maddie making faces through the glass. 'Why are you here?' I ask her as I open the door, standing in front of it in the vain hope she'll get the hint that I want her to go away.

'Yeah, I love you too,' Maddie says, slipping past me. 'You stopped answering my messages.'

'You were being boring. And demanding. And I was in hospital.'

'You were in *hospital*? And you didn't *tell* me? Your *literal* best friend in the whole entire world? Who you hung up on a few days ago?'

She turns away and gives a howl of fury. It cuts off abruptly when she realises that Ren is leaning on the counter, watching her.

'Good job she's not a drama queen or anything,' I tell him wryly.

'When did Maddie turn up?' Dad asks, puttering into the

kitchen. 'Is that why our coffee hasn't been delivered yet? Hi, Maddie, please stop howling. Ven might deserve it, but my eardrums have been assaulted quite enough listening to entries for the festival.' He reaches over, grabs the tray I'd been making up and whisks it away.

On the plus side, Ren has clearly diverted Maddie's attention from her need to howl. On the 'oh shit' side, Ren has Maddie's undivided attention. She shoots me the world's least subtle look. Just when I thought today couldn't possibly be worse than yesterday . . .

'Hi, new boy,' she says, springing up onto the nearest kitchen stool. 'My best friend didn't mention you'd be here. I am very interested in your presence.'

'You know his name, Maddie. Don't be rude in my house.' I try to keep my tone jokey, but I can feel fury and hurt and panic rising up the back of my throat.

Don't tease me, Maddie. Not about this. Not about him.

'Only Ven's allowed to be rude here,' Maddie stage-whispers. Then she turns back to me. 'It's RUDE – with a capital everything – not to tell your best friend you're in hospital.'

'It was only for a few hours.'

'Did you know?' Maddie demands, turning on Ren.

Stop talking! You're going to say something you can't take back and I will never forgive you if you do.

'After the fact,' Ren says, backing away and tipping his hair even further over his face.

Maddie opens her mouth to say something unintentionally

awful – she always gets oblivious to the rest of the world when she's cross. And maybe it'll just be something embarrassing, but maybe it'll be about how much I must fancy Ren to behave this way, which would literally kill me with humiliation. I already know he doesn't fancy me back – I don't need to have him tell me to my face.

'Don't,' I say, and my voice nearly cracks. 'Can't I claim medication-induced amnesia?'

'No,' Maddie says. 'No, you mayn't, Venetia.' When I wince, Maddie gives me a smug look. 'Serves you right.' Then she heaves a sigh and subsides, dragging the cookie plate over. 'So, what's your excuse for being here?' she asks Ren.

'My first essay in your weird British version of high school?' he says, turning it into a question. 'What's yours?'

'I need Ven to make Pip cry.'

'She doesn't mean it literally,' I explain to Ren. 'She's just being a wuss about taking charge and Pip's a bulldozer so nothing's getting done. Which isn't my problem any more,' I add, turning back to Maddie. 'I'm busy. You make her cry, or get Ashley to do it.' I cut my eyes pointedly in Ren's direction.

Maddie's face immediately takes on a 'cat got the cream' look. 'Ten years as your best friend and I did not know helping the new kid was your idea of a fun-packed Sunday.'

'Only when I've been in hospital.'

'You can't use that as a "get out of jail free" card *when you didn't tell me*,' Maddie points out loudly. 'Also, Pip is being a nightmare and I hate all of them. Even Sam, and I thought that was impossible. I'm not good enough at being bossy without the others getting cross.'

'They were always cross with me.'

'Only briefly. They always got over it. Mostly because you made us so tired we couldn't hold a coherent thought, let alone a grudge. And also because it worked. I can't make anything work. Today they were all slouching. They'd never have dared slouch at *you*,' she wails, then turns to Ren, pointing her half-eaten cookie in his direction. 'You didn't hear that. I am not pitiful in public.'

'Ren doesn't count.' I wish he didn't count.

Ren shrugs. 'I'm not here. Just ignore me entirely.'

Yes, I'm doing a marvellous job of that, aren't I?

'Go away,' I tell Maddie. 'I've got English and The Singers to deal with. PopSync's your problem.'

'You need to come to rehearsal, Ven. Enough's enough and—'

The look on my face freezes her mid-sentence – but only for a moment.

'Come *on*, Ven. We need you. I know it's not the same, but stop trying to throw everything away just because—' She rubs at her forehead. 'Gah. You know what I mean.'

'Finish that sentence,' I dare her.

'No. That's not fair. You know there's nothing I can say that doesn't sound awful, but it doesn't mean I don't have a point. I know that your health stuff is happening to you and not me, but it kinda is happening to me too—'

'Yeah, because you totally took your share of the fifty hours

I spent with a dislocated shoulder blade the last few days. Sorry, Mads. Totally forgot about that. So glad we're in it together.'

'Don't be a cow.' Maddie's face goes tight with hurt. 'Just . . .' She rakes her hands through her hair. 'Look, you're obviously busy with your new boyfriend—'

Tears set the back of my throat aching, but I channel it into spite and fury.

'Now who's the cow?' I sneer, though my heart is pounding hard enough to hurt. 'Ren's not freaky enough to think that is what's going on here, so will you just butt out and leave me one relationship that's not a massive drama?'

Maddie slithers down from her stool. 'So glad I came to my best friend for help and left feeling happy and supported. Have a wonderful time with your essay,' she says and slams herself out of the back door.

I press the heel of my hand to my forehead, not looking at Ren as I say, 'Apologies for that not at all awkward display with my best friend . . .' Then I turn around and promptly trail off because I have absolutely no idea what to make of the look on his face. I was expecting embarrassment, maybe even a little distaste, but this is something else entirely. 'You don't know the context so leave off judging me. Or Maddie,' I add peevishly.

Ren gives a nasty bark of laughter. 'Yeah, 'cause freaks like me aren't in any position to judge anyone.'

While my mouth is still in the process of falling open, he slings his bag over his shoulder and storms out of the front door.

Mum steps into the corridor, blinking at the door then at me.

I fling my hands in the air. 'Everyone's crazy today. It's all I need.'

Then I stomp upstairs and slam my bedroom door (why should I be left out of all the slamming?) and give some serious thought to whether or not I should cry.

I don't, though I make a few embarrassing and pathetic noises in the process of working it out as I curl into my duvet, trying not to think about the fact that right now I sort of hate Maddie and, instead, applying myself to figuring out why Ren thinks I've called *him* a freak. Wasn't he listening?

After Lunch

(i.e. – far too close to *Monday* for comfort)

Following my busy morning enraging both the boy I fancy and my best friend, the afternoon brings Aunt Jinnie like a proverbial ray of sunshine – if sunshine were rainbow-coloured and talked endlessly at not quite the speed of light. After we have all been thoroughly hugged (she never skimps on me, even now my whole body is determined to disjoint itself), she sends Mum and Dad off to 'make some bleeding decisions about the line-up – yes, go away, piss off, don't want to see your faces till it's done' and settles beside me at the kitchen table.

'Why don't I have chosen charities or numbers for the merchandise?' she demands. 'Is my favourite niece learning to slack off at last? It'd better be because of a boy – or a girl, if your interests are finally widening. You know you mustn't be afraid to consider all possibilities, my darling, because—'

I groan, dragging over the computer and pulling up the merch folder in a vain attempt to derail that particular topic of conversation. 'I'm not interested in *anyone* right now. My hips are too busy dislocating for romance to be all that appealing.'

'I'm sure there are loads of things you can buy nowadays that could help. Let's do some research after we sort out the camisole numbers.'

Just kill me now.

'Let's not do research on sex aids, Aunt Jinnie. Not ever,' I say.

Of course, I immediately think of nothing else. I have no clue how sex will work with my stupid, idiotic body. It's not like I have prior experience to draw on. Is there a position in which my hips physically *can't* dislocate? What if you just have to go for it and assume everything'll be OK, but then it's not? It'd be soooooo romantic having to pause sex to undislocate myself . . . and what if I didn't really fancy finishing the sex afterwards? And that's if the person I'm with isn't running for the hills anyway.

Though maybe it'll be a non-issue because, really, who's ever going to want to sleep with me in the first place? I mean, would I want to sleep with someone like me if I were still normal?

With that gaping well of despair yawning in front of me, I quickly turn to my laptop and bring up the database with last year's merch details. I'm tired and miserable and everything hurts but there's nothing I can do about any of that, so I do the one thing I can – throw myself at sorting out the festival.

'Aunt Jinnie,' I say, when we're halfway through the stock numbers (and a packet of M&S extremely chocolatey biscuits), 'you know how I made Maddie swear never to tell anyone at school about the festival because literally everyone would want me to give them free tickets, but you and I talked about telling PopSync once we were sixteen so we could come and do a workshop class, only then ...' I gesture at my leg, currently propped up on a chair with a Tubigrip supporting my ankle and another around my knee.

Aunt Jinnie's eyebrows rise in surprise. 'If you're OK with it, I'm happy to review a recent performance and put them on the schedule *if* I think the quality is right *and* I approve of the workshop plan.'

I clear my throat, nibbling at a biscuit so I don't have to look at her as I say, 'Actually, I was wondering about The Singers – you know, the choir I've joined for my music coursework? We're rubbish right now, but they've agreed to let me take over—'

'Ah,' says Aunt Jinnie succinctly.

I give her an unimpressed stare.

She just leans over and presses a big smacker of a kiss on my forehead.

'Gross,' I tell her. 'An-y-way, we need to record a performance for our coursework, and it would be incredible if that could be at the festival. I mean, how many other A-level music students can say that in their portfolio? A public performance has got to boost our grades – not to mention I will literally die before I submit a repeat of last term's assembly debacle as part of my coursework.'

Aunt Jinnie helps herself to another biscuit, dunking it in her nearly cold tea (vom). 'OK,' she says. 'Same terms and conditions – your group auditions like everyone else and I say no if the audition doesn't cut the mustard.'

'Deal. I'll just say I've got an opportunity we need to audition for, and I'll let them know what it is if we get it, then no one will be super disappointed if doesn't go anywhere.'

'Probably for the best,' Aunt Jinnie says. 'Now, camisole numbers, O Best Beloved Niece.'

Stock numbers done, we discuss suppliers, then spend a happy hour internet-surfing upcoming fashion trends in order to pick the clothing colours for the year.

I almost forget I'm in pain.

I almost manage not to stress over Maddie and why Ren thinks I've called him a freak.

But then Aunt Jinnie asks, 'Is there a reason we're doing this together as opposed to you just presenting me a *fait accompli* as usual?'

I prop my head in my hands. 'I hate my body,' I say, because I'm not ready to talk about the rest, but I need to get something off my chest at least.

Aunt Jinnie is my favourite aunt because she doesn't tell me I'm beautiful and perfect or any of that crap. She just waits for me to tell her more.

'I used to like how I looked, but now I'm losing all my muscle tone and because my stupid body won't do anything I want it to, I can't do anything about it. How can I when I'm so tired I literally can't walk from the car into school some days, let alone exercise?'

Aunt Jinnie puts her hand over mine and squeezes gently. 'It'll be better than this, darling. One day it'll be better than this.'

I try to believe her, but it just makes tears cloud my eyes. How am I ever going to have a relationship? What sort of a career will I be capable of? If it's already this hard with Maddie, how long will it be before I lose her too?

If I just had one thing to give me direction – something on the horizon that I could get a sense of accomplishment from – maybe it would feel like my world is still big and wide, not getting smaller and darker every day.

The best I've got is The Singers, which just says it all.

Still, something is better than nothing. With that, I start formulating a new to-do list.

Monday

(the inevitability has yet to soften the blow)

Item 1: *fix thing with Maddie (again)*
Item 2: *The Singers – cajole/command/kill (delete as applicable)*
Item 3: *mention the festival audition without mentioning it's a festival audition*
Days to festival: 108

When I catch Roksana's eye in the corridor and she nudges Orla's shoulder, I expect a smile or even a nod of approval. It's the least my new favourite dress – royal blue with the outline of the Taj Mahal picked out in gold and silver thread with sequins for the stonework of the domes – deserves. Instead, Orla's eyes narrow in anger and she turns abruptly away.

My face pulls into a scowl as I fix my eyes on the end of the corridor and march past them as quickly as I can (i.e. not quickly at all). I thought perhaps the ice was thawing and they'd realised they'd misjudged me. I might be bossy and forthright, but I'm quite clever and I'm good at organising things so I'm certainly not *all* bad. Though apparently I am a fool, because the sting of their reaction tells me I'd been secretly hoping we would end up friends.

At least it makes it easy not to spill the beans about the audition, I tell myself.

The others are already waiting in the music room, Roksana and Orla slipping in a moment after I've taken my seat, so at least we're able to start on time. 'Be Like Him' is starting to sound lovely enough that, by the time we pause for a break, the atmosphere is almost cordial. Roksana is fiddling with her phone and Benjo is fixing his hair, but no one is giving me the evils. True, Ren is ignoring me, as he has been since the weekend, but I pretend not to notice (this is not the time or the place to sort out whatever it is I've accidentally done to piss him off).

Crossing to the whiteboard, I pick up a marker, feeling anticipation rise in me as I let myself daydream – just for a moment – about what it would be like to perform together at the festival.

'We need to start working out what and where our group performance will be. And, no,' I add before anyone can cut in with the obvious suggestion, 'we're *not* just recording an assembly or some sad school event when we've got to write a critical reflection. What can anyone say about assembly? "The whole school clapped because the teachers glared till they did." Good luck getting above a D with that.'

'Something more like PopSync doing the competition, then,' Roksana says.

I'm about to snap that it's time for her to stop poking that particular sore spot, *thank you very much, and by the way you've just blown my willingness to get us an amazing audition,* but the speculative look in her eyes suggests she wasn't trying to go there.

'I know PopSync did the whole reality-show competition gig, but trust me when I say that the dance side of things is mild compared with the singing programmes,' I tell the others sincerely. 'I overheard some of the runners talking about it before my little PopSync disaster and ... Well, one of them nearly had a panic attack from the memories. On which basis I absolutely veto any suggestion of applying for anything even remotely like *X Factor*.'

We all shudder in unison.

'Great, for once we all agree,' I say. 'Look, I want us to be ambitious with this, but it needs to be the right level of ambition. I maybe have something that would be just a teeny-tiny bit majorly, entirely brilliant ...' I pause to enjoy the little flutter of excitement in my stomach.

And then I realise the gaping flaw in my plan. 'But I've just realised that not only do we need to audition for the brilliant thing, if – and it is a big *if* – we get a yes, we'll need some money to get to the ... performance space where the brilliant thing happens. It's only a few hours away, but we'll probably want to stay overnight if we can.' If it works out, I can't imagine the others won't want to spend a bit of time at the festival, even if they don't stay for the whole three days.

'Anyway,' I say, 'we shouldn't get ahead of ourselves as it's not till June. The point is that now we need to plan for two public performances – an initial one that is both audition *and* fundraiser, then hopefully we get invited to do a second performance at the brilliant thing. If we're sensible, we'll record the first performance so we've got something for our coursework whatever happens with the audition – and we can always donate the money to charity if it's a no.'

'Do we get a hint what this "brilliant thing" is?' asks Fred/George.

His curious grin is infectious and I find myself smiling back.

'I don't want to get everyone's hopes up so let me just say it would be completely on a par with the PopSync competition.'

There's a little stir of excitement. Even Roksana and Orla look intrigued.

'For now I'm not even telling Ms Meade, so it really is a secret rather than me being a jerk. Anyway, get your thinking caps on about what we could do for our audition-slash-fundraiser and we'll talk through everyone's ideas next time.'

Ren is on the far side of the classroom, and I know he'll beat me to the door if he sees me coming, so I slop out into the corridor then lean against the wall, nodding to each of the others as they leave. They all give me a 'you're such a weirdo' look, but that's fair enough.

When it's Ren's turn, I put my stick across the doorway. The problem isn't going away so I might as well face the music – as it were – even though I'm ninety-nine per cent sure the whole thing is Ren's fault, not mine.

'Why are you in a piss with me?' I demand. 'I didn't call *you* a freak, so I don't know what you thought you heard, but that is not what I said.'

He doesn't look at me, merely reaches down to move the stick away. I lean on it, trying to catch his eyes beneath all the hair. He's been worse than usual with it all day. I swear I don't know how he's managed not to fall over.

'This isn't very mature,' I point out.

'Then get out of my way,' he snarls. His voice is so cold and angry I nearly do. He sounds hurt. Really, really hurt.

I reach for his arm, but he stalks back inside to avoid me. 'I know you didn't get the best impression of me in that fight with Maddie, but I don't understand why you're so upset. It's not like we *were* actually flirting with intent, so what's the big deal?' I say, covering the nauseating humiliation with exasperation.

He doesn't reply, though he must be able to hear that I am sorry. With a sigh, I drop my bag and go over to him. He promptly skirts around me and makes a beeline towards the door.

'You can't have been flirting with me,' I say blankly – and unintentionally. It just sort of spills out.

'Why the hell not?' He wheels round so furiously I blink. 'I'm such a freak no girl could possibly imagine I'd dare flirt with her, huh?'

He's gone before I manage to get a word out.

Although I suddenly hurt for him through and through, I find myself laughing in a weird mix of shock and relief.

Just to be clear, I meant that I know no boy in HIS right mind would want to flirt with ME. I was trying to say that I understood you didn't see me like that because only a freak would. It's a comment on ME. I didn't realise you could possibly think it was about you, but I'm sorry you did. I bet you've made yourself miserable about plenty of things that don't actually have anything to do with you. Anyway, that sounds mean, but what I'm trying to say is get over yourself and stop being so cross and hurt when there's no reason for it.

I'm late for English writing this ridiculously long message, but I refuse to go until I've sent it. I just have to hope that Ren, like everyone else, pays not the slightest heed to school rules about not using phones in class.

Ms Walker waves me to the seat next to Ren when I slink into the classroom. I try not to sigh over the fact that he doesn't even look up and he still has his hair fully over his face like a badly groomed Old English Sheepdog. I open my book and try to focus on the lesson, but all I can really think about is Ren at my shoulder, ignoring me.

Then suddenly something pokes my left elbow. I look down and realise it is the prow of a little boat folded out of paper. To my absolute horror, I swear my heart clenches with hope.

Does he ... ? Could he really ... ?

'Isn't origami a bit cliché?' I whisper. 'Why a boat?'

'Why don't you open it and find out?' Ren whispers back, sounding irritated, but at least speaking to me.

'It's pretty. Why would I ruin it?'

What am I saying? goes one half of my brain while the other continues chanting, *Does he . . . ? Could he really . . . ?*

'Oh, for . . .' Ren's mumble dies away as he hunches his shoulder to me and starts scribbling something. A minute later, he slides a note onto my book.

You're ruining it. This is embarrassing now.

I scribble underneath and slide the note back. *Par for the course for self-centred freaks.*

The note comes back. *Too soon.* Though underneath he adds, *Maybe we could have a go at being self-centred freaks who flirt with intent?*

The world seems to white out for a moment.

Is it a joke? It's got to be a joke. He can't . . . can he?

What if I take it seriously and it's some hideous prank?

But I know it's not. Somehow, impossibly, Ren likes me.

He likes me.

It feels as if someone's replaced my blood with lemonade – bitter and sweet and fizzing through me in a way that's so lovely it almost hurts.

As Ms Walker drones on about Shakespeare, I scribble my own note and fold it into a little paper aeroplane and send it sliding towards Ren's elbow. Only apparently I'm really good at paper aeroplanes because it keeps on going, gliding off the next desk and out of the slightly open window.

Ren and I sit staring after it for a moment, then collapse into helpless giggles.

'Is there some reason the two of you think English literature's greatest tragedy is hilarious?' Ms Walker asks. 'Abigail, do you have any thoughts?'

'None, Ms Walker,' says Abigail Moss primly.

'None at all,' I gasp under my breath.

Ren and I make such a noise snorting back our laughter it's a wonder we aren't told to step outside. We spend the rest of the lesson having a very quiet, very gentle elbow war, with Ren periodically asking me, 'What did the airplane say?' and me pretending not to hear him.

Who knew gentle elbow wars made a person's stomach hurt in such a wonderful, wonderful way?

'But what did it say?' Ren whines, as we walk to the cafeteria together.

'Go and find it and you'll see,' I say, letting my arm brush his. I feel the touch rush through my whole body.

'It's raining out there. Do you want me to get pneumonia?' He sweeps open a door with a courtly bow and a smile that makes the back of my neck sting with heat.

'If it's raining so much it'll have dissolved by now,' I tell him nonchalantly.

'Which is why you should tell me.'

'The answer isn't clear enough?' I say, not looking at him, though I can feel his eyes on me.

We walk the rest of the way in silence. But it feels like a happy silence: happy and hopeful and full of meaning, as if every time our eyes meet something important happens.

It's only as we turn from the tills with our lunch trays that I realise the problem that should have been staring me in the face: I don't want to call attention – and teasing – to what's going on between me and Ren, and yet I've been a bad enough best friend lately that I cannot possibly ditch Maddie for him.

'We need to sit with Maddie,' I tell Ren. 'She might be horrible to me – and she is definitely going to comment on you – but there's nothing for it.'

'You haven't made up yet? Should I go and sit pitifully by myself?'

'No, you can come and sit pitifully with PopSync. I assume you know what that is by now because I'd rather not have to explain.'

He quirks an eyebrow. 'I've got the gist.' He opens his mouth to go on, then wisely shuts it.

'Smart move,' I tell him, leading him over to the girls' table. Pip and the others are huddled together, whispering in angst-filled tones about being knocked out of the latest competition in the first round. While Sam and Ashley look up long enough to flash me a smile, Maddie pretends not to see me, even when I jam a spare chair against the side of hers. 'Budge over, lump.'

Maddie sticks her nose in the air. 'Did you hear something?' she asks Pip.

Pip gives me a smirk over Maddie's shoulder, stealing a chip off her plate.

'Move over, Mads. You know you're not cross with me any more, so just shove up and we can pretend we didn't fight, like usual.'

'Maybe I'm developing stamina,' Maddie says. 'Maybe it's coming to me as part of my blossoming as a leader.'

'I guess Ren and I will go somewhere else if you don't want us.'

Maddie looks past me, spots Ren and promptly shoves Pip sideways without even turning to look at her.

It's my turn to smirk at Pip. When I look back at Maddie, I find her gazing at Ren the way she usually looks at fancy shoes. But now, instead of filling me with despair, I'm just excited to see what happens next.

'We met unfavourably at the weekend,' she tells him. 'Don't mind us. Our friendship is actually very happy and fulfilling.'

'I just want to eat my lunch quietly,' Ren says.

'Lovely.' Maddie makes a shooing gesture at the girls along our side of the table. They grumble, but jostle along to make room for the two of us.

Ren has a 'help me' look on the uncovered side of his face as Maddie bombards him with questions about America and suddenly – despite the ache that always comes with being with PopSync – I can't be anything but happy. Which is stupid, because there's more to life than boys. And yet when the most gorgeous boy I've ever seen wants to flirt with intent with me, maybe it's OK that, for the duration of lunch at least, I can't bring myself to care about anything else.

Thursday

(i.e. two days of long, meaningful looks with Ren later)

Item 1: sort out fundraising-meets-audition performance so we can sing at the festival and get the best A-level music marks in history.

Item 2: figure out how this contributes to broader world domination plans

We (WE! Ren and me! Together!) arrive at the music room for The Singers' second free-period session of the week to find the others sitting in the middle of the space. They're all still in their usual cliques, but they're talking to each other.

Ms Meade finishes gathering her papers from the desk at the front, lifts an eyebrow in a silent 'good luck' and makes good her escape.

'So,' I say, as I plonk myself down, 'the person auditioning us has agreed to come and check us out at the mall, so I've applied for a busking licence. With any luck, we'll raise at least some of the transportation and accommodation money we'll need if it works out.'

'Transport where?' Benjo asks worriedly. 'I don't like coaches or buses or aeroplanes.'

'He pukes non-stop,' puts in Twin 1, who I think might be Fred, if Fred is the one who tends to wear blue and is a bit more assertive.

'Seriously, non-stop. It's why we don't do more gigs,' says maybe-George.

Benjo turns his back on him, knocking his bag over and spilling its contents across the floor in the process.

'We can drive – it's only two hours,' I explain. 'But trust me, if the auditioner says yes, you will be OK with puking on any form of transport necessary.'

Benjo gives me a dubious look as he finishes stuffing books and notes back into his bag. 'I'm not convinced this is legit, but, just in case, I will temporarily stop being an obstructive little shit. We can consider it a probationary truce.'

'Lovely,' I tell him. 'I expect that to go for all of you. On that note, everyone's going to be in charge of one aspect of each performance so we all have something different to focus on in our reflective pieces – also so I don't have to do everything.' I turn to Orla. 'Since you always look nice, can you think about what we could all wear that would make us look unified? It's fine if we can't get it sorted in time for the mall performance, but it would be good to have a plan and a budget so we can figure out a rough fundraising target in advance.'

'I'm not wearing anything embarrassing,' Benjo says quickly.

The rest of us stare at him. He's currently wearing a lime-green polo shirt and purple jeans.

'You and the Twins wear bow-ties for performances,' Orla says. 'I've seen you.'

'Bow-ties are the established barbershop-music look.'

'Established fashion crime,' says Orla, but then she makes a 'settle down' gesture. 'Fine. I'll work out something we can all be comfortable in. Roks can help me.'

'Actually, I thought Roksana could be in charge of making leaflets and a banner. You're doing art, right, and you're always carrying around that huge portfolio, so I figure that's probably your thing?'

Roksana looks astonished that I've noticed. 'Sure.'

'I'm going to be on planning, obviously – the busking licence, logistics and all that.'

Possibly-Fred raises a hand. 'I am learning how to edit videos. I want to make us a YouTube channel and take care of recording our performances.'

I blink at him. 'Wow. Yes, please. Social media and publicity stuff isn't necessary for our coursework, but it'll give us extra things to talk about in our critical reflections – and it'll definitely help our fundraising – so sold to ... Fred?' I ask, grimacing, but to my relief get both an eye-roll and a nod. 'George? Any hidden talents?' I ask Twin 2.

'Photography. I'm in for creating an Instagram account and providing any still images Roks or Fred need.'

'Great. Pics will definitely liven up our portfolios and, again, it can only be good for our fundraising. Benjo, since you do the equipment for the trio, could you . . .'

He nods. 'And I can also take care of checking all the arrangements to ensure all the parts keep to a reasonable vocal range. I asked Ms Meade if we could help each other with stuff like that and she said it's fine so long as it's just feedback, not doing changes if they're needed.'

'OK,' I say faintly, wondering if I'm dreaming, because it seems like we're not just getting along but making actual substantial progress. 'Anyone not happy with the plan?'

Silence around the room. I turn to Ren last. He's grinning at me from behind his hair.

'Don't think I don't have plans for you,' I tell him.

His grin widens.

I give him a baleful stare. 'You're in charge of helping everyone put a rock-gospel spin on their compositions or arrangements so the group has a cohesive sound.' I take a deep breath as a nervous heat rushes through me. 'And you and I are going to be a pair for arranging purposes.' I turn back to the others, but not before I see a smile quirk up the corner of Ren's lips. The relief is like a cool breeze.

'I figure it's going to be Roks and Orla, then, Benjo, are you OK to pair up with both Fred and George for a song, since you're big on arranging and we've got an odd number to deal with?'

Wonder of further wonders, absolutely no one argues.

All of a sudden we have a plan.

The Saturday of the Maybe-a-Date

Item 1: *get through maybe-a-date without humiliating myself or making Ren hate me.*

Item 2: *don't waste maybe-a-date angsting about tomorrow and the chronic pain group.*

Item 3: *no, you can't cancel tomorrow – you promised your loving parents you'd go.*

I know the chronic pain group is going to be a bunch of old people with arthritis, and I'm glad they have that support, but I just can't see what they'll have to offer someone my age with my condition. I wish Mum and Dad understood that even with my expectations most thoroughly managed, part of me keeps hoping against hope that there's something out there that will miraculously fix everything: I've had so many new scans, new doctors, new pills, new physio exercises where I thought, *After this, I'll be OK again*, then nothing changed, and yet I can't seem to stop believing that maybe this time ...

But right now I've got better things to think about than false hope.

I meet Ren at the edge of Market Square, as agreed last night, and manage a credible impression of someone who isn't nervous at all as I lead him through the bustle of the pedestrian zone, packed with shoppers and tourists and students, to one of my favourite places in the world. The Tea Party is an *Alice in Wonderland*-themed cafe with cakes that are literally fantasy made real. Unfortunately, we have to go all the way around the block to avoid Abigail Moss and her pack (yes, I know, but being tired and slightly sweaty will put a much smaller dent in my efforts to be cool and collected than facing her and ending up frothing with fury). At least I get to show off my (only pieces of) local knowledge as I point out the seventeenth-century market hall and Elizabethan inn (now a Michelin-starred restaurant).

'So, what *are* your plans for me?' Ren asks as we finally settle into a corner booth in The Tea Party with a tray of tea and mini-cakes. He cuts a line through the middle of the lemon drizzle then pauses, frowning, when he sees me staring at him in bewilderment. 'What?' he says self-consciously. 'I don't know which one's your favourite yet.'

My stomach does a weird fluttery-clenchy-happy thing. I am officially pathetic. 'We could share them all if you like?' My voice has gone weird: high and a bit squeaky. I glance at him just as he does the same and suddenly we're giggling and I'm not nervous any more.

Well, only a bit nervous instead of composed entirely of nerves.

'Before we discuss Singing Group plans, can you just explain how the whole US-military-in-the-UK thing works?' I ask as I pour the tea. 'Is your dad stationed here permanently now or . . . I mean, you are staying through A-levels, right?'

'Definitely,' Ren says fervently. 'I am done with new schools and my mum wanted a forever home, so hopefully this is it. My parents split up last year – but it's fine,' Ren hurries on when I pull a face at the realisation that my attempt at a simple get-to-know-you question was anything but. 'We actually get more time with him now – or at least better time. And it's great not to be endlessly moving, plus we all needed a change after . . .' His hand moves up as if to cover his scars.

I sip quietly at my tea, waiting to see if he wants to tell me about them. 'I'm all ears if you'd like me to be, but since I'm doing a sterling job of asking awkward questions, I think I'll let you decide what you want to say on that score.'

Ren grimaces. 'Maybe another time? This is really . . . nice. I don't want to ruin the moment with all that.'

I nudge the bigger half of the carrot-cake slice in his direction. 'So how about your US friends? Do you keep up online or . . .'

The expression that passes over Ren's face makes me wince. 'Yikes. I'm really finding all the sore spots, huh?'

He laughs, shaking his head. 'I've spent my life making new

friends every two to four years and, trust me, it doesn't make a lot of difference whether you're two hundred miles apart or two thousand. If you're not hanging out all the time, things are just different, you know?'

'Yeah.' I clear my throat. 'You've seen how things are going with me and Maddie.'

'No comment,' says Ren wisely. 'Though you don't seem too broken up about hardly seeing the rest of PopSync any more.'

I snort. 'Clearly I was tremendously subtle at lunch.'

'Unlike the rest of the time when you're so shy and reserved in your opinions?' Then his face falls. 'As someone with plenty of experience losing my whole friendship group, I can say with some authority it's not always the worst thing in the world.'

I tilt my head, wondering whether I dare ask and deciding I do. (You cannot be surprised at this point.) 'So, your friends at your last school – is it more of a Maddie situation or a Pip one?'

'Pip's the one who looks like her middle name is Smug?'

I nearly choke on my tea. 'Oh, I am calling her that in my head from now on.'

'Just don't blame me if you do it out loud,' he says. 'Actually, my friends at my last school were OK.'

'But . . .'

Ren raises his hand to the scarred side of his face once more before he drags it down and starts picking pieces off his brownie. 'My brother's lot were . . . not the best people. That's the real reason Mum decided to move us over here – she said she wanted to be nearer her folks after the split with Dad, but it was really about Tai.'

'Younger brother?'

'Older – two years – so he's finished school.' He puts a piece of brownie in his mouth then busies himself topping up our teacups. 'Now he's … considering his plans. You know, with the move and all. So how about your folks?' Ren says not at all awkwardly. 'Just one of you?'

'No siblings but I have the world's worst cousin,' I tell him. And because I can never mention My Awful Cousin Stef without going on a rant, I proceed to do just that. Thankfully it does the trick and Ren relaxes again.

I break off when I realise he's biting his lip as if he's about to start laughing. 'What?' I demand. 'Do you really think laughing at me when I'm mid-rant is a smart thing to do?'

Ren pulls a weird face.

'Why are you looking like that?'

'I'm trying to assume a "listening attentively" expression.'

I roll my eyes, grab my bag and stick, then stump over to the counter to pay, because if I stay still I might give into the urge to lean over and kiss him and I am not ready to find out how he'd react. 'Do you want a lift home? I've got the car,' I call over my shoulder.

'What are you doing?' he asks, appearing next to me with a frown on his face.

I raise my eyebrows. 'Paying for our tea and cake? You know, like people do in shops? They love me here, but that only goes so far.'

It takes me a moment to realise that Ren is fumbling for his wallet.

'Let me get this,' he says awkwardly, not meeting my eyes.

'You need to pay, do you, because I'm the girl? This was my idea, so it's my dollar. Well, pound, but whatever.'

'Can't I—'

The look I give him shuts him up, but still he shifts awkwardly from foot to foot, clearly not happy about it. 'Are you a sexist pig?' I ask him.

'Of course not. I mean, it's usual for the guy to pay but—'

'No buts. Either you're not a sexist pig and I get to pay since I suggested coming here, or you are a sexist pig who doesn't want to admit he thinks sexist stereotypes about who pays actually have some merit.'

Ren runs his hands through his curls, then quickly drops them, glancing around to see if anyone saw the scars. And just like that all my righteous irritation is gone, melted away by the need to reach out and touch him. My hand acts without permission and does just that, sliding across the back of his where it's clenched on the counter.

He deflates. 'I could at least pay half. That's what actual equality looks like, you know.'

'Or you could pick the next thing and it'll be your turn to pay?' There's a wistful hopefulness in my voice I never intended, and I'm glad of the excuse to turn away as the waitress offers my change. When I turn back, Ren is slouching against the counter, smiling at me from under his curls in a way that makes me understand the phrase 'heart in your throat' for the first time ever.

'Am I allowed to suggest we come here again next time, or does it have to be somewhere new for me to get to pay?' he asks, as he hurries ahead to hold the door for me.

I shrug. 'You just can't think of anywhere cooler than this, can you?'

'It's quite an ask. Hey, is that Roks and Orla?'

I follow his gaze and there they are, standing behind a stall at the edge of the weekend market.

The stall is in two parts: half has jewel-coloured embroidered shawls and loose shirts, and the other has an odd assortment of 'hand-blown, hand-painted eggs' and cheerfully decorated wooden pencil-pots and picture-frames. A sign at the back advertises nail decoration. Roksana turns from her last customer to see us loitering at the end.

'I didn't know you did all this.' I look about admiringly, but Roksana's face darkens.

'What about it?' she demands.

'Nothing,' I say. 'I was just coming over to be friendly. Figured I'd ask your thoughts about perhaps getting The Singers a stall one weekend as an additional fundraising opportunity. We could do a bake-sale or—'

'Has it not occurred to you that we might have something more important to do with what we earn here?' Roksana snaps. 'You may have pocket-money coming out of your ears, but some people have actual bills to pay, not just a "new boots every other day" fund. You're not having any part of my rent or my university savings, thank you very much.' She's puce and panting by the time she's done, shoulders heaving, and hands clenched as if she's about to climb over the stall to fight me.

I realise my mouth is slightly open and close it. 'No,' I say quietly. 'It didn't occur to me. Thanks for bringing it to my attention so nicely instead of being a cow about it.' The moment it comes out I feel even worse, because I *was* being oblivious, I get that, but she could just have pointed it out without making me sound like the worst person ever. And anyway, where does she get off going on about where my money is coming from or how I spend it when she's equally oblivious about what's going on in my life?

I march away before I can make the whole thing even worse, getting a good ten metres before I remember Ren was with me. Does he have to be there every time I get into a fight? I grit my teeth as I imagine smashing a cymbal into Roksana's face. I do not need a new nemesis at school. I'm already exercising those muscles plenty with Abigail Moss.

'Is there some history with Roks I should know about,' Ren asks, appearing at my shoulder, 'or do you just bring out the raging psycho in everyone?'

I turn, ready to let rip, but he's grinning in this oddly fond way that makes all my irritation evaporate. 'I honestly don't know what her problem is with me. We've never had a falling out. I mean, there was some sullen muttering and glaring when I made a few particularly astute suggestions about Singing Group last term, but they were all ignored so . . .' I spread my hands helplessly, pointedly ignoring the content of what Roks just said as I'm not calm enough yet to accept what I already know – that she's being unpleasant about it, but has a point. 'I think she just hates my face,' I say, like the mature, non-defensive nearly adult person I am.

Ren flinches. 'Can't see why she'd care about yours if she doesn't about mine,' he says, voice suddenly tight.

I reach out and pull him to a stop, dragging at his arm until he meets my eyes. 'I know it's complicated and I'm not going to tell you how to feel about any of it but – for the record – I like your face. I like it a whole lot.'

The corners of Ren's mouth twist up, though his eyes are still full of misery. He squeezes my hand. 'Well, I'm glad someone does.'

Before I can stop myself, I'm reaching up to cup his cheek. Suddenly my heart is hammering against my ribs as if I've been running, my breath coming tight and sharp. Should I ask him if I can kiss him? If the answer is no I will literally die so ... No, we're standing here, staring into each other's eyes, my hand on his face, so I just need to woman up and ask ... and then hopefully not topple over going up on my tiptoes to reach his lips – assuming he says yes, *please let him say yes ...*

'Ven! It's so fun you're here!' someone shrieks by my ear, and the moment is broken. I stumble sideways, only realising the shrieker is Pip – whom I want to kill at the best of times – when she catches me. 'We have a new routine and I have *so* many questions for you!' she burbles straight into my eardrum.

How can she still be ruining my sanity even now I'm not in PopSync? I have definitely offended the gods or the fates – probably both, given how things are going.

The Chronic-Pain Party

Item 1: be my best self and give this experience a chance.

I suppose it shouldn't be a surprise, since I'm here for a chronic pain self-help group, but all the disabled parking bays are taken. When I finally find an empty regular spot, it's down the opposite end of the car park and I seriously consider just going home, as walking all that way then feeling rotten seems more self-defeating than self-helping. But although I've been alternately ignoring it and pretending everything will be fine, I need to face up to whether I'm going to manage my normal festival work, let alone if I've got a performance with The Singers to juggle too, so I slop my way progressively more sloppily to the door to see if there are any solutions on the other side.

I am late, a bit sweaty and a lot miserable by the time I arrive at the room the receptionist pointed me to. The group all turn to stare as I shove through the door.

'Sorry. Took me ages to walk from the car park,' I say.

A woman in a pink cardigan one hundred per cent the wrong colour for her complexion beckons me over and fetches a spare chair, setting it next to hers in the circle. 'You must be Venetia.'

'Ven,' I snap. 'I mean, I prefer Ven,' I add in a conciliatory tone.

'We were just introducing ourselves. You'll be at the end so you'll see what to do.'

I fix a smile on my face as I look around the circle. Everyone here is at least a decade older than me and most of them are *old*. Almost all of them are giving me a suspicious up and down – the look that says, 'You seem surprisingly young and healthy for someone who's meant to be in pain', because it's obviously impossible to be young, slim-ish and still have health issues. I already don't like the lot of them. Which is not particularly helpful when I'm apparently here to tell a bunch of strangers about my deepest fears and miseries. I am already regretting the whole thing.

I blank the intros so it takes me a moment to realise the room is silent and waiting for me. 'I'm Ven. I'm here to see if this is for me. I just want to listen today, but if anyone has any tips for managing a solid week's work at a music festival where I need to be on my feet all day, I'll take them.'

The whole group looks at me as if I've farted. Twice. Unapologetically.

'Right,' says the facilitator, with a rather frozen smile. 'Does anyone have any suggestions?'

'When I went to my niece's wedding last summer, I tried a hunting stick – it's like a walking stick, but there's a bit that folds out and you angle it against the ground then sort of prop yourself on it. It's not sitting, but it's better than nothing.'

I give the woman a smile. It isn't going to help at the festival since the end will just skid off the smooth tiles of the building we use for the box office, but it might not be the worst idea for parties where there's a wooden floor or carpet or grass.

'Well, to be honest,' the woman continues, tone suddenly sharp and anything but encouraging, 'the seat bit makes the stick so heavy that by the end of the day I felt worse than I normally do at these events. Took me eight weeks to get over it . . .'

And they're off into a horse-race of galloping accounts of misery and woe. Maybe this is just the World's Worst Self-Help Group™ but within five minutes they're basically just one-upping each other about how bad their pain is and how bad their condition is and how bad their prognosis is. I mean, I get it, but why do none of them want to discuss stuff that they could do that would be fulfilling and enjoyable and help distract them from the pain? Why aren't they talking about how important it is to have achievable goals and what that means when you're dealing with health issues? I'm not living in their bodies or experiencing their lives, but I just can't see how any of this is helping when literally every word out of their mouths just depresses me more than the last.

If there isn't good stuff – like the festival, or acing exams or even growing the world's best pumpkins – what is life for? If this is the best I've got to look forward to when I'm their age, hold the morphine and pass me the arsenic.

I want a life that is good and big and full. I refuse to have nothing but pain.

Which is precisely why I am going to leave before I start screaming abuse at these people – it wouldn't be right or fair and it would only make me feel worse.

'Not feeling well, got to go,' I say in the direction of the facilitator.

'See you next week, Ven?' she calls after me.

But I am busy fumbling at the door. I need out, I need out, *I need out.*

I cannot be here.

I sit in the car and cry. My head is full of cruel, hateful things it almost rips me apart not to say. Why do I want to go back in there and shout at that group of strangers? Why do I want to hurt those people who are hurting already? Why do I feel as if they've hurt me? It's like someone has torn off my skin of niceness and goodness and shown me that everything underneath is rotten with fury.

'I *hate* them,' I hiss at the windscreen. 'I *hate* those people.'

I am literally shaking with fury. What is wrong with me?

'I hate myself,' I whisper.

Shame and rage and helplessness swallow me.

For a while I just sit in the car and cry and shudder and wipe snot onto my sleeves.

Still Sunday

Item 1 (revised): DISTRACTION!!

When nothing works to take my mind off the morning, I grab my phone and message Ren before I can overthink it. *Having a rubbish day. Want to arrange the shit out of some music?*

My brain promptly goes into a spiral of, *What if he thinks I'm being clingy, wanting to get together again when we only had our first maybe-a-date yesterday? Why am I so hopeless?*

My phone pings.

Yours or mine?

Oh. He's inviting me over. We'll both have been to each other's houses. That's got to mean he still likes me, even after everything with Roks and Orla yesterday, doesn't it?

Yours, I type back quickly. *My family is currently having an extended discussion about toilets. I NEED TO LEAVE.* The moment I hit send my brain wakes up. *OMG, why did you say that? WHY?* it shrieks at me.

Don't ask about the loos, I reply frantically, as three little 'typing' dots appear on Ren's end. *Seriously just . . . let me delete that and we can pretend it never happened.*

I'm gutted but will console myself by putting on the kettle and seeing if I can find some biscuits.

I want chocolate ones.

Oh God, that was demanding, not flirty. Why am I like this?

Well buy some on the way then.

Too tired to walk into the shop. Has that saved it or does it sound whiny and self-pitying?

Should I run down to the cornerstore? I might not be back before you get here but if you give me 10 it should work.

No. Don't humour my unreasonableness. But do find the biscuits. It's imperative.

That sounded all sarcastic and collected and not at all bundle-of-nerves-because-I-fancy-him-*way*-more-than-should-be-allowed, right? *Right?*

I make myself gather my stuff and get going before I can start agonising over whether I should change into something nicer first, like different clothes will somehow compensate for my body being what it is.

'I have found chocolate biscuits,' Ren says as he opens the door.

'Well, that's something then,' I say. 'I might have left otherwise.'

Ren rolls his eyes but leads me into the living room, where I peruse the family photos on the mantelpiece. There is a sharp divide between the left-hand side, which is all pictures of a man and two teenage boys, and the right, where the photos show a woman with the same two boys. In the middle, there's one older group shot of the four of them together. Wow. Wonder who came up with this not-at-*all*-symbolic arrangement.

I turn and take in the rest of the room, including the pile of unopened boxes in the corner. 'Love your decorating style.'

'We think of it as Amazon Warehouse Chic,' Ren says, disappearing through the far door. 'Be back with tea.'

It gives me time to go back to the mantelpiece and be extra nosy, though it's a while before I realise what's different about the Ren in most of the photos: his hair is shorter, pushed back from his face, and there are no scars. At most he looks about two years younger, so the scars are a new-ish thing.

I squint into the photo that looks the most recent. Ren's standing on his mother's right, his brother on her left. None of them look particularly thrilled to be having their picture taken. Ren is turned slightly towards his brother and there is a troubled frown on his face. His brother looks like Ren but a bit older and a bit less gorgeous, but also ... taut. I don't know how to describe it. Ren's athletic – tall, big shoulders, strong without being either muscley or skinny. Ren's brother is probably no thinner but it's like someone has pulled all his strings tight. There's something in his eyes that makes me uncomfortable.

'Caffeine, sugar, chocolate,' Ren announces.

I turn and follow the tray to the coffee table, then slump by stages onto the floor.

'The chairs don't bite,' Ren says, raising an eyebrow.

'Comfy here,' I mumble, seizing a plate and two biscuits and stuffing the first into my mouth.

Ren pours my tea and adds just the right amount of milk and sugar. I tilt my head as I watch him, feeling my face heat at the realisation that he'd been making mental notes in The Tea Party. He catches me watching and tips his hair further over his face.

I lean forwards to brush it back, then swerve away at the last moment to take another biscuit, even though it makes me look like a greedy pig. I do want another biscuit, though. It's been a 'three chocolate biscuit' sort of day, in case you hadn't noticed.

I gesture to the corner without the boxes but with a gorgeous baby grand. 'Whose piano?'

'Family piano. Mum and Tai both play too.'

'Are they as good as you?'

Ren's smile is shy and gentle.

It does funny things to my insides. 'Is that what you want to do after school?'

Ren shakes his head. 'I want to compose. Do you like musicals?'

I shrug. 'Sure.'

'That's what I want to do. Big old-school musicals with chorus lines, the works. How about you?'

My smile falls and I look away. 'Still figuring out my new plan since the old one's about as much use as Abigail Moss's brain.'

I startle when I feel a hand on my shoulder, gentle and warm. I turn to find Ren has joined me on the floor. It feels as if I've frozen as he raises a hand and brushes my hair back from my face, his thumb lingering on my cheek.

We nearly kissed in the market and now . . .

There's a crash and a curse in the hallway.

'Who the hell put this here?' demands an angry voice. A moment later, Ren's brother comes into the living room, holding my stick.

'Sorry!' I squeak. 'I thought I'd tucked it out of the way.'

'What's this even for?' Tai looks at me, then at Ren, lip curled in a sneer. 'Even you can do better than the type of halfwit who uses hiking poles in a town.' He glances at my walking stick – black, accessorised with red and gold dragon decals – and scoffs. 'More like a freaking swagger stick. What kinda moron thinks "cripple" is a fashion trend?'

I physically flinch. It's one thing to know the word technically applies. It's another to have it flung in my face. And though I know there should be no shame it in, humiliation burns through me.

Beside me Ren makes a noise like the air's been knocked out of him.

'How about disabled people? Where do we fit into your hierarchy of who's good enough to be in your house?' I snarl as I push to my knees, then my feet.

Tai's eyes, blown wide with surprise, narrow as he turns back to Ren, ignoring me. 'You can do better than mutual pity, bro.'

I turn to apologise to Ren for the fact that I'm about to

verbally eviscerate his brother. But instead of finding horrified embarrassment that Tai would talk to me like that, there's nothing on Ren's face at all because he's too busy looking at the floor. 'Are you seriously not going to say anything?' I demand.

Ren just hunches into himself. 'Tai,' he says, quiet and wretched, 'you can't say stuff like that. Don't you want me to have a life? You know girls aren't exactly queueing up to spend time with guys like me.'

'This,' Tai growls, gesturing at his brother's face, 'is *not* the same as this,' he says, shaking my stick.

Ren wrings his handless helplessly. 'Tai, please,' he whispers. 'You're being awful. It's not fair to drag her into this. Can't you just go away?'

Tai folds his arms.

Ren peers through his hair at me, with a pathetic attempt at a grin. 'He's got a bad case of foot-in-mouth syndrome, but you and I know how it goes with first impressions.'

Everything in me turns to ice: I blaze from the inside with it. 'Oh, right. The problem is him saying the quiet bit out loud, is it? You know what, if he thinks I'm so broken and worthless no one could ever want me unless they're out of options, I'd rather know so I can avoid having anything to do with him. And thanks for making clear you're exactly the same as your charming brother, just better at keeping it PC. I'll leave you to bask in each other's charming company.'

I storm over to Tai, rip my stick from his hand, then slam out of the front door.

Yelling erupts behind me, and for a moment I think Ren is about to come running after me. *Please let him be coming after me/no don't*, says my brain in a way that makes my head hurt as much as my heart because, unlike Ren, I know it's better to have no one than someone who doesn't think you're special, just equally broken.

Guess that's that, I tell myself.

Still, my chest and eyes and throat burn all the way home.

I Actually Wish it Were Monday at This Point . . .

Item 1 (revised): DISTRACTION 2.0 ACTIVATED

Days to festival: 102

I turn my misery into productivity and lose myself in the festival for the rest of the day. Well, almost. Far too much of my brain is busy with the sneaking suspicion that maybe if everyone hates me, I'm the one at fault . . . even though it feels like I'm trying my best to the point where I will splinter into pieces if I pile any more pressure on.

Sometimes I think the pain is getting into my brain, warping me from the inside, constantly looming over everything till I don't know how I can keep breathing because I can't stand it, and yet

I have to because there is no way out ... No way out except the one-way exit.

Subject change! Subject change! Emergency Distraction Techniques Re-deployed!

Thankfully, there are endless things to obsess over with the festival. Today it is merchandise designs, now that Mum has finally picked this year's line-up. My uncle's graphic-designer best friend does our posters and T-shirts as a favour. Unfortunately, as part of the trade, my uncle lets Richard (or Designer Dick, as I like to call him) sell his own range of special T-shirts and posters too, so guess which have the good designs?

'His ones,' you say? *Ding-ding-ding*, we have a winner for this year's Award for Most Obvious Outcome in the World!

As such, I am unsurprised to open the latest design files and find the names of three bands misspelled on the poster that lists all the acts, two others are missed off entirely and several are so badly formatted that they have, effectively, been combined. The result is viral-tweet-worthy for all the wrong reasons. I fire off an email about the errors and remind Designer Dick of the deadline for getting the artwork to the printer. Last year I had to fix it myself. Since I have neither the skills nor the graphics software, only my sheer awesomeness saved the day (and a free thirty-day trial of Photoshop).

You're not awesome – everyone hates you, says my brain.

I will not think about Ren. I will not think about Roksana, I tell myself.

I turn to the logo file for the clothing merch. Although the basic festival logo never changes, we dress up the merch version differently each year to help encourage regular festival-goers to always buy a T-shirt or other item of clothing. Last year we had stars and clouds. This year we've gone for a nature theme, so it's blossom and trees. Or at least it's meant to be. This monstrosity looks like something a particularly angry, art-hating toddler came up with. It's just depressing.

My thoughts drift again to Ren but I wrench them back. *My family is counting on me. I am a good, loving daughter and niece. I am not going to let them down.*

I check the name of the festival for typos (yes, that happened once), attach the logo to the stocklist, plonk in the supplier's email address, then sit with my finger hovering over the 'send' button.

We've had blah logos before, but this particular offering is vile. The merch will probably sell better without it – but of course it's not merch if there's no logo. Maybe nothing will come of stalling, but we do have a bit of time before the order has to go in. I might as well use it to see if I can turn this catastrophe-in-the-making around somehow.

A knock on my bedroom door startles me. I'm expecting it to be Mum with a cup of tea, but it's Maddie. Which somehow makes my heart simultaneously lift and sink. Everything between the two of us is so raw that, though I desperately want to talk to her about Ren and his awful brother, I'm not sure I dare. What if she says something thoughtless because of what's going on in our friendship and I just can't get past it?

'Your mum insisted I bring provisions,' she says quietly,

manoeuvring a laden tea-tray around the door.

There's a dejected droop to her shoulders that sees me quickly move my laptop onto the bedside table and draw my knees up so Maddie can put the tray down between us. She passes me my mug, but I wave away the chocolate biscuits – just the thought makes my stomach twinge after everything that happened at Ren's house. I wait for her to speak, but she just sits there, looking into her tea.

'I don't know what you want from me, Maddie,' I whisper. 'I can't sit on the sidelines, watching. I'm just not built like that.'

Maddie sniffs, then she puts her tea aside, takes my mug from my hands and puts it on the dresser before curling up with her head on my pillow. I lie back with her and let her cuddle into my side and inadvertently (I hope) wipe her nose on my jumper. The fact that I do not ewwww is proof of my deep and abiding love and devotion.

'Whatever I said that's sticking in your teeth, I'm sorry, OK?' I whisper.

'It's not that!' Maddie says in a quavering little wail.

I prod her. 'Then what? Just spit it out, Mads.'

She shakes her head, tears spilling down her cheeks. 'I want to do something awful. You'll hate me.'

'It's theoretically possible but unlikely in practice.'

'Don't snark at me, Ven. Not right now.'

'I won't snark if you *just tell me*.'

Maddie takes a deep breath, opens her mouth ... then turns and sobs into my pillow. I pat her on the shoulder. After five minutes, the pats turn to prods.

'Stop being a drama queen. You're turning into Pip and I really might hate you if you do that.'

Finally, she rolls onto her back and wipes her face with her sleeve. Now we're both snot-covered. If this isn't the foundation of a life-long friendship, then I'm going to be very annoyed about the amount of nose-juice I've been subjected to.

'I hate it, Ven,' she whispers. 'I hate PopSync.' She claps her hands over her face.

She can't possibly mean it – unless I've missed something not just huge but ginormous.

'I thought you loved it. I thought you were just as into it as I was,' I say blankly.

Maddie groans into her hands. 'I was.' She takes a shuddering breath then lowers her hands. 'I loved it when you did all the work.'

I frown. 'But I didn't, Mads. You were always there—'

'Backing you up,' Maddie finishes for me. 'You were the one who got us going and decided what we were doing. You were the leader, Ven, and it made it fun.' She swallows hard, her eyes filling with tears again. 'It was *so* much fun . . . but it's not now I've got to do it all myself.'

I grimace. 'You just need to ask the others for help—'

'Pip doesn't want to help. She wants to take over. And the others . . .' She trails off. 'You probably think I'm pathetic, and maybe I am, but I don't want the responsibility. I don't *want* to be the one who has to make herself get up and rehearse when I'm tired – and then make everyone else do it too because there's always some new competition coming up and maybe this one will be our lucky break, only it's not and . . .' She throws her hands in the air. 'It's always such a fight now, and I hate it.'

'So you want me to come back to do all the heavy lifting – and you think it's fine to ask that of me, even though I don't get any of the fun any more?' I ask, low and dangerous.

Maddie closes her eyes and seems to deflate, even though she's already lying flat on her back. 'No,' she whispers. 'I really thought you'd change your mind and *want* to get back to it. You always seemed to love that bit as much as the dancing and I just thought with a little time . . .' She holds up a hand before I can say any of the awful things now frothing on my lips. 'Don't yell at me, Ven. I get it now. I wasn't trying to be stupid. I really did think you'd change your mind. But I get it now,' she repeats softly. 'I just don't know what to do about it because I hate doing it without you. I think maybe I'd rather not do it at all.'

I'm so surprised I just sit there, staring down at her. The idea that maybe Maddie went along with PopSync because of me, rather than because she loved it . . .

But it *can't* be that. Maddie loves to dance. I fell in love with it because she begged me to go to classes with her back in primary school so she'd have a friend there. It's been our lives ever since – and only more so when we got to secondary school and formed PopSync. I thought we'd never look back but . . .

A quiet sob cuts my thoughts short. I reach out and clasp Maddie's ankle.

'If you want to do dance at uni, then you need PopSync,' I say. 'It would be stupid to quit if you're still even considering a dance career. But,' I add, when Maddie looks like she's about to cut in, 'maybe you could stop doing the bits you hate.'

'But how the hell do I do that if you won't come back?' she snivels, wiping her nose on the back of her hand.

'You let Pip take over,' I tell her.

Now it's her turn to stare at me speechlessly.

'It'd be a whole different set of issues, and I doubt PopSync will be winning anything, unless all the other competitors come down with gastric flu, but you'll still be able to put it on uni applications, and you'll still be able to dance with the girls. And you can bet Pip won't arrange half as many practice sessions as I did, though there will probably be double the number of shopping trips.'

Maddie gives a wet little snort of laughter, then claps her hands to her face when a bubble of snot erupts with it.

'Gross,' I tell her lovingly. 'Moving rapidly on . . . For A-level purposes you're going to have to ditch PopSync and join The Singers. You'll be better off counting our performances towards your grade once Pip's in charge – Ms Meade and the others won't mind. We could do with another female voice and there's still plenty of time to get you up to scratch. Especially since, you know, I'm the leader and all.'

'Do you mean that?' Maddie whispers. 'I thought you'd feel like I was throwing away everything we'd built. Pip'll ruin it. You know she will.'

I shrug. 'So what?' I jostle my shoulder against Maddie's. 'Let her do her worst. I may be the world's bossiest person, but your life is up to *you*, Mads. You can say no to anything you don't want to do.'

'Really, Ven?' She gives me a pointed look, but there's a soft glisten to her eyes that belies the lightness of her words. 'Has saying no to you ever ended well for anyone?'

I stick out my tongue even as I curl my hand into hers. 'Even if we aren't chasing the same dream, we can still do the rest together. It's got to be easier if you're happier and I'm less jealous, right?'

Maddie rolls her eyes, but tucks her head onto my shoulder. 'I'm sorry you don't get to carry on dancing,' she whispers.

'I know,' I whisper back, throat choked with grief. 'I'm glad you do, PopSync or otherwise.'

Then we just sit there together and, though my eyes sting and my chest burns with anger at all I've lost, suddenly it no longer feels as if the grief is wound around my heart.

Monday

(urgh)

Item 1: ignore Ren while turning The Singers into a competent choir – nothing simpler.

It's just as well I patched things up with Maddie or I'd never have been able to face Ren. I think about telling her but decide I can't face putting it into words. It's enough that she'll have my back when I'm ready to explain.

Armed with the confidence of knowing I'm a good enough person to still have Maddie as a best friend, I arrive at school in an absolutely stunning FCUK sculpted off-shoulder denim dress, with a fitted black shirt over the top.

'Hi,' Ren says, sitting down next to me in English.

'Hi,' I say, not looking up from the notes I'm scribbling in the margins of my text. I play it so deliciously cool I'm both surprised and impressed with myself.

'I thought about messaging you but figured I should probably apologise in person.'

I give him a bland little smile. 'Don't worry about it,' I say, and go back to my book.

Although I'd also enjoy strangling him with my stick, there's a surprising amount of vicious satisfaction in denying him any reaction at all. Neither he nor his stinking brother are worth the oxygen.

'So, we're still on speaking terms.' His voice is both relieved and confused, like he's waiting to find out he's the punchline of some strange joke.

'Apparently so,' I say in a tone of unobjectionable mildness. Maybe acting should be my new dream because I am rocking this Ice Queen thing.

Ren opens his mouth then closes it again. Finally, he says, 'So if I messaged you later—' Oh, the delicate hope in his voice, as if he really thinks there's a chance I'm going to pretend Sunday never happened.

'Why would you need to?' I ask. 'Expecting trouble understanding our homework?'

'I should have stood up for you,' Ren whispers.

'That would have been nice,' I agree, shrugging one shoulder, 'but such is life.'

'Could we maybe make a plan for you to yell at me and call me names or—'

'I'll stick with being mature about it. We've got all our subjects in common. Won't be much fun if we can't play nice.'

'I don't like it when you're polite to me.' He does his best to make it sound teasing and charming, but there's a brittle edge. 'Maybe in a day or two I could … I don't know. Bring you chocolate. Make a grand gesture. Find some really good way to get you to forgive me.'

I shut down all the stupid, soft things welling up inside. He doesn't deserve them and I'm done letting this particular boy trample on my heart. He may think I'll do as a potential girlfriend because he doesn't have any other romantic options, but I'd rather be alone forever and at least hope some day a boy will like me as I am.

'I'd rather we just get on. I don't need another Abigail Moss in my life.'

'You'd put me in the same category as Abigail Moss? You wound me to the quick.'

'Look, you can joke all you like, that's fine, but it turns out I don't like you very much.'

Pain flashes across his features, his mouth tightening as he swallows hard.

'Anyway,' I say lightly, 'we're meant to be discussing the play. Could we focus on that?'

Ren and I are polite to each other for the rest of English. He hovers at the end, waiting for me, but I take my time fussing with the stuff in my bag, then taking my pills, and eventually I hear him leave.

I tell myself I am brimming with satisfaction at how beautifully I handled everything. Dignified. Mature. Triumphant.

Only the triumph tastes bitter and I might have confused dignity with sadness because it turns out none of it has made me feel better after all.

As Maddie's already agreed it with Ms Meade, The Singers take the news of her joining us with equanimity.

'We needed another girl,' Orla says, 'so no complaints here.'

'Benjo, do you think you could trade with Maddie on one of the songs you're arranging with the twins so she's got a partner?' I ask, pen poised to correct my list of pairings.

'I'm in if you'll take me,' Fred (I think?) says, giving Maddie a shy smile.

She grins. 'Cheers.'

'I'm the techy one, he's the arty one,' Fred says, pointing to George. 'We're not the same person.'

'We're both funny, though,' George adds. 'Just in case anyone hadn't noticed the odd similarity between us.'

'Next order of business,' I interrupt, 'is figuring out who's conducting, so we're all going to have a turn at "Be Like Him" then we'll vote, OK?'

Although Ren's an excellent conductor, I'm surprised to discover that Benjo's even better – at least when there aren't any music stands nearby for him to swat across the room in the process.

After that we focus on our set list for the fundraising-and-audition performance at the mall. Apart from Benjo and George's coursework arrangement (I can't believe they're already finished when the rest of us haven't even started), the songs are all four-part rock-gospel arrangements of pop songs that Ms Meade found for us when we explained what we were after. It may be a little uninspired, but doing covers takes some of the pressure off so we can focus on being technically strong for the audition.

When no one has a single snippy word to say about our evolving plans, I call a run-through of the whole thing. There's still a lot of work to do – places where our timing is a hair adrift, bars where our individual dynamics don't quite gel – but we're all hitting our notes and our cues, building to crescendos as a group and modulating chords in near-perfect sync. Benjo and George's song is particularly strong, which is both brilliant and daunting – at some stage the rest of us have to not just deliver our own, but come up to scratch. And that includes me and Ren, oh joy unbounded.

When the final chord of our encore song – 'Be Like Him' – fades to silence, I clap my hands and stride forwards. 'Our busking licence has come through, and the person auditioning us is available, so the performance is a week Saturday. Any problems?'

Orla and Roksana have their heads together, whispering furiously. Roksana casts me a murderous look over Orla's shoulder.

I knew it was too good to last. 'Raise your hand now if you're unhappy or can't make it.'

Orla and Roksana ignore me, still muttering under their breath. It's Ren who raises his hand.

I cross my arms. 'What's the problem?'

'Oh,' he says quietly. 'I'm just unhappy. It's not singing-related.'

Benjo sniggers.

'Don't you start,' I tell him.

'Sir, yes, Sir,' Benjo says, and gives me a haphazard salute.

'I could get used to that,' I tell him, 'so don't tempt me. For now I've had enough of the lot of you. See you next time.'

'Wait!' Orla calls. 'Quick announcement. It's my birthday and I'm having a party on the first Saturday of the spring holidays. You're all . . . well, I wouldn't go so far as to say welcome, but you can come if you like and I won't chuck you out. Riverside Community Centre from eight. Bring drinks and snacks. Tokens of appreciation and admiration welcome too.'

I linger by the door, relieved when Orla and Roksana are the last to leave. 'Don't bite my head off for asking, but I can see you're unhappy with me, per usual, so I need to know – are you actually going to turn up to busking?'

Orla turns away, nibbling at a nail. Then she catches herself, lowering her hand with a curse as she inspects the end.

Roksana tosses her hair haughtily. 'We might ditch if it were just you, but we wouldn't do that to the others.'

I take a deep breath that makes my shoulder pull threateningly. 'Why do you hate me so much? I know I'm not everyone's cup of tea, but this just seems way OTT considering I'm the one doing all the heavy lifting here.'

'That's the whole *point*. You're making these decisions as if we're all living the high life,' Roks snarls. 'I'm so tired of your privilege.'

'Yeah, I'm one hundred per cent living the high life,' I say, raising my stick. 'I had *no* idea what I was missing before I started spending every second of my life in pain, but now I have all the luck.'

Orla ducks her head, flushing all the way down past the collar of her top, while Roksana flinches back, face torn between fury and shame. She swallows heavily. 'Look,' she says, voice suddenly low and gruff, 'it sucks what you're going through, but it doesn't mean you get to think you're the only one struggling. And being disabled doesn't mean no one else gets to criticise you—'

'When the hell did I say you couldn't criticise me?' I snap, then take a deep breath and continue more calmly. 'But fine. You tell me what part of my suggestion is *such a mega problem*,' I say, adding some jazz hands, 'that isn't just you being difficult for the sake of it and I'll listen and, if you've got a point, I'll come up with something new.'

'Even after you saw us at the market on Saturday did it never enter your head that maybe Orla and I have to work at the weekend? That maybe we actually *need* that work and the money we get from it?' She looks away, jaw clenching. 'We're going to figure out how to be available for the busking session, but that means sacrifices that have apparently never entered your brain because all you seem to need money for is an ever-expanding wardrobe.'

I want to snarl and snap, because one or both of them could just have told me this earlier, but I get that it's hard to admit sensitive, private stuff to people, let alone people you don't like. 'OK,' I say, when I've given myself a moment to think. 'First off, I'm sorry I didn't realise the Saturday thing was a problem.'

Then I pause again, gritting my teeth as, with spectacular

timing, my shoulder blade grinds out of place. When I've just about got control of the pain, I add, 'But I shouldn't have to guess stuff like that any more than you should automatically be expected to know that I've just dislocated my shoulder blade and need to put it back in, so we're going to have to hit pause.'

Orla makes a little whimper when my shoulder pops audibly as I force it into place over the back of a chair. (It's the left shoulder, so at least it goes quickly, with the first attempt.)

'Does that hurt as bad as it sounds?'

'Yes,' I say tightly.

'I've seen you do that before,' Roksana says, an almost-courteous tone in her voice as she sits down a few chairs along. 'And something with your leg.'

'My hip goes out too. And my fingers and my thumb and sometimes my jaw and occasionally other bits too. We all have stuff to deal with. I don't expect you to know about mine, even though you can literally see some of it. I'm sorry I didn't put two and two together about your work commitments, but, like most people in the world, I'm a bit self-centred at the best of times and right now things are shit so I'm fairly oblivious about everyone else. I'm not trying to be a dick, but it's hard to be considerate when you're in pain. And I'm in pain all the time. It's not an excuse, but it is a reason.'

Orla is back to nibbling at her nails. Roksana knocks her hand away from her mouth.

'So, tell me about this busking thing. Is it possible, because I'd rather know now than later?'

'We'll make it work,' Orla promises. 'We just need a plan.'

'Can the rest of us help? Like . . . what exactly is the issue?'

Roksana sighs. 'If we're not on the stall, Mum has to be there, but then there's no one to look after the kids because Orla's mum's got a Saturday job in the library and obviously the two of *us* are singing, so we'll have to fork over cash for a babysitter or a few hours at the crèche.'

'Or you could bring the small people to the busking session and I can get Maddie to babysit. She's not ready to perform with us yet, but she wants to be there so it's win–win.'

Orla's head comes up. 'She'd really do that?'

'Of course. I'll owe her chocolate cake afterwards, but sure. She loves kids.' I shrug – carefully. 'And by the way,' I add, 'I *don't* have new boots every other day, but I do give myself five to ten quid per week to go on eBay and bid on something fun since I'm not putting fifteen pounds into the PopSync fund any more.'

I don't tell them that the reason I've been buying a lot of new stuff recently is that it's the only way I can feel even a little bit better about how much I hate my body.

'Also, for the record,' I add, 'I work bloody hard for that money, though I concede I'm very lucky that my parents can afford to pay me for what I add to their business.'

'Ten quid per week?' Roksana scoffs. 'Think you should check your bank statement because you've had new boots twice in the last month and I don't believe for a heartbeat that they're second-hand.'

I grin. 'No, they're brand new. Those maroon ones with the three gold buckles? £8.99 including postage.'

'No way,' says Orla.

'The benefits of size three feet. There are a lot of bargains, especially off season.'

Roksana laughs then. 'I am both impressed and infuriated. Truce in return for finding us a babysitter so we can busk without being out of pocket?' she asks, offering a hand.

'Done,' I say and we shake. Then I wince and undislocate my fingers.

Orla turns away, covering her mouth and trying to pretend she isn't dry-heaving.

'Also, I demand to go on eBay with you,' Roks adds, 'because I am completely jealous of the shoes. Plus I need you to help me find something awesome for Orla's birthday.'

Orla jostles her shoulder. 'That's Roks's way of saying that, now we're sort of seeing eye to eye, you should come to my party.'

The party, despite being a month away, is the talk of the cafeteria. It is quickly becoming apparent that no one in our year cares whether they've been invited or not. I've already told Maddie she's going to be babysitting for Roks and Orla when we go busking, so she's entitled to make an appearance. Just as well, since she spends the whole of lunch burbling on about what we're going to wear. I ignore the fact that PopSync immediately pile in as one. While I knew Pip would be delighted to take over the group (she is currently glee personified), I wasn't sure how the others would feel about Maddie stepping down, especially knowing she wouldn't have done it without my blessing. Thankfully, while Sam and Ashley eyed me cautiously when Maddie and I first sat down, they quickly relaxed into talk of the party and are currently bent over their phones, flipping through the ASOS catalogue and occasionally flashing us a glimpse of potential outfits.

Maddie and I give a particularly hideous yellow jumpsuit a joint thumbs down.

'We need to go shopping – as in actual, physical shopping,' Maddie says. 'Hey, how about after busking next Saturday? We'll already be in the mall. Come on, Ven! If I have to babysit, the least you can do is shop with me. Oh, there's Ren.'

I grab her hand as she goes to wave him over, then end up gasping with pain.

'What did you do?' Maddie asks as we lean over my hand as I try to straighten it. 'Your finger isn't meant to look like that. I'm going to puke.'

'Shut up, Maddie. Just don't look.'

She slaps her hands over her eyes then immediately peeks over the top. 'Horrified fascination,' she explains.

'If you puke on me, we are not going shopping because I will murder you with your fork.'

'Understood. Fix your finger, Ven.'

'I'm going to. Give me a sec.'

'Fix it, fix it! Fix it quick!'

I take my right index finger in my left fist, then I clamp the bottom of the finger firmly and wiggle the top with the rest of my fist. Wiggle – *grind* goes the joint. Wiggle – *grind* goes the joint. A firm jerk to the right – *crunch* goes the finger.

Maddie does a little retch that I don't think is put on. 'I heard that. Oh my God, that is so disgusting.'

'Thanks for the sympathy and support, Mads.'

'Yeah, whatevs,' she says. 'Why did you pull your finger out of joint to stop me calling Ren over?'

Of *course* she hasn't forgotten about that.

'Ren and I aren't friends any more.'

Maddie flops back in her chair with a dramatic sigh. 'I don't believe this. We patch up our friendship after months of arguments and what do you do? You withhold vital information.' She sits forward and pokes a finger into my face. 'Now tell me about the boy, Ven. Tell me all about the boy.'

'Not here,' I whisper, sliding my eyes sideways.

Maddie looks over my shoulder to see Sam and Ashley pretending they aren't listening. 'Right. Desperate times, desperate measures. We'd better go to the library.'

We both have a free period next so we were headed there anyway, but we go early. It's horrible telling her about Ren and Tai. My throat closes up and my voice goes all weird when I repeat what he said at the end.

Maddie tucks her hand into mine and glares so poisonously at our lovely school librarian when she heads in our direction to tell us to stop talking that she does a military about-turn and leaves us to it. (Note to self: apologise to the librarian later.)

It startles me when Maddie hands me a tissue. 'What's this for?' I ask.

Maddie looks up to the ceiling and takes a deep breath. 'For crying.'

'I'm not crying.'

'More's the pity. Crying's normal, you know, when boys stomp on your heart.'

'Don't be a drama queen. It's no big deal.'

Maddie throws her hands in the air. 'Would you stop telling me lies? If you bottle anything more up, you are going to explode.'

'I've got bigger things on my plate right now and I'm doing really well at being proactive and positive and productive . . .'

'Yeah, that's what I'm worried about. You're going to productive yourself into an early grave.' Maddie's face scrunches up. 'Bad wording. Very bad wording. But honestly, Ven, I think you need to quit pushing yourself so hard and figure out how to strike a healthy balance.'

Right on cue Ren walks through the library door. He squares his shoulders when he sees us and gives me a tentative little wave-and-smile. I fix a polite expression on my face and wave back then bend over my books. I only look up again when I realise there is a weird sound coming from Maddie. I think she might actually be growling. Ren registers the look on her face and hurries off.

'Mads, I told you I'm being grown-up about Ren.'

'No. We hate him.' Her expression goes speculative. 'I'm pondering how you'd handle things if a boy did that to me.' Her face brightens. 'Shall I tear his throat out with my teeth?'

The Weekend of No Rest for the Weary (Part I)

Items 1–7Ø million: Box Office Weekend

Days to festival: 96

Box Office Weekend is a solid two days of preparing the mail-out of all the tickets ordered direct from the festival to date. The whole endeavour is fuelled by a mix of solidarity, desperation, caffeine and cake of all varieties (i.e. the best kind of cake). I love every endless second of it. For hours my brain is so tied up it can't think about how much everything hurts.

Having managed to basically avoid him all week, I even forget about Ren.

I almost feel like I used to – full of energy, busy conquering the world. For once, none of the problems are because of my stupid, hopeless body. Instead, it's all down to My Awful Cousin Stef living exuberantly up to his name.

Aunt Jinnie once told me, 'God invented Stef so that the rest of us would always feel adequate by comparison.'

Harsh, you might say, never having met Stef.

True, you would say if you'd ever had that displeasure.

Stef works part-time for the festival and part-time doing exactly what he does for the festival but for someone else – i.e. not very much but with a lot of whining. That's bad enough, but the real killer is that Stef will never, ever offer solutions to the problems he creates. You can literally stand and wait ten minutes (I've timed it) after asking him, 'Well, what are you going to do about it?' and he'll just droop pathetically until you give up and sort it out yourself.

Case in point, Mum has just asked Stef to move some ticket-stock into the kitchen. So of course he's knocked over the coffee table and dropped everything everywhere. Now he's standing there, looking at the mess as if trying to remember the words to the magic spell that will clear it all up.

Uncle Geoff looks over, clocks the situation and hightails it to the kitchen with a mumble of, 'More caffeine, I think.'

'Aren't you due to check out that new marquee supplier, Stef?' says Aunt Jinnie in a cheerful voice with a clear undercurrent of threat.

Five minutes later, he's gone.

'Blessings be upon us,' Aunt Jinnie breathes.

It says it all that within half an hour Aunt Sarah, Stef's long-suffering mum, is humming joyfully under her breath as we plough through the Ticket-Form Binder of Doom (currently volumes one through twenty-five).

By the time we break for lunch we are officially all Grumpy and Frustrated. I love this bit too. It is the grumpy frustratedness of busy people wrestling their way through an almost insurmountable task. When I was little, I used to pretend days like this were skirmishes and the festival a battle. We would emerge shattered but triumphant, having created a place where magic and music came alive for a few days only to melt away into a plain green field at the end, like an enchantment.

It's why I even love the bits I hate. I used to feel like that about dance too. Now I'm worried it's going to end up just the same. How am I going to manage to run the box office when I'll be tired enough just walking to and from the loos? If I can even do that this year. It was bad enough last festival.

The run-up was OK when I could drive the seventy metres from the box office to the loos, but when the barriers went up for the three days of the festival itself I had to choose between a dehydration headache and hanging on till I was desperate because that tiny distance suddenly felt like a mountain hike. By Sunday lunchtime, I was only managing ten steps at a time, meaning it took nearly half an hour to get there and back – time I didn't have. Given that I only managed by the skin of my teeth last year and things are worse now . . .

And then there's the performance. It would be amazing for our portfolios, but I've allowed myself to pretend that's all that matters instead of facing up to the fact it'll also make the week even more stressful and exhausting, and give me a whole new way to let everyone down – not just my family, but Maddie and the others. The truth is it's asking for trouble – and I've already got enough of that.

Before I can get sucked into a whirlpool of angst, Aunt Jinnie squishes herself onto the sofa beside me.

'Don't dislocate her hip,' Mum says, frowning at us.

'Fiss-Fuss,' Aunt Jinnie says. 'We can fit.' She puts her arms around me and plants a kiss on the side of my head. 'We're being a United Front because you're looking grim and scary.'

Mum heaves a sigh, but leaves us to it.

Something about Aunt Jinnie just sitting quietly with me makes me need to breathe slowly and gently so I don't cry.

After a moment, she leans over to press another kiss to my curls. 'My bestest girl,' she whispers.

It brings a lump to my throat that's half gratitude and half grief because I don't feel 'best'. I feel like I'm a millimetre from failure – it's at my heels and I'm not fast enough to outrun it any more.

The Weekend of No Rest for the Weary (Part II)

Sunday dawns with us still neck deep in the *Ls* of the Ticket-Form Binder of Doom (volumes thirteen to twenty-five), which means there's still technically more than half the alphabet to go. Still, everything is coming along nicely until my thumb slides out of joint. I throw my pen down in frustration, grasp the thumb firmly and shove it into place. Only it won't go.

I growl and try again. No crunch. No rush of pain then relief, just more pain.

'Ven?' calls Mum.

'It's fine,' I say, lowering my hands below the table and going for attempt number three.

Nothing. Nothing. Nothing.

Gritting my teeth, I pick up my pen. But I can't seem to grip it.

'Ven, darling, let's see your hand,' says Mum softly.

I let the pen fall and slam my way upstairs, where I put ibuprofen gel on my stupid thumb and force it back into place. But it still won't go. Why won't it go?

Everyone looks up when I reappear in the kitchen doorway. Stef is in my seat, writing out the envelopes. Between Stef's suitably awful handwriting, and his imaginative approach to spelling (he's not dyslexic, just useless, BTW), he has been banned from writing ticket envelopes since I got big enough to do them instead. This has been MY job for about ten years now. But thanks to my stupid body, even Stef is more use than me right now.

I snatch up one of the binders randomly and take it into the sitting room to find something useful to do, like making sure all the forms have a tick to show payment's been taken. I expect someone to follow me, but no one does and I can't tell if that's good or bad. There's nothing anyone could say that will cheer me up and we're all too busy anyway, especially now The Grand Stefer Upperer is involved. It's Stef's role to let everyone down, not mine. It's not my fault, but that doesn't change anything.

And how about The Singers? If I can't even hold a pen, how am I going to make it through the festival and a performance there? It'll be the disaster with PopSync all over again. Maybe I really should tell Aunt Jinnie not to bother coming to the busking session on Saturday. The others don't even know what the audition is for, so I can just tell a little fib that it fell through and they'll never know. After all, today is practically a neon sign telling me to turn back while I can. But how could I do that to the others?

I clench my left hand around my right and force my thumb into place. This time it goes.

Busking Saturday

Item 1: *ensure The Singers perform brilliantly and raise enough money to go to the festival.*
Item 2: *pretend to have forgotten Ren and I ever flirted with intent.*

Maddie spends most of the week talking about shopping after the busking session because even she doesn't know how much is riding on it. I mean, obviously she knows all about the festival, but I haven't told her Saturday is effectively an audition to perform there because she'll get so nervous on our behalf she will definitely end up spilling the beans.

I pretend to be enthusiastic as she goes on about all the shops she wants to drag me through – the last thing I want is to rain on her parade. I even gush about how I've no idea what to get Orla for her birthday, let alone how I'm going to help Roks find something too.

The week disappears in a whirl of last-minute rehearsals.

Come Saturday, sunshine spills through the glass roof of the mall, yet I'm cold all over, even in this space that's almost as familiar as my home given that PopSync used to rehearse just around the corner and we always ended up piling in here for drinks and shopping after. We even performed out in the parking lot a few years ago for the summer fete. That was the day I entered us in the TV talent competition. If only I could recapture some of that confidence now.

It'll be fine once we get going, I tell myself as I make a desultory attempt to get The Singers into position, doing my best to ignore how ridiculously hot Ren looks in his plain black slacks and royal-blue shirt (until we've done our fundraising, there's no budget for outfits so Orla told us to come in the school colours – black trousers, blue top – so at least we're vaguely coordinated).

A few people glance over, and an elderly couple sit down on a bench by a fake flowerbed. A mother with a toddler and a child in a pushchair stop at the cafe, choosing the table nearest to us.

I glance to the side where Maddie is standing with a collection bucket, babysitting Orla and Roks's brood of siblings. Well, Roks only has the one, but Orla has *five*. Of course none of them are a match for Maddie, who has them working in teams: two handing out flyers, two jingling collection tins and the other two taking turns colouring in a design Roks has drawn up on an A2 sheet of card purloined from the art department at school. We've asked permission from the bookshop behind us and they've agreed to let us stick it to the shop window, once it's done, as a backdrop.

'All change!' Maddie yells to the kids.

They promptly scurry into action, trading jobs and bending back to their tasks with an intensity born of greed – I have made myself a Favourite Person by sourcing a set of cheap mini lightsabers 'for any small people who behave and listen to Maddie'. Also sequins, bubble-blowers and chocolate. I am a Big Hit, though Roks gritted her teeth when she saw it all.

'I'm doing the Fairy Godmother thing, which is all about bribery,' I said, holding up my hands. 'Just go with the flow. They're not going to expect this from you just because they got it once from me.'

'If they do, you are financially and logistically responsible,' she warned, but has since been mollified by how quiet the kids are.

I look around one last time, then turn to the others. 'Let's skip the intro speech. We'll do it once we've gathered a crowd.' Ignoring Ren's attempts to meet my eyes, I put a broad smile on my face, despite the sickening flutter of nerves in my stomach. 'Time to go.'

Ren moves to the front, while Fred hits record on the tripod-mounted camera he set up earlier, then scurries into place. I slug down a painkiller in an attempt to head off the inevitable cost of standing up for too long. Thankfully, there isn't time to dwell on the fact that 'too long' is now all of twenty minutes. I programmed the set to include a water-break after the first five songs so I'd have an excuse to take the weight off for a few moments, but though I'm starting to wonder if that's enough to make it manageable, it's too late to change things now.

While I take my place, Maddie and the kids quickly stick the banner behind us, hurrying away as Ren plays our starting note on his phone. He counts us in then we're off with our first song – a four-part spin on Carole King's 'You've Got a Friend'.

The acoustics are weird, as you'd expect with all the glass and metal and reflective surfaces, but it amplifies our voices, making them echo so that we sound like a crowd. More importantly, we sound good. The chords are true and we hit our beats, though I make a note that some of the lyrics aren't clear enough and there are a few places where our voices don't blend smoothly. And yet the music fills the air, fills the space, and suddenly I am happy.

I am part of something wonderful. I can't dance any more, but I can do this – and it's good. *We're* good. Together, we're beautiful.

People are stopping. The toddler is staring at us in awe. The baby is jiggling in the pram. Shop assistants come to their doorways, customers with them, to listen. Out of the corner of my eye I spot Aunt Jinnie and Ms Meade lurking behind a hedge of fake shrubs, making notes. It's probably just as well I can't see them properly as it makes it easier to focus on the music.

By the time the song ends, we have everyone's attention.

I step forwards. 'Thanks for stopping to listen to our first public performance. We're students from the local high school and we're here today to raise some money to fund a bigger, fancier performance for our A-level music portfolios, so if you have any spare change and you enjoy what you hear, every little will be much appreciated.'

I nod to Ren, careful not to meet his eyes, then move back into place as he plays our next starting note.

'Hey, dorks, you got something from this century?' a boy shouts.

'Yeah, who do we complain to about the hearing damage I'm suffering listening to this shite?'

I turn and see Abigail and a sub-set of her pack: two girls from school, and three boys – one I recognise and two who I'm pretty sure are strangers. I set my shoulders back, ready to march over and sort them out, but Aunt Jinnie and Ms Meade are already converging on them. Abigail and the pack promptly scuttle off.

'You know you're a hit when you've got hecklers,' Ren tells the crowd, who laugh encouragingly. A few people even clap, though they go silent when he plays our starting note and we launch back into song.

By the end of the second number (a close-harmony version of Al Green's 'Lean On Me'), we draw a smattering of applause and, when I look around at the others, it's to find that everyone's smiling. The jolt of memory of performances with PopSync is sharp but, for once, not painful; there's nothing like the type of belonging that happens in the moment of creating something together. The feeling that I'm part of something bigger goes straight to my bones and lodges there, like a light turned on inside.

For each song, the crowd builds and so does the applause. When we pause for our water-break, I slump down by my bag and top up both the caffeine and painkillers in my system. Then I get back up, because if I let myself think about how tired I already am, and what hurts (let alone how much), it's all going to be over.

I'll just have to trust the adrenaline to get me through, though God only knows how I'll survive Maddie's post-performance shopping plans.

Thankfully, although I was worried people would leave if we stopped singing, instead a bunch come up and put money in the tins, while Maddie takes the bucket round to the rest. At the end of her circuit, she peers inside and beams, only to jump when Ms Meade suddenly leans in to look too. We all hold our breath as we await her verdict.

'Knew you could do it,' she says. 'Keep up the good work.'

We do another four songs before I tip Benjo the nod.

'Do you all want an encore?' he calls.

There's a resounding 'YES!' so we give them another two numbers. There's a gratifying cacophony of clapping and whooping at the end. I thank the crowd, give Fred a thumbs up to turn off the recording – and we're done.

For ten minutes we buzz and talk and rehash what was brilliant, and which cues we missed, and which pauses we fluffed, and speculate about the money we've raised ... Then, almost in unison, we sag.

'Great work, team. I'll let you know the news about the secret performance opportunity as soon as I hear anything. Now go and enjoy your weekend,' I tell them, and suddenly it's over.

I look around for Ms Meade and Aunt Jinnie, but both are gone, while Ren is deep in conversation with George, scrolling through George's snaps from the day. When I turn back, Roks and Orla are in charge of the kids again and Maddie is pushing the collection bucket into Fred's hands with a cheery, 'Tag, you're it! Look after it for me until our arranging session, OK?'

She dives on me, tucking my arm through hers, then leads me over to a quiet table in the corner of the cafe. 'Let's have a cup of tea before shopping,' she says. 'Get your boots off and put your feet up. I'll be back with provisions.'

I blink at her as she scurries away. I love Maddie but this is not usual. She should be dragging me into the nearest shop, oblivious to how tired I am. She should certainly be asking for cash for the tea and cake. It takes me until she returns with a laden tray to work out that Aunt Jinnie must have given her money to make sure we were fed and caffeinated after the performance.

'What's wrong with you? You look all chill and happy,' Maddie says, reaching to feel my forehead. '*Ew.* You're kind of wet and cold and slippery. Is fish-skin a symptom of something?'

I raise an eyebrow. 'First, you snotted all over me the other day, so you do not get to *eww* at me. Second,' I say, raising three fingers and then stopping. 'I don't remember what's second and I'm confused about where three comes in, so maybe we should just stop there.'

'Eat the chocolate cake. Eat it instantly,' she says, digging a fork in then raising it towards my face in an attempt to be solicitous. I'm sure part of it is genuine concern for me, but part is worry that I'll flake on our shopping session if she can't get me to perk up.

I snatch the fork from her, accidentally catapulting the piece of cake across the entire cafe. We watch it land in a potted plant where a toddler pounces on it and stuffs it into his mouth before his horrified grandmother can stop him. Maddie and I clap our hands over our mouths to muffle our laughter as we turn away, pretending the whole thing is nothing to do with us.

'You were awesome by the way,' Maddie says through a mouthful of millionaire's shortbread. 'You should be a group manager as your career.'

I make a face. 'PopSync and The Singers are bad enough. Imagine working with pop stars.' We pause to do just that. 'Nope,' I say. 'There's enough pain and misery in my life already. I don't need it in external human form too.'

'Yeah, fair,' agrees Maddie. 'Hurry up with your tea. I've been kind and considerate for ages and now I need to shop.'

We make it around two shops – Maddie tries on a handful of things while I sit and breathe deeply and try to think happy, pain-free thoughts – before it becomes clear I am more than flagging. I'm so tired I think I might be ill if I don't stop.

It's not fair that I'm meant to be having fun with my best friend and the whole time I've been thinking longingly of it being over so I can go home and lie down so it doesn't hurt as much. But it's going to hurt tomorrow too, and the day after that, and the day after that, and every day after that, and I don't want that life. But there's no way out, there's just this, every day forever and no way out except—

Abort thought! Emergency new thought deployed! Distraction procedures initiated and ... Let's look at what's in this shop window.

'Hideous much?' says Maddie, looping her arm through mine

in a vain attempt to pretend she's being affectionate instead of just towing me from shop to shop.

We only get four steps before I stumble, dragging us to a stop.

'Are you ... ? Oh, you don't look right,' Maddie says, face falling.

I sigh. 'I need to go home.'

Maddie, to give her credit, nods and starts towing me in the opposite direction.

'No, Mads. You stay here,' I say, trying to disengage my arm from hers. 'I'm sure I saw Sam and Ashley having coffee. Why don't you go join them?'

'Don't be silly. It's just shopping.'

'And I'm just going home. Seriously, Mads. I appreciate it – I really do – but you stay. Send me pics, OK?' I say, doing my best to smile instead of grimace. My rubbish body doesn't need to ruin the day for both of us and I'm done making Maddie feel bad about being able to do stuff I can't. 'Please?'

'If you're safe to drive by yourself then I'll stay,' she concedes. 'But you have to message me the minute you get in. And no "I was tired, I forgot".'

'OK,' I say, rolling my eyes. 'Have fun. Buy something short and ridiculous.'

As I slop doggedly from the lift to the car my steps get shorter and shorter until I can barely think beyond shuffling forwards. All I care about is reaching the car and Sitting Down (insert chorus of Hallelujah).

Then suddenly I register that something more than the pain is wrong. I stop, swaying on the spot. My brain is saying, *Warning – Problem – Warning*, but doesn't seem willing to supply any further information.

Gritting my teeth, I look around.

Voices. They're not loud but there's something in the tone – jeering, aggressive – that makes me freeze. Listening closer, I catch another voice, tight and controlled: the voice of someone trying to defuse a situation about to turn nasty. Fear washes through me – the instinctive urge to freeze so the danger doesn't see me warring with the need to run or hide. But then . . .

Ren's voice. That's Ren's voice, teetering on the edge of either terror or fury.

My lips are drawn back in a snarl of pain by the time I hobble my way past the big van blocking my view. Ren is walking towards me, head down. Three boys about our age are dancing round him. As they come closer, I recognise them as the ones who were with Abigail Moss earlier and, sure enough, mincing along at the back, grinning in delight, is Little Miss Snake-Face herself, though the other girls are currently nowhere in sight. My blood is thumping so loudly in my ears I can't make out what they're saying, but I catch the word 'freak' and the word 'monster' and . . .

'Hey, dipshits,' I call, and the volume of my voice surprises even me. I didn't think I had enough breath left to shout. 'Get the hell away from him or I'm calling the police.'

My heartbeat feels like an elastic band snapping against my

ribs, my breath is short and choppy, but they're just bullies and they aren't going to turn me into a coward.

'Oooo, a girlie freak! How cute,' one of the boys sneers.

'Whatever,' I drawl, putting as much bored disdain into the word as I can. 'Look, you've had your fun. You've called us some names. Now go away. Come on, Ren.'

I step forwards, trying to get between him and at least one of the others, but the tallest boy steps right into my face making me jerk backwards, stumbling when my leg threatens to give way before I've got my stick down to support my weight. They all howl with laughter, though I note that the one I recognise from school hangs back, presumably not wanting to cross the line and get reported to our teachers.

They're just bullies, not dangerous, just bullies, I tell myself as I swallow down the fear, forcing it off my face before it can tempt them to more than thuggish posturing.

'Gotta worry, mate, when you need a cripple-girl to fight your battles,' says the tallest boy, clearly the leader.

Ren turns and shoves him. The leader surges forwards again, but his mates pull him back.

'They're not worth it, Ren,' I say when the two of them stand there practically growling at each other, hackles raised.

'Thought you were all high and mighty about how people shouldn't get away with calling you names,' Ren hisses, chest heaving with fury.

'These jerks?' I say, my voice full of disbelief. 'Why would I care what some random moron says?'

'Say what?' demands the stockiest of the boys, turning on me. 'Want to repeat that, you little—'

Ren punches him.

It knocks him into the third guy, making them stumble back even as the tallest one steps forwards, shoving Ren away – right into me as I lunge to drag him clear.

I fold over, dropping to my knees, as Ren's elbow connects with my solar plexus, knocking the air out of me.

'Oh, smooth moves, lover boy,' the stocky boy gloats as Ren swings round in horror.

The lead bully smirks at us for a moment, then turns, draping an arm around the shoulder of the boy who got punched and pulling him away.

'You two deserve each other. What a power couple,' Abigail Moss sneers over her shoulder as she hurries after her friends, leaving me burning with the wish that Ms Meade would magically turn up in time to see Abigail with her mask of faux-concern ripped off and all the venom underneath exposed . . . But of course that would be far too convenient.

'Dammit, Ven,' Ren says, crouching beside me. 'Why did you . . . I was fine. I didn't need your help.'

I just wheeze and gasp, eyes squeezed shut as I wait for the pain to subside, hoping that when it does I won't realise that I've managed to dislocate something in the process of thumping down onto my knees.

'Should I call an ambulance?' Ren asks in a very small voice.

'No, you shouldn't call a bloody ambulance,' I grit out. 'I need you to get me on my feet then piss off as quickly as you possibly can.'

'How do I help?'

I finally manage to take a deeper breath, then, because I've got no other option, I turn and grab his arm. 'Get a grip under my elbow and shoulder and pull me up when I go.' I make it an order. A surly, spitty, ungrateful order.

I spend a while swaying when I'm upright. Ren holds on and keeps his mouth shut. It's the best thing to happen in the last two hours.

I want to turn my back on him and march away – make a dignified, haughty exit – but I know I'll just fall over if I try. Not to mention that I dropped my bag and there is absolutely no way I will manage to pick it up without blacking out. I'm still trying to come up with a solution when Ren sees where I'm looking. Checking that I'm steady enough without his help, he walks over and grabs it, brushing away the dirt.

'I'm sorry I knocked you over, but you shouldn't have gotten involved,' he says, low and angry. 'It would have been fine if you hadn't gotten in the middle.'

Given how Ren backed down from his brother, and how he barely speaks in class, it seems a bit much that I get the full force of his occasional ability to be confrontational. Maybe he's right and I really do bring out the raging psycho in people.

This thought naturally does wonders for my temper. I give him the most scathing look I can summon. 'For your information, I wouldn't have left *anyone* in that situation. I'm not that sort of coward. So don't flatter yourself. It's not about *you*, Ren. It's about who *I* am.'

My face burning with anger and humiliation and adrenaline come-down, I wish with everything in me that a hole will open in the ground and swallow Ren up because I do not need an audience for the fact that I still can't breathe right and my vision is going loopy.

'Why are you still here, anyway?' I ask wearily.

Ren's hands clench into claws by his sides. 'I'm not going to walk away and leave you alone in this state. Especially since it's my fault.'

'I'm not in a bloody state,' I lie, looking him straight in the eye through a tangle of hair.

'It doesn't matter if you hate me. I'm going to get you home or to a doctor and that's that.' Then his shoulders slump. 'Though I really wish you didn't hate me.'

'You know how to fix that? Learn the difference between having a dick and being one.'

Twenty(ish) Minutes Later

Item 1: *get to car.*
Item 2: *sit in car.*
Item 3: *figure the rest out later.*

Ren gets me to the car. It's messy and pathetic and so slow that by the time we make it a bunch of people have come up to ask if we're OK. Where the hell were they half an hour earlier?

I can barely limp-hobble, let alone walk, and my vision has gone grey. Ren ends up carrying my bag and almost carrying me. He leans me against the car and holds me there with his hip while he gets the door open. With much difficulty, I end up in the driver's seat with it pushed back from the wheel and tilted ridiculously low. Wedging my feet up against the side of the windscreen, I lie down while Ren climbs into the passenger side.

'No bloody ambulance,' I say at one point. 'Just shut up and give me a minute.'

It takes a lot longer than a minute. After a while, my phone starts buzzing.

'Is that important? Should I answer it?' Ren asks.

'Probably my parents. They can wait. Shut up.'

Miracle of miracles, he does. I'd be grateful if I weren't almost too tired to breathe. It's hard work not to just sink into a stupor that might become sleep, but I need to get home. And I need to message Maddie because I'm not ready for us to be in another fight, even though it is truly not my fault this time.

But everything hurts so much I just can't – can't anything. Because I need it to stop, stop, *please stop*, and I know it'll be better soon, but what if one day this is what it's like *all* day, *every* day, on and on . . .

Slowly everything ebbs. I stay still, still, still . . .

Eventually it recedes a bit more . . . Until finally I manage to take a deep breath and open my eyes.

'I'll drive you home,' I say, slowly pulling my feet down from the windscreen, then turning stiffly, with some pained grunting, to get the seat-back winched into a position that lets me see above the steering wheel.

'I'll walk from yours. Seriously, I'm not getting out of the car until I've seen you safely into your house. Are you sure you can drive anywhere?'

I scrub at my eyes. 'I wouldn't if I wasn't safe. Can you reach my bag?'

Ren drags it between the front seats and puts it carefully in my lap. I rip into a mini Mars bar, alternating with slugs of Gatorade.

'That looks foul,' Ren says, gesturing at the lurid blue liquid.

'Apparently it was formulated by an American cardiologist for people with blood-pressure issues like mine. Afterwards, he realised that athletes and people doing sports can suffer similar symptoms through overexertion, so then he made a fortune re-inventing it as a sports drink,' I explain between sips. 'It doesn't fix what's wrong, but it helps in an emergency. It just tastes like liquidised highlighter pen mixed with air freshener.'

'They should put that in their ads.'

'It's nothing compared with the taste of morphine, which is kind of what I imagine petrol and horse piss would be like if you mixed them with golden syrup.' I chuck the bag into his lap then put the keys in the ignition.

'I really am sorry,' Ren says, face pinched with shame. 'I'm *not* my brother. I don't *do* stuff like this – get into fights, punch people . . . You have to believe me, I never meant to—'

'It's fine. Shut up now, so I can concentrate on driving,' I tell him. I'd be too tired for this conversation even if I were ready to forgive him, which I'm not.

When we pull up outside my house, Ren is around the car before I've even got the door open. He offers a hand.

I shake my head. 'Just take my bag if you want to be useful.'

He hovers behind me as I inch my way out of the car then

shuffle towards the front door. Mum pulls it open while I'm still only halfway up the path.

'What's she done to herself now?' she demands of Ren. 'I told you it was too much to go shopping after the busking,' she tells me. 'You shouldn't have let Maddie guilt you into it.'

'It wasn't the shopping.'

'That's not what Maddie implied when she called asking why you hadn't let her know you were home safe.'

'It's my fault,' Ren says, offering Mum my bag.

'I fell over in the car park and Ren feels bad for not catching me,' I lie, glaring at Ren when he looks as if he's going to come clean. My parents worry quite enough without knowing I've just got myself involved in an unfair fight. They'd be simultaneously proud and even more stressed out about me going anywhere by myself. Thankfully, Ren wilts almost immediately, though his jaw is tight as he stares down at the pavement.

'I'm going to soak in the bath,' I announce, 'and you are going to stop fussing as if I've come home missing a limb.'

'First you text Maddie,' Mum orders. 'She's coming over for dinner, though I've already told her that she's to sit quietly with you on the sofa and make sure you rest, otherwise I will chuck her out on her ear. Ren, do you want a cup of coffee?'

'No. He's going home. Will you give him a lift?' I ask as I contemplate the front step.

'It's a twenty-minute walk. I don't need a lift. Um ... I'll message you later?'

'If you have to.' I could have made it into a joke but my tone makes it quite clear that I'd rather he didn't. I believe he feels bad, but it doesn't change the fact that he agrees with his horrid brother that my biggest selling point as a romantic interest is that I'm broken too and no one else is ever going to want either of us.

'See you at school?' he asks quietly.

I don't bother answering. To be fair I *am* otherwise occupied. I totter inside then crawl (yes, literally) up the stairs and into the bath. While it fills, I message Maddie. *Sorry. Not my fault. Explain later. Am only semi-dead. Will recover. X*

I've just turned off the water when Mum puts a cup of tea and a slice of cake down on the side, orders me not to lock the door, and warns me she'll be checking I'm awake and undrowned every ten minutes. Then she leaves me to it.

I expect to lie there and brood. Turns out I'm too wrecked even for that. Instead, I just slump in the water and wait to see if I'll live or die.

Spoiler alert: I live.

Maddie creeps into the living room a few hours later, carefully picks up my feet and settles them in her lap. When I open my mouth, she puts her finger to her lips and points at the TV.

When the movie finishes, I wriggle round to look at her, but she's staring at the credits, her eyes all teary. With a groan, I topple sideways to lean against her shoulder.

'I didn't mean to make you sick,' she whispers. 'Why didn't you tell me I was making you sick?'

'You didn't. I make my own choices, Maddie. Sometimes I

need to just do stuff and pay for it later because otherwise I'd never have any fun at all. And if you say one word about respecting my limits, I am going to make sure Abigail Moss turns up at Orla's party and then I'm going tell Orla it was all your idea.'

Maddie sinks down so she's resting the side of her face against my hair. 'This sucks, Ven. I know it sucks a thousand times less for me than it does for you, but I want to make it not suck and I'm angry that I can't. And I'm angry that you're always pushing yourself. And I love that you do and you always will, but I wish you wouldn't too, you know?'

'I'm sorry I made you worry.'

'Stupid,' Maddie says. 'The bit you should be sorry for is not being honest with me that it was too much to go shopping.'

'It's pathetic to be a teenager and too tired to spend a few hours out,' I say, feeling my eyes prickle. 'If it's like this now, what happens when I'm older?'

I don't say old. My condition isn't necessarily 'life limiting' as they call it nowadays when you're going to die young, but sometimes I wonder. Sometimes I even wonder if that would be such a bad thing.

A while back I made a silent pact with myself: I'm going to make sure there's so much good stuff between now and the time when no more happiness is possible beyond the pain that I'll have earnt the right to choose to say I've had enough. I really hope the law's different by then because I've written a letter about what I want.

I did it when I finally figured out why I hated those people at the self-help group so much: they scared me. Then I realised that as long as I get to decide for myself what living means, it doesn't matter what choices they make.

That's what the letter on my desktop says. Now I just have to tell someone it's there. Not because I think it'll be needed any time soon – hopefully not for years and decades to come, if ever. All the same, I should tell someone about it, just in case, so I can stop worrying.

Monday

(but a relatively good one as Mondays go)

Item 1: SHARE GOOD NEWS!

Item 2: use happiness from good news to get stuff done.

Days to festival: 87

'I have something to announce,' I say the minute all The Singers are gathered for our next meeting. 'The person who came to watch us busking is from a music festival.'

'What?' says Benjo, jerking up so violently from fiddling with his phone that it sails into the air.

Fred grabs it and hands it back without even looking away from me.

'Before I go on, I'd really appreciate it if you could keep the next bit a secret because the last thing I want is half the school petitioning me for free tickets, but my family runs a not-so-little festival that happens over three days in June about two hours from here. You might know our motto – "Putting the Family into Family Festival".'

There's a sharp intake of breath from George, while Benjo looks as if he's about to faint.

'You mean . . .' whispers George.

'Seriously?' says Benjo. '*How* did you sit on this? Most of my favourite bands played their first major gig there! Can you imagine being there right from the start with . . .' He shakes his head. 'You don't even have to, do you? I can name any act I worship and you've probably met them.'

'There are certain perks to go along with all the work,' I say, grinning as I flick a glance at Ren – even he is looking impressed. 'Now, before your shock wears off and you start talking about family favours,' I add, 'I will remind you that we had to audition, like everyone else. The nepotism was getting the opportunity, not getting a yes.'

'So you're saying the answer is no,' Roks says in a small voice.

Benjo groans.

'Actually, my aunt – she's the one who came to listen to us on Saturday – messaged me last night with her verdict.' I break into a grin. 'And it's a resounding *yes* to a workshop with a mini-performance at the end because she was – and I quote – really quite impressed.'

There's a hushed silence.

'Wow,' says Orla, staring at me. 'That's like . . . a Thing. A whole Thing. Oh my God.' Then she shakes her head. 'This is a joke, right? You're getting us back for being mean to you at the start.'

I shake my head, letting my smile speak for me.

A moment later, the whole group's on their feet cheering and hugging me, each other, cheering some more and hugging some more. I even spot Maddie and Fred high-fiving.

When I turn to find Ren in front of me, we both freeze.

'This is amazing, Ven. Really,' he says quietly, digging his hands into his pockets.

I find a smile for him. 'Thanks.' Then I'm being pulled into a hug by Benjo. Of course he promptly drags me off balance and only Ren reaching out to stop us toppling over prevents a nasty accident.

'OK, OK!' I shout, once I've got my feet back under me. 'Can I tell you the details now?'

They scuttle into their seats and turn their earnest little faces to me.

'It's on the Sunday afternoon of the festival and we have fifty minutes, split equally between a workshop – where we'll talk a little about the history of gospel music and teach the audience a song – and the performance itself. It's only a workshop tent, so it's not a massive audience and it's anything but fancy, but it *is* still a major national festival with' – I allow myself a proud smile – 'real name recognition, so if we don't all end up getting amazing A-level grades I will be both astonished and very cross indeed.'

'Does Ms Meade know?' Fred asks.

'I had to get her agreement – and theoretical agreement from the school since it's after exams but still officially during term-time – to be there to chaperone and assess our coursework, so that's fine, though we all need permission from a parent or guardian too. Now, before we get carried away, we've got a lot to do if we're to be ready, so get your music out. The real work starts now.'

For the first time, I end a session beaming. I want to kick myself for tempting fate when Roksana calls after me as I go to follow the others off to lunch. I turn back apprehensively.

'Look, I know what you're going to say. That this whole thing is just me showing off my privilege, and of course it is an incredible thing for my family to—'

Roks holds up her hand. 'I think the whole thing is fantastic and I am just grateful that one of us has the contacts to get us this once-in-a-lifetime opportunity. I'm sorry I was a bit off with you before, but I'm over it. I called you back because I was hoping you meant it when you offered to help me find something for Orla's birthday.'

'Oh. Um, sure,' I mumble, waiting for the catch. 'Over lunch?'

When I start slopping towards the door, Roksana follows at my heels, nearly treading on me when I have to stop as my knee threatens to turn inside out.

'Sorry,' she says, jumping back.

'Why don't you go first?'

Of course this doesn't work either as Roksana gets halfway down the corridor before turning to speak to me and realising I'm still ten metres back.

'Do you want to grab lunch and I'll catch up?'

'Would you prefer that?'

I groan. 'Look, this is awkward because it's literally impossible to walk naturally with me when I'm having one of these days so just ... pretend it's not happening. Actually, even better idea.' I reach into my pocket and slip out my phone, tapping through to my draft of the world's longest email, written in a frenzy of excitement last night after Aunt Jinnie messaged me with the happy news about the audition. 'Read that and tell me if it's possible for anyone in The Singers to be unprepared for the festival.'

It gives Roksana something to do while I slop my way along the corridor. At the end, she holds the door for me, still reading as I eye the next hallway balefully.

'Well?' I grunt.

'If there is any more detail to add, I'm not convinced we'd all survive it. I can safely say you've covered everything.' She blinks down at the phone. 'Even the fact that we should not come in see-through clothing.'

'You might think it doesn't bear saying, but bitter experience has taught me otherwise.'

Roks lowers the phone. 'Tell me you're joking,' she says, half awed, half horrified.

I purse my lips and shake my head. 'There was an ... incident.'

'Wow,' is all Roks gets out. 'By the way, I like the tip about bringing a change of shoes so you're putting pressure on different bits of your feet. I'm so going to use that at work.'

Getting our food and picking a table in a quiet corner is

characterised by what I'd call 'courteous shyness' if it were anyone but the two of us. *Is she nervous too?* I wonder. *Could Roks actually want to be friends after all?*

The others beckon us over as we turn away from the tills, but I wave them off and cross to an empty table, trying to ignore the looks of surprise. As soon as we're seated, I open my laptop and start asking what sort of things Orla likes.

It only takes ten minutes to find the right thing. The delight on Roks's face warms me all the way through, even before she whispers a soft thank you.

'I didn't think I could afford anything halfway good enough, so this is . . . yeah.'

'You're welcome. Got time to help me find something to wear?'

'I take it that means you're definitely coming to the party, then?'

'It was a done deal the moment Maddie heard the word *party*.' I think about telling Roks that it's the first party I've been to since things got bad with my mobility and how I'm not sure I'm going to manage if there aren't seats. Even if there are, if it's just one or two in a corner, I'll have the option of falling on my face or being left out because how am I going to join in a conversation if I'm the only one sitting?

'It's quite the sacrifice, you know,' I say instead. 'My parents are having a weekend away for their anniversary and I'd have had the house all to myself, but instead I'm going to drag myself out to ensure your festivities aren't bereft of my scintillating company.'

Roks groans. 'What I wouldn't give for a night alone. Don't get me wrong, I love my family but peace, quiet and solitude are so not a thing in my house.'

'Chances are they won't be in mine either. I don't put it past my parents to change their minds and make my aunt stay the night. They can't seem to grasp that I'm sixteen and, honestly, what sort of disaster do they think's going to happen if I have a little alone time?'

Yes, I know. Famous last words and all that.

The Saturday of the Party

Item 1: *have fun and bond with The Singers.*

Item 2: *figure out what to do about having to arrange a song with Ren.*

The Easter holidays get off to an excellent start with Maddie coming over for a lazy day of movies before we get ready for Orla's party. For a little while it feels like old times, if by old times I mean 'times when I tried to have fun despite having the flu'. I've been tired and achy all day. That's obviously not unusual, but I've got this weird back-ache and I never get back-ache. I must have been sitting wrong because of my hip, though that's actually not so bad today – I haven't had to put it back in once, despite wiggling into a bunch of outfits before settling on what I already knew I was wearing.

I think about telling Maddie how worried I am about standing up for long enough to have any fun, but why ruin the night in advance?

Instead, I try pinning my hair up and then Maddie does one of those 'loose braid around the front' things for me, and both are terrible but great comedy value. The important thing is that we laugh at lot, sing along to various ancient songs we wouldn't be caught dead admitting to liking in front of anyone else, and Maddie talks about the various boys she fancies and how likely it is they'll turn up tonight. I poke gentle fun at whether 'nice arms' are the key to lasting love and try not to dwell on how much I wish I'd got the chance to run my fingers through Ren's dark, tousled curls before I realised what a jerk he is.

Maybe it'd be worse if we'd kissed, but I can't make myself believe it – at least it'd be some evidence that I've got a shot at romance, rather than the likely scenario where I stand on the sidelines for the rest of my life, watching Maddie falling in love.

And with that happy thought, I slap on 'It's Raining Men' (the original, thank you very much), pumping the volume up till I can't hear myself think.

Determined not to be unfashionably early, even if we're probably going to be neutrally on-time, we do final checks in the mirror, then it's time to leave. Only, when I go to do a wee there's this sudden nasty yank somewhere in my belly as if an elastic band has snapped inside.

We're about to go out the door when I have to hare back to the loo because, dammit, I've got some sort of sudden-onset urinary infection. Just what I need – normal-people health problems on top of being me.

My stomach aches and seems determined to bloat out to twice its usual size: exactly the look I was going for. I stop in the kitchen to gulp down some cranberry juice, take a third trip to the loo and finally we're off.

Things are already in full swing when we arrive at Riverside Community Centre only fifteen minutes late.

'Wow,' says Orla. 'I didn't know you did any sort of late, let alone fashionably, Ven. Has someone sedated you or something?'

I make a face at her then hand over a present and a card. 'This is all Roks's idea, so if you hate it blame her.'

Orla surprises me with a hug. 'Come on. I'm rounding up the gang for a birthday song.'

The gang. Huh. The thought fills me with a pleasant buzz of warmth that almost offsets the pain of the bloat and the need to wee again. I am astonished to find myself between Roksana and Benjo a moment later, arms over each other's shoulders as we sing happy birthday and Orla blows out the candles on her cake.

Soon I'm passing plates as Orla carves it into sloppy pieces. Benjo promptly drops frosting down his front then stands pouting as I do my best to clean him up with napkins dipped in lemonade.

'Here,' says Orla, shoving a plate into my hands at the end. 'Payment for your top-class cake-passing and guest-blotting services. Now, excuse me while I go and deal with the horror that Roks has decided belongs on the sound system.'

I look at the cake, grimace and put the plate aside.

'Don't tell me you're on some crazy no-cake diet,' Benjo says. 'I thought you were too sensible for that. Not to mention I was hoping you might agree to drop some down yourself in solidarity.'

'I couldn't even touch your level of cake-wearing prowess. Seriously, you've got some on your shoulder now.'

I set to with a fresh napkin.

'Are you sure you don't want that?' Benjo asks, eyeing my discarded cake longingly.

'All yours,' I say, because eating anything, even cake, is literally the last thing I want right now. Yes, I know – it might as well have been a warning sign with flashing lights.

'You probably think I'm being a pig.'

'I am literally dealing with how little of the first piece you actually ate.'

Benjo heaves a sigh. 'I don't know if that's better or worse.'

The need to wee is back, so I leave him to it as Maddie whirls over from chatting to Fred. Unfortunately, Pip, Sam and Ashley catch me before I've gone two paces so I spend an agonising five minutes making small talk about how everything's going with PopSync. Thankfully, Pip is so busy gushing about what a natural leader she is I barely have to do more than smile to make her happy.

'We miss you, but we're doing OK,' Sam whispers, when the need to go forces me to excuse myself. She presses my arm, then laughs when I pull her into a hug. Behind her shoulder I see Maddie and Benjo deep in conversation.

When did they get to be such good friends? I wonder, as I

hurry off to the loo. I mean, yes, Maddie's been rehearsing with us for a while now (and even doing some conducting), but when did they have time to bond like this . . . and why haven't I, when I've been with them – leading them – for ages longer? *I should have been more worried about my personality than the lack of chairs*, I think gloomily as I lock myself in a cubicle.

When I step back out into the hall afterwards, need-to-wee addressed but jealousy still bitter on my tongue, the first thing I see is Ren looking around as if searching for someone. Then he turns and spots me.

There's a weird look on his face. Sort of shy. And nervous. But also hopeful and excited. Though it's mostly just weird. And what is he wearing?

'What do you think?' he asks, twisting his arm to show me a huge pink, yellow and white heart pinned to his sleeve.

'Um,' I say, trying to work out what sort of response he expects.

'Read it, Ven,' he says in this quietly pleading voice.

I'm not feeling well and most of my attention is devoted to the fact that I desperately need to wee *again*, so I lean closer without really focusing and read, *Please can we go back to snarking/flirting with intent?*

It takes me altogether too long to put the pieces together. By the time I look up, Ren has turned away, his mouth flattened into a line, his hands pushed into his pockets.

'You're such a dork,' I tell him, trying not to smile when he swings round, looking hopeful again. And, though I always thought it was just a particularly stupid cliché, I swear my heart tries to skip a beat when his eyes meet mine.

'A cute, forgivable dork?' he ventures. 'A dork who's really, truly, incredibly sorry for his previous incarnation as a total jerk?' He shrugs helplessly, but there's a smile tugging his lips up. 'Could we write it up to the fact I'm a teenage boy and being a jerk is basically the final stage of male puberty?'

'That,' I tell him pointedly, 'is sexist nonsense. Being a jerk is not inevitable for boys any more than being nice is inevitable for girls. It's a choice.'

'Did you seriously just "not all men" me?'

I fold my arms.

'Come on, Ven. I am literally wearing my heart on my sleeve here.'

He is! For me! The most gorgeous boy I've ever seen in my life is doing that for me. In front of most of our year group. And I know I need to be firm and strong and stick up for my principles, but I also really, really want to run my fingers through his hair and . . .

'Grand gestures do not fix bad, recurrent behaviour,' I tell him (and myself) sternly. 'It's Feminism Rules for Relationships 101. No amount of candles or red roses substitute for a boy who treats you well.'

He runs a hand through his hair, forgetting for a moment that it's exposing the scarred side of his face. But just as he freezes, ready to let his curls hide the scars once more, he stops and, looking me straight in the eye, rakes his hair back anyway. 'I can do better?' The way he says it makes it into a question. 'Like you said when I thought you were calling me a freak, I'm . . . I'm kind of screwed up about stuff and when Tai's involved . . .' He swallows hard. 'It's really complicated – and I'm not just saying that as an excuse. I know it sounded like I was dismissing how he was behaving, but he knew he'd put his foot in it and when that happens he gets . . .' He closes his eyes for a second, looking pained. '. . . mad defensive and I didn't want things to escalate so I . . . I focused on him instead of you and I'm sorry and I'd really love it if you could help me get my shit together about this, like you did about the "freak" thing,' he ends, all in a rush.

'Sounds like an absolute blast for me,' I tell him witheringly, despite the fact that everything in me is shouting, *Yes! Yes to all of the above! Especially if it comes with snogging!* 'You think because I've got my own stuff to deal with I'll be fully trained and ready to help with yours? I'll understand it all, will I, because broken people need to stick together?'

'No,' snaps Ren, then forces himself to take a deep breath. 'I'm a mess but I'm not broken and you . . . You're whatever you want to be, Ven. All I know is that there isn't anyone I enjoy spending time with as much as you. At least, when you don't hate me,' he adds in a small voice. 'Could you maybe not hate me? I really miss you for whatever that's worth.'

'You barely know me.'

It's true, even if sometimes it doesn't feel like it. But I refuse to let myself get carried away by a paper heart or those huge dark eyes.

He shrugs again. 'We could change that if you'd stop hating me.'

Oh my God, he's so gorgeous, says my brain. *So, so gorgeous. And clearly very, very sorry.*

Then it adds, *But I really, REALLY need to wee.*

'I really, really need to wee,' I say before I can stop myself. And because I really, really honestly do, I turn and pretty much bolt into the loos (well, my equivalent of bolting).

I should be figuring out what to do about Ren and his gorgeousness and his tendency to be a complete jerk, but I am entirely occupied by how much it hurts to wee. And by the fact that even after I wee, I don't get up because I feel like I need to wee some more. My life is now complete: I'm stuck on the loo in the middle of a romantic crisis.

I close my eyes and try to think happy thoughts, then I flush the loo and go to wash my hands. Only I really need to wee some more.

My wee is pink. I didn't think cranberry juice did that. It is officially gross: the humiliation cherry on the degradation cake.

I wash my hands again, still trying to figure out what to say to Ren because I can't just leave him standing there and I seriously don't want him to think I'm hiding in the loos, because that would be pathetic but *Oh my God, I need to wee.*

When I finally make it out of the loo, Ren is nowhere to be seen. I sag against the nearest wall, swiping at the cold sweat prickling across the back of my neck.

Orla and Roks are dancing with Benjo, Fred and George a few metres away. Behind them, Pip and Sam are attempting some sort of ballroom move that ends with them both laughing on the floor. Ashley catches my eye and beckons me over, but I just wave back and give her a thumbs up, gesturing towards the drinks table. I need to sit down, but the chairs are all the way across the room. I could just sit here on the floor, but then Orla would probably feel she had to stop dancing to check on me and I don't want to interrupt them. Adding Party Pooper to Bossiest Girl In The World doesn't seem like a recipe for social success.

Ren seems to have disappeared. He can't seriously have thought I'd hide rather than just reject his apology outright, can he?

I take out my phone, finger hovering over the message icon, but when I glance round once more, there he is. I step forwards eagerly, then the crowd parts and I see that he's dancing with Maddie. Her face is turned up to his as Ren spins her out then draws her in again. I watch as she throws her head back, laughing, before she leans in, whispering something to him. They part, then attempt a travelling return, only Ren spins at the wrong point, tripping her so that he has to lunge forward to stop her falling. They cling to each other, laughing.

I thought Maddie wanted to tear his throat out with her teeth for me.

I thought he barely knew who she was.

I thought he'd wait for me.

I don't understand what's happening. Surely I can't have wrecked things just by needing the loo. *Oh my God, I need the loo, need to go now, now, now, now, NOW.*

I turn and stumble frantically back into the toilet, nearly crying when I spot an empty cubicle. I make a weird sob-type sound when I wee more pink cranberry wee.

Finally, I manage to wash my hands and leave the toilets again.

Maddie is standing by the drinks table now, winding her hair about her finger as she chats with Fred. Ren is gone.

I wish I weren't so sweaty and shaky. And why is it so hot in here? No, cold. It's cold. I'm cold and sweaty and shaking and teary, though I sort of want to laugh without knowing why and . . .

Oh.

I am stupid.

And ill.

I need to go home.

First, though, I need to tell Maddie, because if I leave without a word she is going to go nuts. Thankfully the drinks table is on the way to the door because a detour is so not on the cards right now. I don't know whether it's a good thing or a bad one that Ren's nowhere to be seen again, but at least it means I don't have to deal with why he and my best friend were dancing just a few minutes ago.

'Ven!' Maddie squeals, when I tap her on the shoulder. 'Where have you been? I . . .' She trails off, her face falling. 'You look *awful*.'

'I'm sick,' I say. 'Weeing issues,' I whisper very, very quietly.

Maddie makes a face. 'Give me five minutes to say bye to Fred and Orla and I'll meet you at the car.'

'Don't be silly. Just have a nice time and give me all the gossip tomorrow. I do not need an audience for the fact that I'm going to spend the next hour or two on the loo. I'll message you later, but I've got to go before I end up stuck in the loo *here*.'

I turn away while she's still protesting. 'Say bye to Orla for me!' I call over my shoulder.

By the time I pull into my drive, I just want to sit and rest, but I really, really need to wee. It's a relief that, for once, no one's home to watch me hobble in tiny, painful oh-my-God-I'm-bursting little steps. This time it stings fiercely, although I barely have any wee left to wee. When I turn to flush, I see I've progressed from pink-tinged wee to a strong rosé-wine colour.

I manage to lie down on the sofa for all of five minutes before I have to head back to the loo. This time I just stay there, weeing progressively pinker then redder. It's around this time that I realise it's probably not cranberry juice but blood that's causing the problem.

It stops me cold for a moment, but then I reason that in the scheme of things it can't be a lot of blood. Nothing to panic about. It's obviously not good, but it's not an emergency yet. Probably.

I'm feeling a bit woozy as I head to the kitchen, keeping a careful hand on the wall.

Get a grip, I tell myself firmly. *It's not nice but it's not going to kill you. If it doesn't stop, you can call the NHS helpline and see if they think a doctor should come out.*

In the meantime, I've got the shakes something rotten and my breathing's a bit weird and my heart's all fluttery so I fetch myself a Gatorade. Then I put the kettle on because, although I'm kind of clammy-sweaty, I'm also freezing cold – so cold my teeth are starting to chatter. Is this normal? Maddie had a UTI once and she said it was horrid, but she never mentioned this.

'Just a bit shocky,' I whisper, but there's no comfort in the words when my voice sounds so thin and hoarse.

Forcing myself to focus on what I can do to fix things – get warm then lie down with a hot, sweet drink and sip it slowly – I set my wheat bag heating in the microwave (it's literally a fabric bag of hard wheat grains that can be heated up then draped over a sore shoulder or knee – like frozen peas, but cosy). As I lean against the counter, my eyes fall on the phone.

Maybe I should call Aunt Jinnie. I mean, I'm handling it so I'll probably be fine in half an hour, but maybe it would be sensible to let someone know, just in case ...

On the other hand, I don't want to bother her when I'm ninety-nine per cent sure I'd be wasting her time. After all, if things keep going as they are, there will be plenty of SOS calls in my future and I don't want to have cried wolf so often I've used up all my rescues before things get really bad.

As I stand there, trying to figure out what to do, I realise that the edges of the kitchen have gone wavery and grey. Then suddenly everything's spotty. The spots keep getting bigger and bigger and I suddenly feel really sick and ice cold.

I should have called Aunt Jinnie, I think.

Then the world turns over and swallows me whole.

A Little While Later

'Ven?'

Shh. I'm sleeping. Go away. Tired. Sleeping.

'Maybe she's in bed. You don't want to wake her if she's sick.'

Yes. Sleeping. Go 'way.

'Ven, are you in your room?' Someone stomps upstairs, then down again. 'Did you check the living room?'

It's Maddie. Maddie's the one stomping and waking me up.

Why is my bed so cold and hard?

Not in bed.

Why am I not in bed? Isn't it night-time?

Doesn't matter. Need to sleep. So tired ...

But something's not right. The tone of Maddie's voice says something's not right.

'Maddie?' I mumble. My voice is broken. I can barely hear myself.

Footsteps coming closer. Good. She'll let me sleep when she sees how tired I am.

'Ren!'

What's Ren doing here? Why is Ren here when I'm sleeping?

'Ven, wake up!'

There's a warm weight against my side and soft, cool hands on my face and warm breath on my skin.

'Ven, please wake up.'

I'm awake. You woke me. Oh, but I've got my eyes shut.

I open my eyes. Everything's fuzzy so I blink.

Maddie is kneeling beside me, bending over so her hair tickles my nose.

A moment later, Ren is on my other side. His beautiful face is full of fear.

I feel a smile tug at my lips. It's nice that he's worried about me.

His hand closes on my shoulder. 'I'm calling an ambulance,' he says. 'Good job you already hate me, I guess.'

'Don't hate you,' I whisper. It comes out weird and slurred, but Ren smiles as he dials.

'Ven, what's wrong?' Maddie is saying, stroking my hair back from my face.

'Think I'm bleeding.'

Her eyes scan me.

'Something inside. Kidneys? Maybe kidneys. Didn't think it was too bad. Was going to call Aunt Jinnie . . .' I trail off with a groan. 'Don't need an ambulance. We could go in the car.'

Maddie snorts and a big fat tear plops onto my cheek. 'I am so unbelievably cross with you. You need an ambulance, Ven. Shut up, OK?'

'Don't call my parents,' I whisper, closing my eyes because the kitchen is starting to turn around me like we're on a merry-go-round.

'Of course I'm—'

'Let them have their anniversary, OK? Don't need to ruin *everyone*'s night.'

'Our night wouldn't have been ruined if you'd just let me come home with you instead of being all stoic and stupid and leaving me to find you passed out on the kitchen floor,' Maddie says. And I know she means it to sound angry, but it just comes out small and scared.

'Sorry,' I whisper. 'Didn't think it was a big deal.' I sigh. 'It definitely isn't a *big*, big deal.'

'We note your complaint, but you're still going to the hospital,' Ren says, leaning over me again, phone to his ear. 'They said the ambulance will be here soon. And they said we should definitely call your parents or at least a family member.' My face must fall because a moment later Ren is telling the person at the end of the 999 call to hold on as he sets the phone aside and reaches out for my hand. 'Obviously we're going to the hospital in the ambulance with you, but they need someone from your family to meet us there.'

I close my eyes and squeeze Ren's hand. 'Call Aunt Jinnie. Then maybe you could help me to the sofa.'

I think there's a silent conversation going on over my head because after a moment Maddie scrambles away with Ren's phone to one ear even as she taps out a message on mine with her other hand. Ren settles down against my side.

'Maddie's getting you a blanket but you're staying where you are till the paramedics get here.'

'I hate hospitals. I hate doctors. Tonight sucks.'

'One day we'll look back on this and laugh.'

I squint an eye open and give him a doubtful look.

'OK, maybe we won't, but we're getting to spend some quality time together on your kitchen floor. I figure there's a rule about not entirely hating someone after that, no matter how much of a jerk they've been.'

'I wasn't trying to avoid you earlier.'

Ren smiles. 'I figured that out when Maddie came running over to tell me she was a terrible friend but she wasn't going to let you down again so I had to help her check you weren't dying. She said she was too worried to wait for a lift or taxi so she was going through the park and she'd do it alone if she had to, but she'd rather not because she actually has some sense of self-preservation . . .' He trails off meaningfully.

'I'm just sick,' I say, closing my eyes again.

'You need to learn to ask for help, Ven.'

I hum and roll onto my side so I can huddle against him. He's all warm and when he eases down so we're sort of curled into each other I drift off into an almost-sleep thinking that at least there's been one bright spot to the night.

A Lifetime of Humiliation Later

Because we're all underage, they let Maddie and Ren ride in the ambulance with me. Maddie holds my hand and Ren latches onto my ankle and it'd be kind of nice, if I didn't feel so awful. I try not to think about what I saw at the party, why they ended up at my house together, and what it means that they suddenly seem like a united front. Under other circumstances it would be impossible to ignore, but there are quite a number of rather pressing distractions that put it out of my head for whole minutes at a time.

Aunt Jinnie arrives twenty minutes after we get to the hospital and promptly sends Maddie and Ren off in a taxi. That done, she settles at my side and starts insisting that every possible test is run immediately. There are a *lot* of tests and pokings and proddings and a great deal of Things We Will Not Discuss, but which are deeply embarrassing and gross. However, at the end of it all I am allowed to go home. Aunt Jinnie and I get back at the same time as my parents. Soon I am installed on the sofa after which everyone alternately fusses over me and yells very quietly.

The only upside is that I no longer desperately need the loo all the time. It has been an entire two hours since I last weed. What delight!

Sometimes it's the small things in life.

I want to burrow into the sofa and pretend absolutely nothing happened, but I know it's asking for trouble. So, since I am tough and brave, I message Maddie.

I am still among the living, but my family are making me wish I weren't. Come over tomorrow and save me? Also you can get the yelling over with. The suspense isn't good for me. xx

Then I compose and edit and re-edit and delete and rewrite a message to Ren, finally settling on, *Thank you for last night. I will snark you in a day or two when my brain has unmushed itself.*

I have the world's longest silent debate with myself about whether to add a kiss. I don't. Instead, I send a spectacularly enticing PS – *Also, we really need to talk about our arrangement* – because apparently my flirting skills are about as developed as my self-preservation ones.

Maddie sends back an all-caps reply composed entirely of swear words. At the end it says, *I love you. Glad you're not dead. Xx*

Ren's reply takes a while. Probably because he's busy rather than doing the writing/rewriting thing, but I can't help but hope otherwise. All his message says is, *Can I come over so we can snark in person tomorrow? I'd really like to SEE you're OK. If you don't mind.*

Yes please, I write back before I can overthink it.

I get a smiley face in return and sit beaming stupidly at it for five pathetic minutes. I blame this soppy behaviour on emotional and physical exhaustion.

Then I remember that Ren and Maddie were at my house together – right after that thing I witnessed at the party – and now I've gone and invited them both tomorrow. Suddenly I don't feel sappy at all.

Monday

(but the Easter-holiday type)

Item 1: convalesce.

Item 2: apologise to Maddie.

Item 3: find a way to ask (without making it weird) why she was at my house *with Ren* when I collapsed, instead of him just dropping her off, given that she lives almost around the corner.

I was hoping Maddie would arrive early enough to get her yelling done before Ren joined us, but when she lets herself in Ren trails her down the corridor. I blink at them. Did they come together – again – or did they just arrive at the same time? What exactly went on in the half hour I was stuck in the loo after Ren made his grand gesture?

'I'll let you fight while I figure out your kettle, OK?' Ren says, barely giving me a wave before he disappears into the kitchen.

I stare after him open-mouthed. I still don't know how they

had time to make friends and start dancing together let alone *this*, whatever *this* is.

'Oi,' Maddie says, plopping down next to me and poking me in the arm. 'You need to focus for this. I spent yesterday preparing.'

I give her my most pleading, wide-eyed, helpless-invalid look.

'Not a chance,' she says. 'You told me you were OK. You didn't call for help when you needed it. You left me to figure it out for myself and use my spare key to find you passed out on the floor. I cannot emphasise enough how cross I'm going to be if you ever do anything remotely like it again.'

'So noted.'

'Shut up. I've only just started.'

I really want to ask what happened with Ren and why they're suddenly besties, but I know my role is to sit quietly and be lectured.

Maddie is in mid-flow when there is a pointed cough from the doorway some ten minutes later. Ren is standing there with a huge tray of steaming mugs and enormous pieces of cake. 'Ven's parents say you've got to have a tea-break in yelling at her.'

'I wasn't yelling,' Maddie protests. 'I was informing her of the many and varied ways she has caused trouble and distress to those she professes to love. It's a guilt trip, not a shouting session.'

Ren raises an eyebrow. 'It's a very loud guilt trip.'

Maddie huffs at him and points at the coffee table.

Ren puts the tray down then passes me nearly a quarter of a Victoria sponge cake. 'Your mother said to make you eat this by any means necessary if I don't want to face the consequences.'

I look at Maddie. 'This is a stupid amount of cake. Tell him, Mads.'

'Eat the bloody cake,' my loving best friend tells me.

'Everyone's punishing me for being ill,' I say sulkily.

I am met with matching glares and quickly devote myself to the cake.

'Do you think she's the most infuriating person you'll ever meet, or just the worst you've met yet?' Maddie asks Ren.

'I'm trying to get her not to hate me, so can we return to the question when she's decided she's stuck with having me around?'

I peek up to find them sharing a conspiratorial look. What is going on between them?

All too soon the cake is gone. I put the plate aside to find Maddie grinning at me like the Cheshire Cat.

'Since I had all the cake, could you consider finishing your rant early?'

'No. There's lots more. Right, the next bit goes—'

'How about I put on that musical I told you about?' Ren interrupts.

'The *Bandwagon* one or the *Brigadoon* one?' Maddie asks. 'Or that series about Broadway?'

'I bought them all,' Ren says and Maddie squeaks with delight.

When did they talk about musicals?

'We could let Ven pick?' Ren suggests.

'Ven doesn't deserve to pick. Shut up,' she tells me, though I've made no effort to speak.

I scrunch down in my blankets.

'Ren, go make film things happen,' Maddie orders.

Ren barely rolls his eyes as he gets up to oblige. This is incredibly un-Ren-like behaviour. Something *must* have happened between them. Something significant. Obviously he bumped into Maddie after I had to dive into the loos, but then what? He told her I'd rejected him, grand gesture and all, and she forgot how he'd treated me, and how she hated him on my behalf, and fell into his arms instead?

No, I'm just jumping to stupid conclusions. Maddie wouldn't do that to me . . . would she? I mean, she wouldn't if she knew how I felt, but what if she believed me when I said I was completely done with him.

A hand settles on my knee. 'I know I yelled and guilted a lot,' Maddie says, voice suddenly gentle, 'but you're not going to cry, are you? I want you to be sorry – very, VERY sorry – but I don't actually want you to cry. You almost never cry. She almost never cries,' Maddie adds to Ren as if he didn't hear the first time.

I sniffle and swipe at my eyes. 'Just yawned. Made my eyes water.'

Maddie clearly doesn't believe me and squishes up against my shoulder. 'It was really, really awful finding you on the floor like that. You know that, right?' She doesn't look at me as she says it, staring across the room with her mouth a thin, quivering line. 'I know I can be stupid and inconsiderate about you being sick, and I haven't quite sussed out how to spot when you're pushing your limits but . . .' She stops with a sharp little intake of breath.

'I haven't sussed it either, Maddie,' I say softly.

'You don't want to, you mean,' she says testily. 'You've never had any common sense when it comes to your well-being, but now you can't afford to be like that.'

'OK,' I whisper as she puts her arms around me.

When I pull back, I realise Ren's gone.

'We've got a deal that he buggers off if we need a moment,' Maddie explains.

They've got a deal. Oh.

'Ren!' Maddie screams, and I wince as my eardrums protest. 'We're done now!'

He reappears with an enormous bowl of popcorn.

'Oooo, gimme,' says Maddie, snatching it from him.

I want to think Ren picks the armchair at her end of the sofa because of the popcorn, but I don't really believe it.

Having angsted over Maddie's role in all this, my mind turns to Ren and how he can have performed a grand romantic gesture for me one minute then switched affections within the hour. If that's what happened and I'm not just panicking over nothing. But what other explanation is there? It makes sense that, if he thought I'd rejected him and Maddie was super nice and comforting, he might have figured it was just serendipity.

Why didn't I say something to him before I rushed off to the loo? Now it might be too late and I can't even blame it entirely on my stupid body being stupid. Some of the stupid is just pure me.

My chin starts quivering dangerously and I quickly disentangle my legs from Maddie's, levering myself upright.

‘Where are you going?’ she demands.

I turn so she can’t see my face and point towards the bathroom.

‘Oh, OK. Don’t take too long or I’ll come and find you.’

But I do take my time, splashing water on my face and adjusting my make-up then finger-combing my hair, which just makes the whole frizzy mess worse.

Of course Ren’s decided he likes Maddie, and why wouldn’t she like him? As I stare into the mirror, I want to rev myself up with anger at them, but I can’t. All I feel is misery that I’ve lost something I wasn’t being careful enough with, not realising how much it meant to me.

I can hear the two of them whispering together as I pause at the top of the stairs.

‘But she’s so quiet and placid and *nice*. Are they sure she shouldn’t still be in hospital?’ Ren is saying.

Great. He thinks I’m only nice when I’m ill. Another reason for him to like Maddie better.

‘The hospital said it’s something to do with one of the kidney valves, but the organ itself is fine and she’ll be fine too with some antibiotics. Hopefully it’s just a one-off, but we’ll have to see.’

I feel my skin flame with heat. Why does Maddie know all this? I haven’t told her. Why is she telling Ren? It’s my medical information, not theirs.

‘So should we tell her about . . . you know?’

‘Not now!’ Maddie hisses.

‘But what if she’s angry we didn’t tell her earlier? Don’t you think—’

‘This is *not* the time.’

‘Do you at least have a plan for when?’ Ren asks, and there’s a teasing note in his voice that wouldn’t be there if they weren’t together.

I try to think good thoughts about two people I care about making each other happy.

And when that doesn’t work, I try telling myself that it’s just raw and new but soon I’ll be fine with it.

And when *that’s* no good, I try to focus on the fact that I love Maddie and the most important thing of all is that our friendship is back on track.

But it still feels like I’ve dislocated my heart.

Centuries* of Misery Later . . .

(* a good two hours at least)

Everyone puts my near silence down to tiredness, so Mum and Dad pointedly usher Maddie and Ren out after the movie.

'See you tomorrow?' Maddie calls over her shoulder.

'See you,' I say, trying to make my voice bright.

But Maddie is already talking to Ren. 'Can you pick me up from Fred's at two? We should be done arranging by then and it'll give the two of us an hour before we said we'd be back here.'

I mustn't think about what their plans are for that hour. I must be a good best friend, even if part of me thinks Maddie's broken the Code. I don't really believe in stupid codes, but . . .

I scrub my hands over my face and stomp into the kitchen.

'Why the hell are you telling Maddie about my medical stuff?' I growl at my parents, slamming a mug onto the counter next to the kettle. 'It's private.'

'We didn't realise you'd mind,' Dad says. 'And we need Maddie to understand about your condition—'

'I'm not a child. It's up to me who I tell and what I tell them! I know I was stupid and I broke your trust by not calling for help when I needed it, but I didn't *know* how sick I was. It was an accident, or at least a mistake. An honest mistake.'

But they're both looking at me in this sad, solemn way.

Dad shakes his head. 'I know that's true to a point, Ven, but it's not the whole truth. You're always so busy being brave and indomitable that sometimes you make pretty foolish choices.'

'I'm just trying not to behave like an invalid! If I panicked every time some awful thing happened with my body, we'd be calling an ambulance three times a day.'

Mum reaches out but I step away.

'I don't always know my limits, but that's not my fault. Even the doctors don't know. They say one thing, then another, then they try me on these meds, then those ones and they don't really *know*.'

Mum rubs at her eyes behind her glasses. 'We've been discussing things,' she says, glancing at Dad in a way that makes my stomach lurch, 'and maybe you need a year off school to focus on getting well. We know how hard it is – all the time for doctors' appointments and the energy it takes to go to so many different hospitals and recover from all the tests—'

'And you think I want to spend a year stuck in that nightmare with nothing good to keep me going?'

'If your health is better afterwards—' Dad tries to cut in, but I stop him short.

'It's not going to be better.' I deflate into a chair. 'I know you've been reading up about it all – I have too. Maybe there will be new treatments in the future but right now this is it, so the important thing is that I'm coping. But I won't cope if this is all I am – all my life is.'

I let Mum wrap herself around me, patting her arm when I realise she's crying. Then Dad joins in. I probably cry a bit too.

Let's just say we spend a while being weepy and miserable.

When we finally quit being maudlin, Mum sends me off to soak in the bath. By the time I come down in my pyjamas, Aunt Jinnie's in the kitchen with Mum and Dad and there's the hushed, concentrated feeling of a big festival day, though I didn't think we had anything on the To-Do List of Doom for this week.

It turns out they're not doing festival stuff at all. They're researching me. With a sigh, I join them.

We don't find any amazing solution, but we do learn some interesting stuff. Some of the things my body does that I thought were completely normal (as in normal for normal people) are actually symptoms of my condition. We also find a handful of tips that improve symptoms for some people and are so easy and low-cost they can't hurt to try. The most promising involves avoiding seemingly random types of food that are actually all things that ferment quickly in the body, which is bad for stomachs like mine – turns out 'an apple a day' might be the worst possible advice for people like me!

Finally, if reluctantly, when Mum asks for the fifth time if I couldn't re-consider the chronic pain self-help group, I sign up to a Facebook group for teens with mobility issues. As Dad said, I don't have to talk to any of them if I don't want to, but who knows? Maybe there will be some useful tips. Or maybe I'll think of a question I want to ask. And at least if I hate it, I can just close the laptop and that's that.

'We really need to pick this year's charities for the festival,' Mum says tentatively. 'Maybe it could be a few of the organisations that do research—'

'No,' I say, when I realise why she's looking so nervous about her proposal. 'We're not making it about me. I want to focus on someone else's problems for once. I promise I'll have a decision soon.'

Pushing myself to my feet, I make tea for everyone while the adults settle down to some festival work. My parents barely look up when I deliver their caffeine, but I manage to catch Aunt Jinnie's eye and nod towards the living room. She raises an eyebrow, but silently follows me next door and settles on the sofa with me.

'Spill,' she orders.

So, I slide my laptop in front of her, wiggling the mouse till it whirs softly to life, then I click open the letter on my desktop.

'This isn't for now,' I say, when Aunt Jinnie's eyes fly to my face in panic. 'It's just in case. Because I need someone to know what I want, if I can't tell them. And I'm not depressed or, like, freaking out about what might happen or anything like that. I just . . . there's never a good time to discuss this stuff because the right time's too late.'

I take her hands in mine. 'You always, always stick up for me. And, if it ever comes to it, I know you love me enough to do what's right for me. This just makes it really clear what that is.'

Aunt Jinnie squeezes her lips together, but still her chin quivers. She lets go with one hand, reaching up to tuck a curl behind my ear. 'My bestest girl,' she whispers.

I fall into her arms and she holds me tight, pressing a fierce kiss to my hair.

Over dinner, the four of us outline some ground-rules about what different people are allowed to know about my health, then I gather up my pudding and the merchandise folder.

'And now you're all going to leave me in peace,' I tell them, 'because if you don't we're stuck with Designer Dick's monstrosity of a logo blown up to show off its true vileness across all our merchandise. Up to you.'

Reader, they left me in peace.

One Hour Later

Item 1: save this year's merchandise.

Days to festival: 73

I'm no graphic designer, but it doesn't really matter at this point. Designer Dick's effort is a disaster. Any improvement is better than nothing and, at the end of the day, the design just needs to be good enough that it doesn't stop our merch selling – not exactly a high bar. Still, a doodle on a piece of notepaper isn't going to do it.

I sit staring at it, then suddenly I know exactly what I need to do. Smiling, I take out my phone and message Roks.

Need a massive Photoshop-related favour in the next twenty-four hours. Will trade time spent sorting graphics emergency for babysitting. Will also throw in online boot-shopping expertise and a graphics credit in the official festival programme.

I tag my address onto the end.

Roks's reply is almost immediate. *Deal. See you in 10.*

When she arrives, we sit on the sofa, my laptop on the coffee table in front of us, and politely sip the mocktails Aunt Jinnie made us 'to help the work along'.

'So, um,' I say articulately after five minutes, 'do you want to start with boot-shopping or are you OK if I launch in about the merchandise design?'

Roksana raises one perfect eyebrow and suddenly we dissolve into giggles.

'Let's just stop being polite to each other, OK?' she says when we finally get our breath back.

'Why are you the second person to say that to me in the last month? Rhetorical!'

Roksana snorts, shifting to tuck her feet under her as she gestures at the laptop. 'Let's focus on the graphics, though I am *so* keeping you to the offer of boot-shopping help. But I warn you – I've got all of a tenner right now, because I bought an art book I shouldn't have.'

'Is that what you want to do at uni?'

She shakes her head. 'My thing's art history, but *if* I go to uni, I need to study something sensible. Anyway, it probably doesn't make sense to go at all. It's such a lot of money, and I'd have to stay living at home to help with The Brood . . .'

I frown. 'I thought you just had the one sister and The Brood was really Orla's lot.'

'They are. It's . . . complicated.' She shifts uncomfortably.

I keep my face open and my curiosity to myself.

It's obviously the right move because Roks relaxes again.

'The point is that family stuff keeps me busy, which would eat into my study time, and I'd have to work too so ...' She darts a glance at me. 'Before you tell me it's my life, I get that. It *is* my decision. But my decision is that I love my family and they come first.'

I want to say something supportive and wise, but I'm coming up blank on what that might be.

'Actually ... you know you said you'd trade design help for babysitting?' Roks says before I can think of something. 'I really want to go to a university open day, just to see, but I'm meant to be with Orla on the stall this weekend. Is there any way you could help with this instead? It'd be way more than a few hours so is there any chance we could just agree I owe you some more graphics time? I promise I'll make it up eventually.'

I roll my eyes at her. 'Roks, this is a *massive* out-of-the-blue favour. I am delighted to trade it for a day on the stall. That's totally fair, no extra owed.'

Roks groans, scrubbing a hand down her face. 'It's really not. I appreciate it, but I don't like taking advantage—'

'Oh, come on,' I tell her.

Roks gives me a look that's half grateful, half angry. 'I'm fed up of being the person who always needs help,' she grinds out between her teeth. 'You already bailed us out with Maddie babysitting at the mall. It's not fair if we keep dumping on you just because we're friends now.'

I stare at her, warmth blossoming in my chest and a smile breaking across my face. 'Friendships aren't tit-for-tat,' I say, my voice only a little hoarse. 'I'm not planning to keep a balance sheet. Are you?'

She heaves a frustrated sigh. 'I don't even know why I want to go to the stupid open day when I can't do the degree anyway.'

I reach out and knock my slipper against her foot. 'Because you want to see what your options are. You deserve that. Anyway, it's a done deal, don't want to hear any more about it.'

For the next while, we focus on the laptop, but it's not uncomfortable. Roks is smiling – just a little – and so am I. My chest feels tight with hope.

Something-day

(no school so it really doesn't matter)

Item 1: learn to work with Ren without imploding if it turns out he and Maddie are together.

Deciding there really is no time like the present, I suck up my pride and message Ren to ask if I can go over to his to work on our arrangement.

The fact that it's Tai who opens the door when I ring their bell does nothing to improve my mood at having to spend the morning with my-best-friend's-maybe-but-hopefully-not-new-boyfriend-who-I-have-a massive-crush-on.

'Ren and I have music coursework,' I say instead of hello, because that feels like less of a concession while still being polite and dignified because I am not a complete turd – unlike some people.

Tai opens the door wider, rubbing wearily at his eyes. He's unshaven, a greyish tint to his skin. 'He's in the garden,' he says, voice rasping as if he hasn't used it in a while – or has spent the morning puking.

I consider starting a conversation – very loudly – in appreciation of his hangover. Instead, I am a literal saint and merely shuck my shoes in the line by the coat rack then march past, feeling Tai's eyes follow me until I turn into the kitchen. Let him look at my stupid slopping gait if it pleases him. At least I can't help that, whereas he could probably do *something* about being a total git.

Ren is fussing over a pair of loungers shaded by a little apple tree in the tiny back garden. There's lemonade (actual freshly squeezed lemonade with lemon slices floating in it) and glasses on a wrought-iron table.

'Hi,' I call as I step down onto the grass.

He swings round, looking like I've caught him doing something dodgy. 'Hi!' he squeaks.

'Tai let me in,' I tell him inanely.

'Oh. Good.' He shakes himself then gestures at the loungers. 'Is this OK? I thought it might be more comfortable than sitting at the kitchen table, but if you're cold—'

Why is he so nervous? I'm the one who needs to make sure I'm being perky and entirely jealousy-free. 'This is great.' I dump my bag by the nearest lounger and make a show of settling down.

'Can I get you something? Cup of tea? Coffee?'

'Lemonade's perfect for now.'

He hurries to pour me a glass, spilling it over his wrist. He shakes it off with a grimace. 'Well, that was smooth. But look' – he reaches over and hands me a plate of biscuits – 'I made absolutely sure we had chocolate ones.'

I manufacture a smile. 'Thanks!' I chirp, helping myself. 'Shall we just dive in with picking the song we're going to arrange?'

'I thought maybe . . . a mash-up?' he says tentatively.

'I've no idea how to do one, but sure,' I say, nodding so enthusiastically I have to put my shoulder blade back in.

And so it goes for the next glacial, terminally awkward hour as we toss around ideas for songs we can put a rock-gospel spin on. When we finally run out of steam – we've got some possibilities but nothing that quite chimes with either of us – Ren excuses himself to make tea. I scroll on my phone for a bit, then realise I need the loo and pad over to the door, only to pause at the lintel.

'I thought the meeting started at eleven,' Ren is saying in a low, furious voice.

'I spent the last four hours upchucking. I'll catch the afternoon one.'

'You mean you'll leave the house and head straight to the nearest pub.'

'Really appreciate the faith and encouragement,' Tai growls.

'Because last night merits that, does it? Mum didn't even want to go to work today, but you promised you'd go to a meeting.'

'I'm trying, OK? I messed up – *again* – but I'm trying! What more do you want from me?'

'I want you to stop. Just stop. Mum's working all the hours under the sun to pay for this move to get you straightened out.

It's time to show her some appreciation and stop crapping your life up – and mine.'

There's a horrible, leaden pause.

'And there it is,' says Tai, cold and hard and miserable. 'Because what's really gonna help me choose not to go out and drink again is reminding me how the worst thing I've ever done is going to be staring me in the face for the rest of my life.'

'Well, it's better than it *being* your face – I'd take that happily,' Ren spits back.

Someone goes stomping away down the corridor, then pounds upstairs.

There's a sound like a stifled sob. 'So would I,' Tai whispers, his voice wrecked with grief.

I dither by the back door until I hear the radio go on, then put a smile on my face and step into the kitchen because, in case you missed it, I'm constitutionally incapable of avoiding problems.

'Any chance of a cuppa?' I say cheerily, as if Tai hadn't said things I'd happily defenestrate him for the last time we met. I'm starting to suspect that his truly impressive rudeness was less to do with prejudice and more to do with whatever's going on between him and Ren . . . and possibly withdrawal symptoms. 'Ren's done a runner and my caffeine levels are depleting rapidly,' I add when Tai stands looking at me so blankly I wonder for a moment if he not only forgot I was there but who I am.

Finally he shakes himself, putting his phone down, and moves to fill the kettle. I slop over to lean against the counter. His phone is still playing the video I mistook for the radio and I realise it's a clip of two kids running about a garden. The bigger one is blowing bubbles from one of those pots you get in party bags and the little one is chasing them, snatching them from the air with shrieks of delight.

When I look up, Tai is staring down at the phone too, his face tight.

I wince. 'Sorry. Didn't mean to be nosy.'

Tai swallows hard. 'I'd be hours blowing bubbles for him and he'd just chase them and chase them like the frigging Energizer bunny.' His face twists between emotions too fast for me to identify as he looks down at the phone. Love and guilt and misery and rage, then back to guilt. 'When did it get so complicated to be happy?' he asks, then snatches up the phone and clicks it off. 'Tea? Coffee?'

'Is caffeine on offer?' Ren asks, appearing in the doorway. His eyes sweep from me to Tai and back again, shoulders relaxing when he sees there's no blood-spatter on the kitchen walls.

I watch him and Tai move around each other, fetching milk and sugar, coffee grounds and teabags. Ren always stands on Tai's left, so the scarred side of his face is away from his brother. Yet every time Ren turns away, Tai stares after him, his eyes full of pity and horror.

The Next Day

(Wednesday? Let's go with Wednesday)

Item 1: figure out the mash-up while there's still time for The Singers to rehearse it before the festival.

Thankfully, Orla and Roks's arrangement is done, and Maddie and Fred's just needs tweaks, so we're two steps closer to a well-rehearsed set list for the festival. Still, it's embarrassing to be the last pair to finish our arrangement when I'm meant to be the leader – not to mention that the whole reason I took over The Singers was to ace my coursework, and if Ren and I don't have a song for the group to perform ...

Desperation provides the courage to invite Ren over to continue where we left off yesterday. If you've seen *Pitch Perfect,* you'll know the scene where one of the characters starts a song and another holds a matching beat then effortlessly breaks into a different song but the two fit together perfectly. That ... does not happen. We get as far as deciding to use 'Chandelier' and stall on what song to pair it with.

When Maddie turns up mid-morning, we break gratefully, squishing onto the sofa together so I can show them the final artwork proofs for the merch.

'I'd buy that for thirty-two quid,' Maddie says, squinting at the proof of the festival hoodies over my shoulder.

Roks has worked wonders and my far-from-professional doodle not only looks a thousand times better than Designer Dick's disaster, but, done up properly, is actually quite good.

'I *will* buy that for thirty-two quid,' Ren puts in, leaning over my other shoulder.

I freeze, not sure what to do with myself.

Ren sighs, his breath warm on my cheek, then moves away.

Maddie gives me an odd look, so I quickly excuse myself to take some pills.

'What the hell did you do to her?' I hear Maddie ask the moment I'm out of the room.

'Nothing! What did you do? Did you tell her?'

'Of course I didn't tell her, moron.'

'Then why's she all quiet and meek?'

'Why would she be quiet and meek if I *did* tell her?' Maddie hisses back. 'When I asked if you thought what we're doing is OK, you told me she'd think it was great, so what—'

I go to the kitchen and pour myself some morphine from the little plastic travel-shampoo bottle I carry around with me. The big brown glass bottles the prescription comes in are super heavy and the lids always get jammed because liquid morphine may look like water but it's actually spectacularly sticky. Decanting it into the travel bottle stops me dislocating my thumb every time I need a dollop of extra pain relief to stay functional – and this is definitely one of those times as the day has already involved my hip going out, my jaw, my knee and a partridge in a pear tree.

The afternoon drags into evening. Ren and Maddie keep sharing these silent-conversation looks and, every time they do, I get quieter in an effort not to snap at them collectively or individually. I don't do jealous snits.

Apparently, however, jealous sulks are right on brand.

I need to get over myself before they figure it out. 'So, what have the two of you planned for the rest of the holidays?' I ask, trying to sound cheerful and accepting.

They give me matching looks of bewilderment.

'You're never happy when other people do the planning,' Maddie says, reaching out to check my forehead. 'Not feverish,' she reports.

'I'm . . . expanding my horizons.'

Maddie looks offended. 'There's something weird going on. What aren't you telling me?'

'Nothing! What aren't you telling me?'

Maddie lifts her hands. 'Nothing. Oh, well, almost nothing.' She glances at Ren.

I grit my teeth. 'Why don't the two of you just spit it out. I'm your friend – both of you. I don't know why your "big secret"' – I make little air quotes, hoping it looks nonchalant – 'needs to be a secret at all.'

'Look, I don't know what Mr Big Mouth here,' Maddie says, glaring at Ren, 'let slip about our surprise, but why wouldn't it need to be a secret? You get that the secrecy bit is pretty important in surprises, right?'

Ren glares back at Maddie, folding his arms. 'I didn't tell her anything. What do you think you know?' he asks me.

'That, well, you two ...'

'Oh my God,' says Maddie, and there is such laughter in her words that I nearly bite her.

I want to curl into a ball – anything so I don't have to look at them – but that would be pathetic, whereas I am a person of profound dignity ...

... for at least ten minutes a day. And, today, those minutes start right now.

'She thinks you're into me,' Maddie tells Ren.

Ren turns to me, disbelief and incredulity on his face then ... delight. Absolute sun-through-the-clouds delight. 'You're jealous,' he says.

O Gods above, please strike me dead with lightning or snatch me into oblivion by way of a handy one-woman cyclone, whichever will be faster.

Only ... Ren's look isn't one of smug, nasty, ha-got-one-over-on-you delight. It's honest and shy and flattered and ...

They're not together.

'So,' Ren says, 'can I take it my grand romantic apology worked after all and flirting with intent is back on the cards?'

I have absolutely no words to reply. My head is whirling with relief. *He's not with her. She's not with him. He still likes me, not her. She didn't betray me. He didn't pick her.*

'For the record, she's never been jealous of anyone ever before, so I'd take it as quite the endorsement,' my traitor of a best friend informs Ren. 'Yikes! That look,' she adds as she sees my face. 'Maybe I *should* tell you about our surprise.'

'Distraction isn't going to work here, Maddie. Face it like a girl,' Ren advises, as he heads for the door.

'How come you're running away?' she calls.

'I'm facing it like a boy,' echoes Ren's voice from the corridor as I fix my most terrifying smile on my best friend.

Maddie gives me her most winning look.

I hit her in the face with a pillow then belabour every part of her I can reach.

'Oh the cliché,' Ren drawls, as he comes back in with one of my vile electrolyte drinks and sets it down on the table beside me.

'Some things are clichés for good reason. What else are you allowed to hit your best friend with, especially if you need to hit her a lot?'

Maddie uses my moment of distraction to make a strategic retreat.

'So,' says Ren.

'Mm,' I reply. Then, because someone really, really needs to be a grown-up here, I manage, 'Do you want to do some more arranging tomorrow at yours then maybe come back over here and make dinner together? I know it's a bit simple and basic but—'

'Yes,' he says, sitting down beside me on the sofa. 'To dinner. And arranging.'

Slowly, checking my expression, he moves his hand across the cushion so his pinkie brushes mine. Then somehow our hands are turning over in unison, fingers entwining.

It turns out that simple and basic absolutely rocks.

Pretty Sure Today's Saturday

(still the holidays, so who cares?)

Item 1: help Orla on the stall while Roks is at her open day. Do not screw it up or piss anyone off.
Days to festival: 68.

Working on the stall is much like being on a merch point at the festival. Most of the time is taken up by people asking questions that range from the frankly bizarre to the gobsmackingly stupid.

By midday a rictus smile is frozen on my face, though for once my joints have decided to stay put.

'Stop that!' pleads Orla. 'You're scaring my customers.'

'I'm being friendly!'

'You look as friendly as a velociraptor. Why don't you go and get us a cup of tea?'

'Because I exhausted myself walking from the car. Why don't I pay and you do the fetching?'

Orla pulls a face. 'Roks said that I had to buy you food and drinks when you're working for us for free.'

'What she doesn't know won't hurt her,' I say, but Orla just shakes her head, and stomps away to fiddle with the display on the other side of the stall.

I blow out a long, frustrated breath.

Thankfully a string of customers turns up, giving me half an hour to work out exactly what I've done now. Maddie and Orla are quite similar, though Orla lurches between sweetness and abrasiveness in a way I'm learning has nothing to do with her personality and everything to do with a complete lack of confidence. The current problem finally dawns on me when I realise that, though she glares at me every time she looks over, her mouth is set in a line of misery rather than fury.

'I won't steal your best friend if you don't steal mine,' I tell her in a gap between customers.

'Wow,' she says, flushing. 'I'm so subtle, huh?'

I make a 'buttoning my lips' gesture and she laughs, slouching back against the edge of the table. 'I am sorry I'm being . . . less than grateful. It's really nice of you to do this for Roks.'

I shrug. 'Today may be for Roks, but if either of you ever need a hand the world probably won't end if you ask and, if I'm sick, I'm sure *someone* in The Singers will be able to help.'

Orla ducks her head. 'It'd really be something to have more people to count on – that's what Roks said the other day. You rub her up the wrong way, but she trusts you all the same, and Roks doesn't trust people much. It's a pretty big compliment.'

I look down at my feet. 'Yeah, I get that sense.'

Orla shrugs. 'Seems like maybe Roks isn't the only one who needs to learn how to trust other people enough to ask for help.'

I groan theatrically, holding up my free hand. 'Too many emotions too early in the day.'

Orla laughs. 'Fine. As a peace offering, I'll go and get tea.' She turns to grab her bag then freezes, face blanching. A moment later, she drops to the ground and scuttles under the table. 'Look away!' she whispers. 'Pretend I'm not here!'

I blink at her, then turn to see what's behind this bizarre behaviour. Everything looks normal. There are several mums with prams and a father with a giggling, bouncing toddler clinging to his hand. An elderly couple are strolling arm in arm, beaming at each other. And an ordinary-looking bloke in a T-shirt with a dribble of sauce on it is leaning against the burger van, smoking as he waits for his order.

I flick my eyes down at Orla.

'Shh!' she hisses, when I open my mouth. 'The man by the burger van. Tell me when he's gone. No, don't stare at him!'

'Why not? Hang on, here comes his food.' I watch the man immediately spill fresh ketchup down his shirt.

Orla just huddles into an even tighter ball, arms wrapped around herself.

'I think he's going ... Nope, he's dropping even more of his lunch down his front. Yikes – he's worse than Benjo. Oh, now he's going . . . Going . . . Going . . . Gone.'

Orla doesn't move.

I can't tell whether gentle teasing is what the situation calls for or the worst idea ever. Still, sarcasm is my go-to response, so I say, 'If you think I'm letting you off rehearsals because you're permanently balled up under the stall . . .'

She sucks in a breath, then peeks over the table before emerging, her shoulders hunched and fists clenched.

'Who was that?' I ask as gently as I can.

'Friend of my dad's,' she says absently, then winces. 'It's . . . complicated. I just really don't want my dad to know where I am.'

'Orla—'

'I'm not in any danger.' She flashes me a grateful smile, wrapping her arms around herself. 'Everything's fine if he didn't see me.'

'That doesn't sound fine to me.' There's a horrible hollow feeling in my stomach and even though I don't know any of the history of what just happened, I sense I understand everything that matters. 'Please don't yell at me,' I say, making my voice as soft as it'll go, 'but do I need to call the police or something?'

Orla rubs the heel of her hand against her temple, shoving the edge of her jumper into her mouth and gnawing at a loose thread.

'You don't have to tell *me* anything, but *someone* needs to know what's going on. And I don't just mean Roks. I mean a grown-up.'

'Everyone who needs to know already does,' Orla tells the pole holding up the stall's canopy, though her eyes quickly drift away to where the man disappeared into the crowd. 'What's he doing here?' she whispers.

'He was wearing flipflops. He's probably on holiday and it's just bad luck you saw him at all.' When I turn back to Orla, there are tears spilling down her face.

'I'm sorry,' she gasps, trying to brush them away. 'God, I'm—'

'I'm going to take a leap here and suggest you need a hug, so unless you say other—'

Orla is hugging me a second later, clinging with every muscle tensed. I rub her back, making an apologetic 'Could you come back later?' face at a customer.

My brain keeps churning through all sorts of horrible possibilities, but I know that if Orla wants to tell me why she's so scared of her dad finding out she works at a stall in the market, she will. I just hope she's telling the truth when she says she's safe. Whatever's going on, it's too big to get it wrong.

I'm still trying to figure it out when Orla pulls away to blow her nose. 'This really isn't what you signed up for,' she says wearily, deflating onto her stool.

I shrug. 'I also didn't sign up for us becoming friends, but I'm not sorry about that either. In fact, it's one of the nicer surprises the world's thrown at me lately.'

Orla doesn't say anything, just reaches out to squeeze my hand. All I can do is grip back and hope she understands everything I don't know how to say.

Fun and Games with Music Arranging

Item 1: talk to Ren about The Thing.

When I turn up at Ren's the next morning, once again it's Tai who opens the front door.

'We've got to stop meeting like this,' I tell him.

A reluctant smile twists the corners of his lips. 'Ren said you were ballsy.'

'Ren did not say that.'

Tai shrugs. 'Same difference. He wanted me to keep you occupied for a minute.'

'Because that's obviously a great idea based on our widely successful interactions so far,' I point out. 'Why am I being kept occupied?'

'He baked. Is baking.' He leans against the wall, yawning. 'It mostly looked like making a mess Mum will definitely kill him for when she gets home, followed by a whole lot of peering into the oven as if stress is part of the recipe.'

'So the baking is not a usual occurrence.'

'First time he's ever cooked for a girl. Even before the scars—'

Insert awful pause.

Thankfully, a series of crashes from the kitchen – is Ren trying to build a tank or take something out of the oven? – provides a distraction.

A moment later Ren pops his head into the hall. 'Fresh chocolate-chip cookies await,' he says, gesturing me grandly into the kitchen.

I don't need a second invitation. Some of the cookies are a little scorched, and some are mysteriously undercooked, but I appreciate the thought – and the chocolate. Especially as work on the mash-up continues just as well as previously – i.e. terribly.

'The problem is "Chandelier". It doesn't speak to either of us.'

Ren stretches his arms over his head, rolling his shoulders. 'Let's go for a walk and see if it'll clear our heads,' he says around a yawn, then freezes. 'Please could we ignore that lapse into monumental stupidity?'

'Don't be so bloody sensitive,' I tell him. 'Actually, that's a useful change of topic. I've figured out something I need to do but it's going to be weird and awkward and I just . . . I wanted to talk to you about it.'

Ren swivels round to focus on me as I take a deep, steadying breath.

'The thing is, I don't want a life where all sorts of basic stuff just isn't an option any more. It's bad enough that I'm never going to hike up a mountain or dance again. I was really good, you know. I wish I could show you.'

He doesn't say he's seen PopSync on YouTube or that he wishes it too. That's not what I meant and the fact that he gets it makes my stomach tighten. If you could turn sunshine through raindrops into a feeling, it'd be like this.

'I can't even go to the cinema because it's too far from the disabled parking, so how am I going to manage the festival when it was a close enough thing last year? Truth is that I'm not, unless something changes, so I need to get over myself and . . .' I blow out a frustrated breath. 'This is going to sound stupid, because obviously I can walk, but I think I need to get a wheelchair. Not a fancy electric one,' I hurry on. 'Just a basic folding one, then if I can't walk somewhere, I can still go. But obviously I wouldn't be able to self-propel with my hands and shoulders being stupid too, so I'd need help and . . .'

I press my fingers into my eyes. 'Would you be OK playing chauffeur? Not that I'd expect you to go everywhere with me. And, for the record, if you're not OK with it, I'm still going to do my own thing and make my own decision. I'd like you to help me pick something out and maybe come with me the first time, but it's OK if you think that's weird and way too much given we've only just . . . you know. I can always ask Maddie, so . . .' I run out of steam and breath at that point.

'Have you finished?' Ren asks.

I nod.

'Good. I think you might have used up most of the world's word supply.'

I'm too wound up to laugh or snipe back, but Ren doesn't give me time to fret over it.

'For the record, I think it's a really smart idea. It'd give us more options for fun – give you more options for everything. And that's all it is, Ven. A way not to be limited when you don't have to be. Since you're about the least limited person I know, it seems a good fit.'

I look up at him then and there are things in his face that make my eyes go all blurry. I sniff and he strokes my cheek with his thumb, looking like he might be the tiniest bit damp-eyed himself.

'Is it wrong that your take-charge-of-everything, nothing-stops-me thing is incredibly admirable and amazing and a bit ego-denting for mere mortals, but also totally sexy?'

I laugh, leaning into the hand against my face.

'And, er, not to spoil the moment or rush things,' Ren hurries on, 'but I really, *really* want to kiss you and it'd be really great if you could say yes.'

I've kissed boys before, but none of those times were anything like this.

This kiss starts with reading each other's faces: my surprise becoming delight and his nervousness becoming happiness. And then we're both leaning in and his breath is whispering across my lips, everything in me turning to hope and joy and heat.

I've just had one of the hardest conversations of my life, but suddenly all that is gone. It may sound stupid, but the kiss is like a reward. Like the universe looking down and going, 'Wow, things really have been shitty. Here, have a huge dollop of happiness.'

I'm not sure when I end up in his lap, but even then it doesn't become one of those awful face-eating snogs – wet and slimy and too full of teeth.

Soft and gentle, this kiss is as much stopping and looking at each other.

It's like saying hello all over again when you're already a little bit in love.

Adventures in Babysitting

(the reality not the movie)

Item 1: deadline for ordering merch TONIGHT.

Item 2: deadline for deciding this year's charities for the festival ALSO TONIGHT.

Days to the festival: 65.

When Roks says she's got to bring The Brood if she's to come over for final touches to the merch designs, I'm apprehensive, to say the least, as I know this means Orla's five siblings as well as Roks's one. Although I'm trying not to make assumptions about their situation, I'm pretty sure they're all living together, with Roks and Orla expected to do their share of the childcare. Anyway, it's not the why that matters but the how-the-hell-am-I-going-to-cope-on-my-own-with-six-kids, which, in case you've missed it, is a lot of kids. Especially with a body like mine.

As it turns out, either The Brood are unusually nice, or I'm unusually good with them, or we're all on our best behaviour, because when I plonk the small things in front of the TV they stay there, glued to the screen, long enough for me to show Roks the artwork proofs and explain what tweaks are needed. Then I lead the kids out to the garden, hoping (likely against hope) that this is not just the calm before the carnage.

To begin with, I make them cover their eyes while I set up a treasure hunt so I can lie quietly in the shade as they rush around screaming. Then we play Happy Families at least five billion times.

'Can we play chase now?' asks one of the littler ones.

'Well, you can and I can watch, but I can't really run about. How about a round of hide and seek, then a little more TV?'

'OK!' she says, beaming. 'ONE!' she screams directly into my face, then turns and legs it, still counting.

'You've got to cover your eyes, silly,' one of the older ones instructs me solemnly.

I count louder and louder as they go progressively quiet(er), though I can still tell where most of them are purely from the giggles and whispers.

I take my time finding them, then we collapse in front of the TV with fruit-juice ice-lollies for the kids and caffeine for me. It's surprisingly undreadful. Who knew kids responded so well to sardonic teasing? According to Roks's sister, I am 'uber cool'. (Well, I *am* wearing the most gorgeous LindyBop dress with a Cinderella-goes-to-the-ball pattern and little triangular cut-outs around the neckline.) The unexpected compliment is almost as lovely as how revolted Roks is by the whole thing, especially when none of them want to leave when Orla turns up to take them home.

'Come on. She's had enough now,' Roks says, flashing me an apologetic look.

I wrinkle my nose. 'Actually, they're all super-cute and they hug me a lot and I am a little disgusted by how much I'm enjoying it. Apparently, I'm going soft.'

Roks bites her lip. 'Yeah, you've really mellowed.'

'If you're not nice to me, I'll fill them up on sugar and caffeine just before you pick them up next time,' I tell her.

'This friendship is being contracted under duress,' Roks snarls.

'Yeah, yeah, we all know you're secretly quite fond of me now.'

'Come on, you snot-nosed brats – out!' Orla bellows, at which there is a chorus of sighs and fervent promises (threats?) that they'll visit again soon.

Roks waves once then closes the door on them.

'Well, that was significantly less atrocious than I was expecting,' I say, sinking into the sofa with a relieved groan. 'I really wouldn't mind a repeat visit if you need someone to watch them for another open day or something. How was it, by the way?'

Roks rubs at her forehead. 'It was great,' she says dully, 'but I really don't want to talk about it.' She heaves a sigh, giving me a rueful smile. 'If I change my mind, I promise you'll be the first person I consult to see if there is some genius strategy to make doing the degree possible.'

As she settles back in front of her laptop, I think about asking how she gets any homework done with The Brood around, and whether she ever resents having to structure her life around childcare not just for her mum but Orla's too, but I don't even know where to start. Instead, I say, 'You know, if you – or Orla – ever need somewhere quiet for coursework or revision, you can always come over. And, no, that's not pity talking. It's just . . .' I blow out a breath, then make myself tell her the truth. 'Sometimes it's nice to have something to take my mind off . . . well, off the pain.' I glance up to find Roks giving me a piercing look, trying to spot the lie in my words.

When she can't, her face softens. 'I suppose I could come and be your official tea-maker if you're tired and—'

'Lonely.' I clear my throat. 'Sometimes I'm lonely and I never used to be. Now, while we're doing excruciating honesty, should I be worried about the thing with Orla in the market or is she really OK?'

Roks flops back onto the sofa with a groan. 'You've probably worked out my family and Orla's family live together, and you're probably wondering how all that fits with her freaking out in the market the other day . . . Well, the reason we're all together is that our mums moved into the same shelter on the same day and they bonded, and we bonded, and The Brood bonded, because, when it comes to domestic violence, it turns out it's exactly the same whether a man's from Ireland or Pakistan – it doesn't matter what colour his skin is or what religion he practises or what excuses he gives, the bottom line is they all think they own their wives and kids.' It leaves her out of breath, eyes blazing.

I hesitate for a moment then reach out and squeeze her arm. 'I'm sorry that happened to you.'

'It's why Orla and I are the way we are – we went through this thing together and . . .' She stops, raking her hands through her hair. 'It was the biggest relief to know we would be living this totally different life, without our dads, but it meant we had to move away from everything and everyone we knew. It meant new schools and not talking to any of our old friends and not keeping in touch with anyone from back home. Some people act like it's the end of the world going from one house to another in the same town when their parents split up, and maybe it is for them, but they have no idea what it's like to suddenly have everything change and know you won't see any of the people from your old life ever again. Even people in your family who were lovely.'

Her breath hitches, but her voice is even when she goes on. 'If Orla hadn't been there, going through it all with me . . . It's tough sometimes, worrying about rent and figuring out tax credits instead of just being a kid, but it's sort of cool, knowing I can do that stuff.' The look she gives me is shy but proud. 'It makes me feel important. Anyway,' she says, suddenly back to business again, 'that was a bit bull-in-a-china-shop TMI, but then you're that type of person too, and at least it's over with now.'

‘No, I’m not!’ I take a breath to protest further. ‘Yes, I totally am,’ I admit.

Roks laughs. ‘I love Orla like the other half of my heart, but she is so sensitive and I *cannot* tease her, ever. It’s nice to have someone I can insult a bit.’

‘Thanks … I think?’ I say, elbowing her gently. ‘Look, as we were talking, I had an idea, but if I’m overstepping could you just say no and not bite my head off?’ I stop, blinking. ‘Scratch that, I’ve now got a second, sort-of-related idea, but same sort of problem …’ I shake my head. ‘Details later, questions now. Idea One would mean The Singers going away for nearly a week after exams instead of just overnight. Is that even possible for you and Orla? Maybe you think I should know, but I don’t and obviously I haven’t had time to think it through since it literally just came to me, so …’

Roksana clicks her tongue. ‘Asking questions! What a novel idea.’ She blows out a breath, then nods. ‘It wouldn’t be easy, but it’s not impossible – especially if it’s for something suitably amazing.’ She grins. ‘So, no decapitation needed on the basis of Idea One. Wanna see if you’re on a roll with Idea Two?’

‘Well, truth is I’ve got two deadlines tonight,’ I say, before I can chicken out. ‘Obviously the first one is the graphics, but maybe you can help me with the second too … which is to nominate two charities to collect for at the festival, and I was just thinking maybe it could be ones that deal with domestic violence. If that’s OK with you. And you don’t have to say which refuge you were at. I can totally do some research on reputable organisations and—’

Roks reaches across to catch my hand. 'Orla and I would love that,' she whispers. Then she sniffs. 'My name's not actually Roksana, you know.'

The look she gives me makes me sit very still.

'It's Roshan. Roksana is the Anglicised version – well, the Polish/Russian one. I didn't want to change my name completely, but we needed to make it hard for anyone to find us. You know, when we . . . left.'

'Do you want me to call you that?'

Roks shakes her head. 'No. Better not. Anyway, I like being Roks now.' She flashes me a tremulous little smile. 'It makes me feel like I can be a different person. Not that I'm not who I was – it'd be stupid to pretend you can change your name and the past just disappears – but Roksana's confident: she's bolshie and sharp and loud and in your face and I like this me, you know?'

I raise a shoulder. 'Not really? But I can imagine. Like if I called myself something different so it was easier to leave the Ven who was all about dancing behind.'

'And at least everyone can say Roksana, or at least Roks, because of course Roshan – being all of *two entire syllables* – was just *so* hard. Honestly, the number of people who just couldn't cope with the trouble it put them to.' She rolls her eyes. 'I just . . . I wanted to tell you,' she says nonchalantly. Then she pauses, shakes her head and says quietly, 'It feels like the type of a thing a real friend should know.'

It is, but it's also a gift: one I'm determined to live up to.

Quiet, Please: Musical Geniuses At Work

Item 1: finish the mash-up or die trying.
Days to the festival: 64.

'Well, you're the picture of good news,' says Ren, when he opens the door the next morning to find me vibrating on the mat.

'Yes!' I accidentally slam the door in my excitement, then grimace at the noise. 'Sorry! I just . . . I had the best idea last night, only I was worried that Roks and Orla wouldn't be able to do it, but Roks was there to help with the festival graphics so I asked her and she said maybe, so then I asked my parents and they said yes, so I checked with the head and she said yes, provided Ms Meade and Aunt Jinnie chaperone the whole time we're away and everyone's parents agree. But Ms Meade's already in – she says two of her favourite bands are playing so she was already trying to think of a way to go down early. And of course Aunt Jinnie said yes too, not least because it means extra pairs of hands to help. So it really looks like it's going to work!' I beam at him, panting.

'Great,' says Ren, grinning. 'So what's happening with us and Ms Meade and the festival?'

I blink at him. 'I explained that so much better in my head.'

Ren laughs, gesturing me down the hall. 'You need caffeine.'

'I do!' I follow him to the kitchen and flop into a chair. 'I have arranged – at least theoretically – that The Singers can go up to the festival a few days early to see all the set-up and behind-the-scenes stuff, then hopefully everyone will agree to be part of my box office crew during the festival itself, and then we top it all off with the performance on the Sunday afternoon.' I press my hands together delightedly, dislocating two fingers in the process.

Ren blinks as I reset them. 'I would pick you up and spin you around, but I don't want to damage you so can I just . . .' And then he hugs me as tight as he dares. 'And we thought getting to perform was incredible!' he says, shaking his head. 'Wow. This is just . . . wow.'

I grimace. 'Well, some of it will be awesome, but the trade-off for getting to see all the behind-the-scenes stuff is that we'll also have to help out. And by "help out" I mean work – a lot. Some of it is super fun, like dropping off important guests backstage, but there's also cleaning the box office floor, which is all the glam.'

Ren laughs. 'I can't believe this is a normal summer for you. Trust me – for mere teenage mortals, even cleaning the box office floor is glam when it's for a festival like this!'

I sigh, deflating. 'I just hope everyone's parents say yes and Roks and Orla can figure it out. I don't think I could bear it if it doesn't happen now.' While it's true that without help to manage the massive workload of the festival I don't know how I'll cope, it wasn't what prompted me to invite everyone. It'll be an amazing bonus, but it was thinking about how much fun it would be to share the whole festival – from prep to closing – that sparked the idea.

'Did you save the news to tell me in person, or am I the first to know – well, apart from Roks, apparently?'

I grin. 'I wanted to see your face. I emailed the others as soon as I got the basic go-ahead from my family and the school.' I reach out and snaffle a biscuit. 'I'm just going to sit here checking my phone every two secs to see who's in unless we do something, so . . . mash-up time?'

Ren sets our mugs down and climbs onto the next stool with a groan.

'I know, but everyone else's arrangements are done and sounding great. We don't even have something to rehearse yet. But I was thinking, what if we use "Chandelier" as a complementary track and we pick a different main song?'

'But then we're back to the same problem – we need a song that says something important *and* mashes up effectively with "Chandelier".'

'Well, what are we trying to say something *about*? The meaning of life?'

We lapse into silence. Ren is hopefully thinking Great Thoughts. I'm just thinking about Ren. About us.

Oh. Of course, that's the song.

'"All of Me". You know – the John Legend song? That's the thing we keep telling each other. Not the ... um ...' I trail off, biting my lip, suddenly realising how it sounds. 'I mean, I've only known you a few months, and we're only sixteen, and I'm not making any wild claims about the future ...' I stop and make myself look him straight in the eye. 'But even if we stop going out, I'll always want to know you. I just feel like we're meant to be something to each other, whatever that is and however it changes.'

Ren stares at me.

'God, I've freaked you out. Look, I'm not saying—'

'Ven, can you shut up a sec?' I freeze as Ren laces our fingers together. 'It's the perfect song,' he whispers. '*Yes* to all of the above.'

'Oh,' I say intelligently.

'Under the circumstances, am I OK to assume I can call myself your boyfriend now?'

I lean forwards and kiss him. 'That was a yes,' I say, then turn away and pull over my notes. 'But let's work on the song before we overdose on mush.'

Ren beats out a rhythm on the edge of the table. 'You know,' he says thoughtfully, 'a mash-up doesn't have to be just two songs. What if we took pieces from a bunch of things—'

'We could make it work like a conversation!' I say, my eyes going wide. 'Like a call-and-response song, only the response isn't an echo but something that answers it like a question.'

In the end we take bars and phrases from seven different

songs and, when we're done, it's the start of something that could actually be worth the wait. We won't know until we finish it and start rehearsals, but if we're right then it's The Singers in a single piece of music: together it says more than any individual song ever could. It's the whole reason we raise our voices together.

With a rough first draft of the mash-up finally done, we head to Ren's room to watch a movie on his laptop.

Yes, obviously that is a cover-story for the fact that we're going upstairs to make out. No one is fooled but then that's not really the point, is it?

It starts as slowly cuddling further into each other's space, my hand curled around Ren's arm, fingers making little circles on his skin, then his thumb moving slowly against my neck. His breath in my hair as he turns to press a kiss to my forehead. My breath ghosting over his ear as I turn my face so our lips can meet.

His fingers in my hair, mine in his. My hand on his shoulder, urging him against me. His hand on my back, holding me tight to his body. Our breath coming unsteady as we brush noses, brush lips, sink deep into the kiss, and deeper still. His hand teasing under my top at the back, sliding up my skin, eliciting a gasp. My hand finding the bottom of his shirt.

'OK?' he asks raggedly.

I press my smile against his lips. 'Yes. You?'

He presses himself in for another kiss. Then he freezes.

I pull back. 'Ren?'

And then I realise my fingers have traced the edge of the scar where it spills down the curve of his jaw to his neck.

'Does it hurt?' I whisper.

He shakes his head.

'Do you ... want me to avoid touching you there?'

He opens his mouth, then doesn't seem to know what to say. A moment later, his eyes harden and he moves in as if to kiss me again but I scoot back.

'Not that I don't want to keep snogging, but let's just ... talk about this first?'

Ren groans and flops back onto the bed beside me.

After a moment I curl up next to him. 'Come on. You've got words in there. Try a few.'

'Do I have to?' He sighs, but turns on his side to face me. 'Don't they ... don't the scars feel gross? Because you don't have to pretend—'

'They're not gross, Ren,' I say, though I'd meant to listen without interrupting. 'Seriously, think about our song.'

'It's a lovely sentiment, but—'

'It's not a sentiment, Ren. It's true. I get that *you* think they're gross, but I don't. I just don't.'

'Really?' he whispers, searching my eyes.

'Really. And I don't mean I've learnt to feel that way, it's just ... not a thing for me. It never was. The only feelings I have about your scars are because of how much they must have hurt when you got them and how *you* feel about it all.'

He swallows hard, eyes bright with tears. 'It was a firework.

Tai . . . Tai was drunk . . . more than drunk . . . and he was being stupid, and I was trying to stop him and . . .' He heaves in a breath. 'It's why we moved here. To get away from his friends. Away from his . . . Away from all that. So he could . . . stop.'

'Wasn't it hard to leave your friends when you were dealing with so much?' I ask softly.

Ren shakes his head, staring away out of the window, the tears still standing glassy in his eyes. 'The way they looked at me, all the time. The pity. The disgust. At least here . . .' He shrugs. 'It doesn't hurt the same with strangers.'

I flex my fingertips against his cheek. 'It's still no fun. But I get it. It's why I can't go to PopSync rehearsals. They look at me like my life's over.'

When Ren's tears spill down his face, I lean over him, brushing them gently away, then pressing kisses along their path on one cheek, then the other, scarred and unscarred.

'Our song is not about how at least we're broken and ruined together,' I whisper. 'It's about caring enough about someone – liking enough of who they are – that you like everything about them, and you don't see any of it as ruined or broken, because it's just part of the person you . . . you love.'

Ren's hand winds into my hair, pulling my lips down to his.

We arch into each other. His breath is my breath. His heartbeat fluttering in my chest.

His hand sinks from my hair to my neck to my shoulder and along to the edge of my top, but I pull away, sitting back on my heels.

'Sorry,' he says, flushing.

'Well, that's disappointing,' I tell him. 'I was thinking about taking this off.'

His eyes flare wide.

'OK?' I ask.

'So completely, totally OK,' he gasps. 'The OK-est.'

And I laugh, my head thrown back, and I don't think, just tear my top off.

But before I can dive back into kissing him, he's wriggling up and reaching for the hem of his T-shirt.

'Feeling overdressed?' I whisper. My heart hammers in my chest.

I can't believe I'm doing this. That we're doing this.

Then we're skin to skin and I think briefly about how much muscle tone I've lost and whether I should try to cover the worst bits with my hands, but when I meet his eyes they're full of heat. There's nothing else there at all.

I had no idea until this moment how much I needed that.

I think he's beautiful and he thinks I'm beautiful and it's just as simple as that.

Bridget Jones Meets the Pain Consultant

Item 1: experiment with new and varied forms of pain and misery.
Item 2: learn to accept help gracefully.
Days to festival: 62.

The Easter holidays end with the wheelchair-buying expedition. Dad drops me and Ren off outside the shop so at least we don't have to deal with whether or not there's an open blue badge spot within (my) walking distance. Thanks to a bunch of online research, by the time Dad joins us I've already picked what I want and Ren is wheeling me up and down the pavement to see how bumpy the ride is. The answer is 'quite' but most of the lighter wheelchairs are the same: oh the joys of joints that slop about instead of staying where they should.

People on the street glance our way, but only barely. In the shop, they're brilliantly matter of fact. Dad means well but is … less so.

'No, I am not trying an electric one,' I say through my teeth as I force down the urge to lose my temper. 'If it goes wrong or I get stuck somewhere with stairs and the lift is out, I am completely screwed if I can't bump it along like a walker because it's too heavy. Also, can we please *not* assume my stupid body is going to get even stupider? Can't we just go with positivity? "Yay, Ven, well done for doing this today. I'll get you ice cream now"?'

'I'll get you ice cream now,' says my father. 'Ren can escort you while I pay up.' He turns away, taking out his wallet.

'Hey, Dad,' I say, catching his hand as Ren moves to wheel me past. 'Thanks.'

He smiles down at me, squeezing my fingers gently. 'I'm proud of you, Daughter.'

'And *you* get ice cream too,' I point out, before either of us get soppy.

'And I get ice cream too,' he agrees, then we smile instead of cry and it's just about as OK as this situation could be.

I spend two hours of my last afternoon of freedom before school starts again with my latest pain consultant.

'So,' says the consultant, eyes on my notes, 'the tests show that when you're in pain you get these sudden dramatic falls in blood pressure, causing you to pass out.' He closes my file and smiles across the desk at me. 'Now we just need to make sure you avoid that in future.'

'What do you mean?' I ask, because that can't possibly be a literal statement – can it?

The doctor's smile freezes. 'Well,' he says slowly, as if talking to a particularly stupid toddler, 'you need to avoid activities that lead to pain.'

Gobsmacked silence.

'So, I need to avoid walking,' I say eventually. 'And sitting, especially sitting upright, like all day at school. And lying down's not so good either,' I continue thoughtfully. 'Or breathing. Breathing can be a real problem. I guess I need to hover mid-air and not breathe?'

The doctor looks at Mum beseechingly. She gives him the world's stoniest 'you've made your bed' stare.

'Have you read my notes?' I ask. 'I dislocate. All. The. Time. Shockingly, that causes pain.'

'But what are you doing when you—'

'Sitting, walking, standing or lying down, since I only fly on nights with a full moon.'

The appointment goes downhill from there. Turns out the aptly named pain consultant has a truly extensive repertoire of torture techniques. Case in point is my appointment 'homework', which is to write a diary.

Think *Bridget Jones*. Only instead of calories and cigarettes consumed, I'm going to be recording what bits of myself I've dislocated that day, how many times, how much it hurt (on a scale from zero to ten, where zero means nothing hurts at all and ten is the worst pain imaginable) and any other symptoms.

Since today already sucks, the first thing I do when I get home is sit down and write up my pain diary so far.

7.ØØ: Upset stomach – feels like a squirrel is trying to eat me from the inside out. Brain fog. Pain 5.

7.ØØ–12 noon: Dislocations: jaw, fingers (index and middle, right hand) (twice) each, right hip (twice), right knee (sublux, resolved itself), left hip (sublux, resolved itself).

12noon: Pain 6. Exhausted. Miserable.

13.ØØ–14.ØØ: Pain 6+. Dislocations: jaw, fingers (twice). Dizzy spell.

14.ØØ–16.ØØ: Pain 6.5. Dislocations: hip (twice), shoulder blade. Glooped onto the floor when making tea.

17.ØØ: THE LAST THING I NEED IS TO THINK ABOUT HOW MUCH IT ******* HURTS. THERE IS MUCHNESS OF PAIN AND MISERY. MUCH MUCHNESS OF IT AND MY BRAIN HAS TURNED INTO SOUP.

Unless you're a masochist, we're in exactly the same mood at this point: thoroughly depressed with a sixty per cent chance of tears.

It's bad enough having to deal with it, let alone writing it all down then seeing it there in black and white (well, glitter purple and poison green). I don't need any reminders that even with the wheelchair there is no guarantee I'm going to get through the festival, despite everything now riding on it – everyone's coursework grades, the smooth running of the box office, my sense of self-worth . . .

After that delightful interlude, it's all I need to ring Ren's doorbell and for Tai to answer it, once again.

'Hi,' he says, shoving his hands into his pockets and rocking on his heels in the doorway.

'Any chance of my coming through?' I ask, when he just stands there.

'You're performing at the festival as well as working there, right?' He glances over his shoulder. 'I was thinking maybe I could pop down for the performance. If there are still tickets?'

I summon something that could pass as a smile. 'It just so happens you're talking to the box office manager—'

'God, please don't say you'll kick me out,' Tai says, rubbing a hand over his face.

'Oh for . . . I know you don't like me, but I'd never do that to Ren, so could you just get over yourself? Come to the collection point in the box office and a ticket will be waiting.'

'You don't have to do that,' Tai mumbles.

'I'm allowed guest tickets and you're literally my *only* guest this year so it's not even a favour. Though you'd still better be bloody honoured.'

Tai gives me a reluctant grin and executes a little bow. Then he sighs. 'But don't tell Ren, OK? I need to persuade Mum to let me have the car, and it depends on . . .' He grimaces. 'Let's just keep it a secret for now, in case it doesn't work out.'

I nod. 'Sure. But I hope it does. It'd be really nice for Ren to have you there.'

He nods back, but the way his shoulders hunch as he leads me to the kitchen tells a different story.

'Oh, hey,' Ren says, shedding his headphones as he sees me in the doorway.

Then Tai flashes him a smile and Ren's whole face softens. This is why I'm determined to make Tai like me, even after the disaster that was our first meeting.

I'm sure Ren has said all the right things to Tai about the accident, and I expect Tai has said at least some of the right things back, but though they both want it to be OK, it's not. Ren's scars sit between them, cutting away at every effort to mend things. I just wish Ren could understand that when Tai recoils from the scars it's not because he thinks they make Ren hideous. It's his own ugliness he sees when he looks at them.

Back to School

Item 1: *finish polishing the mash-up and get rehearsing.*

Item 2: *survive – and ace! – exams.*

Item 3: *stay on top of festival work!!*

When Ms Meade comes to check on us in our first free-period rehearsal of term, she stays long enough to gift us with a rare, impressed look and a round of applause. It's so gratifying it almost takes my mind off the fact that this is my first day in school with the wheelchair.

Unsurprisingly, I have mixed feelings about it all. On the plus side, it means that when the lunch-bell rings, all I have to do is pour myself into it and let Ren chauffeur me off towards the cafeteria. I jump, craning my neck to look back at him, when he suddenly swears.

'Left my notebook.'

I roll my eyes at him. 'Dramatic much? I'll nip to the loo and you can pick me up in a minute.'

We're right by the toilet door, so he puts on the wheelchair's parking-brakes, gives me a peck on the cheek and sprints off while I lever myself up and avail myself of the facilities. Things have been OK on the weeing front since Orla's party, but definitely not the same as they were before and I keep having days when I need to go every hour. Joy of joys, Mum's booked me in for an appointment to see a new consultant about it all.

Dithering in front of the mirror, I despair over the mop that is my hair, though at least I'm wearing the most gorgeous top (eBay, of course) – black with ribbons of different shades of pink crisscrossing then gathering together at the shoulders to tie in a multi-strand halter at the back. I needed the confidence of an awesome outfit for my first day using the wheelchair at school. However, despite a near-sleepless night thinking about all the ways people might be mean, turns out the person making the biggest deal about it is me.

I think Maddie and Ren must have messaged The Singers and PopSync about it because all Roks said when I turned up today was 'Loving the blue rims', and Benjo, 'I am in love with that horn,' because of course I got myself one of those old-fashioned trumpets with a squeezy-rubber-bit to make it blow. It's bolted to the armrest so I can honk at people to get them out of my way at will. I mean, do you honestly think I'd have a wheelchair *sans* horn? But the thing that really helps is the others trying not to look at me when I climb in, as if giving me privacy. When I first realised what they were doing, I got momentarily teary that they understood how hard it is for me to accept I need the help.

It's not that any of us are pretending it's not happening or that anyone thinks it's shameful; they're just trying to make it normal, practical – nothing that needs comment or notice.

Obviously Abigail Moss stared as if Christmas had come early when she spotted me this morning. I tensed as she whispered behind her hands to her pack, but all except the two girls and boy who heckled our performance at the mall just drifted away as if not realising they'd left her behind.

Anyway, I'm not going to let stupid Abigail Moss ruin my day. But when I open the door and step back into the corridor, not only is Ren still gone, my wheelchair seems to have disappeared too.

Frowning, I peer along the corridor in both directions, then lean against the wall to wait. After a moment, I slip out my phone, then register that there seems to be a lot of shouting coming from the direction of the cafeteria. Wearily, I take my folding walking stick from my bag, flick it open so that the segments click into place, then set off to find out what's going on.

Which turns out to be Abigail Moss and her inner circle taking each other for joyrides in my wheelchair using the ramp from the outer doors of the cafeteria to the car park. For a moment, my throat closes with rage and humiliation.

Swallowing it down, I start towards the doors again.

Through the glass wall of the corridor, I see Roks and Orla come flying out of the cafeteria. They pelt down the outside steps to get round the three boys who are fending off Benjo and the twins. I am astonished when Fred literally bodychecks one of the pack to the floor. Benjo grapples hopelessly with another, only to trip and take not just the two of them but also George and the other boy to the floor.

I'm still gaping when Maddie charges through the middle, with the whole of PopSync behind her. Together, Roks, Sam and Ashley wrench the girl chauffeuring Abigail away, sending her stumbling into the gathering crowd, while Orla and Pip drag Abigail and the chair to a halt.

As the automatic doors part for me, I stumble to a stop at the top of the ramp, panting, my eyes blurred with tears. But they're no longer of rage.

'Get. Up,' says Maddie. Her face is pure murder.

The moment Abigail Moss is out of the chair, Roks steps forward and shoves her away. The crowd standing behind them parts, letting Abigail tumble to the ground.

'I'd kick you,' says Orla, 'but I'm not getting suspended for scum like you.'

'That's really low, Abi,' adds Pip. 'I mean, Ven's a bit much sometimes but this is just a shit thing to do. I hope you get suspended.'

'Oh, I think that can be arranged,' says a distinctly unimpressed voice, and we all turn to find Ms Meade and Ms Walker standing side by side.

They cross their arms in unison as Abigail and her pack slink to their feet.

Reader, she did, indeed, get suspended. And her little pack too.

Exams and Other Forms of Educational Torture

Item 1: GET EVERYTHING READY FOR THE FESTIVAL! (Ensure everything is planned in life-threatening detail.)

Item 2: REHEARSE, REHEARSE, REHEARSE, REHEARSE SOME MORE!!!!!

Days to festival: 24

My life plunges into an abyss of exams. But for the first time in eighteen months I find it in myself to believe that, even if I don't get tip-top grades, I've still got a shot at persuading potential employers I've lots to offer. Don't get me wrong – I still want the best grades that are in me, but I want it for the satisfaction and accomplishment, not because I think my life will basically be over otherwise. Turns out I'm as excited-slash-nervous to see how much money The Singers raise for the festival's chosen charities as I am to get my marks.

Between all that, rehearsals, final touches to the set list (including endless tweaking of the mash-up), and a metric ton of festival prep, the next four and a half weeks disappear in a disorienting blink. One minute there's a comfortable seven weeks till the festival, then suddenly – *BOOM*: three weeks to go.

Thankfully everyone's joy about our upcoming six-day festival adventure means it's no struggle to get The Singers meeting and rehearsing every other day. It helps that the set list is coming together beautifully – even the mash-up is starting to sound polished.

Now the others wait breathlessly as I scan down my page of workings as I compare our budget with the money we raised from busking at the mall. 'With the festival paying our petrol, and contributing to shared hotel rooms and food now we're all helping out, we have the princely sum of . . . £7.56 for contingencies, but looks like we've got enough to cover our costs.'

Benjo lets out a happy whoop, then nearly falls off his chair. Fred and George steady him automatically.

'Next order of business. Fred, George and Maddie will finish setting up a fundraising page so that anyone who visits our channel or socials can donate via The Singers to the festival's chosen charities.' I get a series of nods. 'It needs to be up and running before we leave because there is just not going to be time once we're there, and we don't want to miss the opportunity of raising extra money with all the new content around the festival.'

More nods! I absolutely do not get the warm fuzzies, not even a little.

OK, maybe a little.

'Right. So that's rehearsals' – tick – 'final touches to arrangements and the set list' – tick – 'and now . . . planning the workshop.' I look round at Benjo. 'I was thinking you might like to introduce us.'

He points at himself (nearly getting his own eye) with a silent, 'Me?'

'Why not start with a mic drop? Set the tone.'

He sticks out his tongue. 'Yeah, yeah, yeah.'

'Seriously, don't drop the mic. They cost a fortune – like seven hundred pounds and up.'

'Yikes,' says Orla, eyes widening. 'I am SO not holding any mics. Stands only, please!'

'All the more obstacles for me to trip over,' adds Benjo with a sigh. 'I will endeavour not to destroy anything expensive – or inexpensive – but I make no promises, because . . . well, dyspraxic.'

I put a tick next to the introduction on my list. 'Next up—'

'George and I want to do a five-minute mini-lesson about the history of gospel music,' Fred announces.

'It's really good,' Maddie chips in, cheeks pinking intriguingly. 'They did a run-through for me when Fred and I were finishing our arrangement.'

'Mini-lesson sold to the twins,' I say, ticking that off my list too. 'Can you . . . ?' I trail off as George passes two neatly printed pages to me. 'Write up some notes, just like these. Moving on, I thought next Maddie could teach the audience something like "Up Above My Head" as a warm-up exercise, though since you're running it, you pick the song. Then Roks, Orla and Ren could divide the crowd into groups to learn a simple call-and-response song – up to you three to agree what that is, but keep in mind we'll want to justify these choices in the critical reflections bit of our coursework, so make sure there's some solid reasoning behind it.'

I get further nods and smiles all round. 'Look at all of us playing nicely together.' Maybe it's the calm before the storm, but I'm starting to think we really can pull this off – working together at the festival and the performance.

Roks promptly gives me the finger. 'Just so you don't start worrying we've been replaced by clones or something.'

'So appreciated,' I tell her. 'Now, what's next?'

Once More Unto the Breach, Dear Friends . . .

See overleaf for to-do list Items 1 to 10,007.

Days to festival: 3

I wake to sunshine spilling through my window and anticipation fizzing through me from head to toe. The others must feel the same because they all arrive twenty minutes early, smiling and buzzing and bright-eyed as can be. Absolutely everything goes smoothly, even deciding who goes in which car. Ms Meade's coming separately, so I get Ren, Roks and Orla, while Aunt Jinnie (who's been staying over with me since Mum and Dad went down to the festival site with the rest of the family) has Benjo, the twins and Maddie, who's fooling no one when she announces that she's going along to make sure the boys behave.

'Thank you for your sacrifice, Maddie,' Aunt Jinnie says, as Maddie and Fred pretend not to be shooting yearning looks at each other as they load their bags into the boot.

All these weeks of work and preparation – endless rehearsals and myriad messages about everything from outfits to external batteries for our phones – have led to this. I thought we'd be irritable and frenzied but we're just happy and excited.

We squeeze together for an 'off to the festival' group selfie, pack the final bits and bobs, then suddenly we're all clicking on our seatbelts – me over my inaugural-year festival T-shirt: a family good luck tradition. It's just enough to steady the bubble of nerves as I realise that this is it, no turning back now. It also helps that I've accessorised my outfit – festival-T, dove-grey jeans with mauve stitching and matching shrug jacket – with amazing footwear for extra confidence: a brand-new pair of mid-calf faux-leather boots with a stacked series of copper-toned buckles running from mid-foot right to the top.

I check my phone is in the console and my stick along the side of the seat, then turn to look at each of my passengers in turn.

'I am in charge of directions and driving, Ren is in charge of music and you two in the back are in charge of passing snacks. Ready or not, here we go!'

It is the single best journey-to-the-festival of my life. Maddie's family usually comes to one day of the festival weekend, but I've never had a friend – let alone seven – there alongside me all the way. It's partly that, until A-levels, there was no chance school would have been willing to sign off on this as an educational experience, and partly because, though I love PopSync, Pip isn't the only one who'd have been far more hindrance than help. But now, although I'm nervous about the million ways everything could go wrong, a bigger bit of me thinks that having The Singers there will make all the good bits of the festival even better, while helping ensure the bad bits – my physical limitations top of the list – are at least bearable.

I have to hope I'm right because there's no way I can manage alone.

Two hours later, we pile into the lobby of our usual hotel in a roar of chatter and rolling suitcases. Leaving the others to pore over the breakfast menu as if it is the most exciting thing ever, I follow Aunt Jinnie to the reception desk, where Ms Meade is waiting to get us all checked in.

'Everyone has twenty minutes to dump their stuff, then meet back by the cars,' I call over the noise as I start distributing keys.

'Don't *you* even think about *that*,' Maddie says, slapping my hand (gently) away from the handle of my suitcase. 'REN!' she bellows. 'Need your muscles.'

He grins delightedly, and presents himself in a superhero pose.

'Oh, for God's sake, Maddie. He used to be so shy and retiring, now look.' I gesture at him.

He quirks an eyebrow as he hefts my bag and his own with ease, while Maddie links her arm with mine and tows me off to the lift. Since we're only going to the second floor, the others beat us there and are already squealing with excitement (Benjo) and exclaiming over the mini shampoo and soap (Orla). I grin at Roks's slightly awed expression, but know better now than to tease. This is probably her first time in a hotel and she deserves to enjoy it snark-free.

'What do you think?' I ask instead. 'Just about up to standard?'

'Are you sure what we raised covers our half of this?' Roks asks, looking around nervously. 'It's . . . really, really fancy. There are flannels and handtowels and two types of big towel each in the bathroom.' She blinks. 'We have our own bathroom. Just us.'

I grin. 'We get an amazing rate because the whole senior team's here every year for at least a week. Just enjoy – by the time we're done, you'll have more than earnt the festival's contribution.'

'Roks!' gasps Orla from inside the room. 'We've got a kettle and, like, four different types of biscuit.'

I wonder if it's fun for them to have this much time away from The Brood, and be free from childcare like the rest of us for once, or whether it feels weird when they're so used to always having to keep an eye out for their siblings. Roks hasn't told me how they sorted things so they could both be away, but the fact that she was excited rather than tense when she told me they could come leaves me hoping their solution doesn't have too many knock-on complications.

I jump when Maddie tugs at my elbow. 'You're lying down till it's time to go,' she says. 'Shh,' she adds, when I open my mouth to tell her I have a million things to do. Then she propels me into our room, where the sheets have already been turned down on the bed.

'What are you doing?' I shriek, when she pushes me onto the bed then kneels in front of me.

'Getting your boots off, stupid. In,' she orders, pointing until I swivel my legs up and lie back. 'Stay. I can unpack. You rest while you can.'

I just lie there watching and thinking that, with my friends' help, maybe I will get through the festival after all.

Forty minutes later, we're back in the car and turning onto the roundabout down to the festival site, Aunt Jinnie and the others right behind us. I'm about to start explaining how it all works when I catch sight of the festival banner, which is upside-down. Who wants to bet My Awful Cousin Stef is behind that?

Groaning, I click the indicator from left to right to go round again.

'You drawing out the anticipation or trying to make one of us puke?' Orla calls from the back seat.

'Someone snap me a pic of the banner,' I say.

We end up going round three times before we finally sail off into the site, the others peering about with matching frowns. I know what they're thinking: where the hell is the festival? The place seems all but deserted, the car parks empty. Then we turn a corner and there it is.

Off to the right a huge, flat plain stretches to distant hills, but in the foreground the marquees are going up. They look so small from here. Even the huge Main Stage and the Big Top. The tepee and rectangular marquees in the workshop area look like Monopoly houses and hotels, though they're like warehouses up close.

The sun comes out, cutting through the clouds and stabbing down in front of the far hills, then travelling onto the field, illuminating the Festival Village just as the banner poles rise up into the sky.

Even so, it doesn't look like much now, but this is the special time. This is what no one else sees: the machinery behind the curtain. How it all *becomes*. Making it happen is the real magic for me.

By the time we pull up at the box office entrance, Stewarding Steve is already removing the padlock and drawing the gates open to let our little procession through.

The building we use for the box office is four square walls of concrete with two counters along opposite sides for ticket pick-ups and sales, while the other sides consist largely of doors leading, at the front, to the car park and, at the back, into the festival. In the middle is a slalom of barriers to funnel all the visitors past the banding station, where tickets are exchanged for wristbands. It all sits under a roof intended to look like a two-pole marquee. In reality it's a dead ringer for an off-white version of Madonna's infamous Jean Paul Gaultier bra. Still, it's my home away from home, so I can't help but smile.

'We're here!' Orla whispers. 'Oh my God, we're actually here!'

'We're going to sing at a festival,' Roks says disbelievingly.

I meet her eyes in the rear-view mirror. Her delighted smile is infectious and, when we all pile out of the cars, we're grinning like loons. Which is purely daft, because we haven't done anything but drive down, check into the hotel and arrive, and yet my blood buzzes with so much energy and excitement I feel like my old self.

The thought brings me straight back down. I can't afford to get this worked up now – I've got two and a half days of prep, then three of festival to survive, and there's no way that's happening if I blow all my energy through nervous excitement.

'Ven!'

I turn to find the others beckoning from the edge of the grass.

'Pics!' orders Maddie. 'Get in here!'

I don't comment on the fact that she promptly pulls Fred in on her other side, though I fully intend to come back to it later. 'We're standing in front of the loo block,' I point out instead.

'We're immortalising our arrival!' announces Orla.

'Technically that's George's job,' I tell her. 'I can see the festival account's already retweeted that pic of the flagpoles, so . . .' I give him a thumbs up.

'He can do the official stuff, but I am literally taking photos of every metre of this place and every hour we're here,' says Benjo reverently. 'This is the best day of my life.'

'Yikes,' I tell him. 'Try to hold on to that thought when we're degriming the box office counters.'

I leave Ms Meade and Aunt Jinnie chatting about how to divide up chaperoning duties so they can each see their top acts, while the others exclaim over the fencing and the tarmac and various blades of particularly wonderful grass. Ducking into the out-building we use as the festival office and HQ, I say my hellos to Aunt Sarah and Uncle Geoff, squeezing past stacks of boxes and crates to collect the box office paperwork. Mum and Dad pop up from the back room, where I can hear the drill going as the festival safe is bolted into the ground. I take them outside to welcome everyone.

'I'm going to drive back to the box office, but you lot are not going to loiter here,' I tell The Singers. 'You are going to follow me like good little ducklings because we have work to do, people, and it starts now. Also, Ms Meade will be behind you, so dawdle at your peril.'

Despite the email I sent round about exactly what helping out at the festival would involve, the others are astonished (even Ms Meade) by the sheer number of tasks involved in cleaning the box office, moving in our equipment, organising the paperwork, then sorting out the initial set-up – and all on our first day. Usually I rope in whichever stewards and family members I can, so it's nice to have a dedicated, if inexperienced, team at my disposal. Plus it makes what is usually a frantic slog into something approaching fun. When we look back, no one will remember the bit where I dislocated my hip twice in a row, but we'll all be able to laugh about Fred, George and Benjo doing a *Mary Poppins* chimney-sweep routine with the mops.

By the time we head back to the hotel, we are all limp and quiet with exhaustion.

'I thought you were lying,' Benjo says, as he collapses into the seat next to mine in the hotel's pizza restaurant. (A big part of why we always stay here is that there's food on hand without having to go anywhere.) 'I thought the thing about changing shoes was bullshit. I thought you were majorly exaggerating just to big yourself up. I thought . . . I'm too tired to remember the words for what I thought.'

I shrug from where I'm leaning against Ren. The box office phone sitting on the table in front of me starts to ring for another last-minute sale. Groaning, I drag myself upright. 'Booking form,' I growl at Ren, who sighs but fishes one out of his bag. 'Pen,' I demand of Benjo. He slams one into my hand as I hit the 'accept call' button.

When the food comes, we take it in turns to slip out into the corridor to scribble down booking after booking after . . .

'And this goes on from now until doors open?' Benjo wails despairingly as he thrusts a completed form at me.

Of course, in the process he puts his elbow in my dessert, nearly knocks over my drink and manages to give himself a papercut, but I'm distracted from complaining by Maddie gallantly offering to accompany Fred on the next call 'to speed things up' even though his brownie is unlikely to melt, while her ice cream mostly certainly will.

'Lines close at ten p.m. tonight – then open again at ten a.m.,' I tell Benjo brightly. 'So tomorrow we'll be doing this all day on top of everything else.'

'I have a new and thorough-going respect for you,' Benjo says. 'And I am so unbelievably grateful for this amazing opportunity, but I also kinda hate you right now, OK?'

'Fair,' I say. 'Now, who wants to see the festival programmes?'

I call, reaching into my tote-bag for the copy I snaffled from Mum earlier. When the others just blink tiredly at me, I add, 'There might possibly be a named credit for everyone to check out.'

They're clustered around me in seconds.

2 Days To Go

Seriously, today's list is twenty pages long. You don't need or want to know the details.

Morning comes all too quickly. While the others are practically glowing with excitement, Roks and Orla's delight at ordering breakfast barely wrings a smile from me as I struggle not to fall asleep in my scrambled eggs. I can't even find the energy to snap a pic of Maddie and Fred making goo-goo eyes at each other.

Thankfully I'd packed a vintage zip-up-the-front tank-top with rainbow-coloured 1960s swirls, a pair of black jeans with silver stitching and strappy sandals with each band dyed a different colour, so at least I look the part as I order The Singers to the cars.

Unfortunately, the day's box office work starts with the discovery of the first major set of Stef-ups. Within an hour, The Singers and Ms Meade have all started using the phrase 'Ven's

Awful Cousin Stef' with the undercurrent of loathing that only Stef can engender in people who've barely met him.

It's the main topic of conversation as we head outside for a break, sprawling on cool, springy grass under the trees next to the box office. From across the fields, I can hear distant shouts as the build continues on the beer tent and tepee. Mum will be supervising with Aunt Sarah, while Dad focuses on the campsite. By the afternoon, everyone will be pivoting to the get-in for the stalls and caterers. Already the early birds are arriving, trundling their food trucks slowly down the slope to their designated spots.

A crackle and pop echoes across the site. 'Hello, Festival Family and visitors!' bellows Uncle Geoff. 'Give Main Stage a shout if you can hear us.'

From all around come whoops and whistles. The sound system hisses then falls quiet again as the teching continues, though I know there will be bursts of recorded music later as our engineers check our noise levels around the festival boundaries.

I let my thoughts drift as I gaze up through the leaves at the blue, blue sky. Maddie is chatting away to Fred on my left, showing him a video of PopSync's latest performance. It's all a bit sloppy, but they look happy and, beyond that, I realise I don't really care any more. Now Maddie's in The Singers, PopSync's just an added bonus for her CV. It's our performances her A-level grades will be tied to, so all that matters is that she's having fun. There's a little pang for a good thing gone to waste, but the sting has gone from the regret.

I feel the last of the sadness slip away as I flop back, pillowing my head on Ren's leg. After a moment, his hand starts moving idly through my hair and I realise that, right now, I am truly happy. Being *able* to be happy feels like something I've achieved, not something that simply happens. It's just as well that when I set my mind to something I'm pretty much unstoppable.

I guess, at the end of the day, that's the thing I'm best at.

'Are you OK?' Ren whispers, his thumb tracing gentle circles on my neck.

I take a deep breath and let it out slowly. 'You know, I really am.'

I put my hand, palm up, on his knee. A moment later his fingers lace with mine and I am amazed again at how that simple thing – being able to reach out and have him reach back – feels like a whole new world.

Plus, I've just eaten two mini Twixes and a bag of Maltesers, so if life isn't good now I'd have to give up all hope.

Twenty minutes later, we're back to work setting up the box office banking system. It doesn't help that we're endlessly interrupted by people needing directions. Stef's meant to be looking after the stall people, so of course almost every single one of them wanders in and just stands there as if hoping for a sign to be lowered from the sky saying, *This way*. It keeps breaking my focus, and then the pain starts taking over.

It's just as well I gave up on the pain/dislocation diary after one entry, because the only thing that could make the whole situation worse is recording every last detail for posterity.

Might as well subtitle it, *A rollicking adventure through one girl's Most Depressing Achievements Ev-er, including her Top Consecutive Dislocation Score and Most Protracted Period of Agony!*

There's plenty of good stuff going on – especially now – and it's *that* I need to focus on.

Trouble is that by early afternoon everything in me hurts. My skin burns, my bones feel stretched, like I'm about to pull apart at the seams and I'm so tired I just want to lie on the floor and never move again. It gets to the point where I'm literally gritting my teeth because I can'tcan'tcan't hurtshurtshurts but I havetohavetohaveto can'tstopcan'tstop . . .

Then suddenly Roks is there. I growl at her when she moves my laptop to the side, but then she puts her hand over mine and the look on her face is so gentle I just sag wearily.

'Come sit with me outside for a minute,' she says.

She makes me lean on her as she leads me out to the grass, then we lie down, side by side, as she talks and I listen and take her hand without meeting her eyes and just hold on as she holds on to me.

In a quarter of an hour, we're back inside, but somehow it feels as if I sank some of the pain into the grass. It's not better, but I feel different inside. It is no small thing to find someone you think might be one of those people who enters your life and never leaves it. Especially when that's the last thing you were expecting.

Ren dumps an armload of print-outs in front of me. 'All outstanding customer queries and issues.'

I stare at the pile in despair until a hand appears in front of my eyes.

'Come and have a break,' Ren says.

'I've just had one,' I moan.

'Have another one.' He gives me a lazy smile.

I slither off the stool and slop around the counter as fast as I can, then show Ren the shady, hidden spot in the middle of the bushes by the gate.

Oh, get your mind out of the gutter. I'm too tired for anything terribly exciting, and, honestly, do I seem like an 'in a bush' sort of girl?

Don't answer that.

For the record we don't, because *if* I were going to have sex in a bush, it wouldn't be at my family's Family Festival. And also because . . .

'I am really worried about sex,' I tell Ren, in a rare pause for air. 'I have no idea how it's going to work.'

Ren blinks at me, opens his mouth, then closes it again.

'Yeah, sorry. Mood killer,' I say, pulling my clothes straight. 'Super sexy, Ven.'

'Hey.' He leans up to wind a hand into my curls. 'I think we can safely say I am in no way underwhelmed by your sex appeal.'

We both flush.

'Anyway, I know it's weird, 'cause I'm a boy . . . No,' he says, cutting himself off before I can. 'That's sexist and you're a feminist so you'll tell me off if I say that . . .' He takes a deep breath. 'I really, really want to – obviously – but . . .' He grimaces. 'I'm not ready yet?' he squeaks.

'Oh,' I say. 'Cool. Good. I mean . . . maybe we just . . . have a lot of fun and see what happens later and, if that involves sex, we just . . .' I shrug. 'Deal with it then?'

Ren's breath gusts out in relief. 'That sounds amazing. Especially if you might be up for some of that fun, like, *right* now?'

He grins wolfishly at me, so I grin wolfishly back, and we have an awful lot of fun indeed.

I stop feeling ugly. I stop feeling sad and angry and ashamed. Not because a boy is paying me attention, but because it's a nice change of pace for my body to be a source of pleasure rather than just pain.

Although there's too much to do and not enough time, I call a halt mid-afternoon and take the others for a site tour (Fred recording a series of short clips for our channel and George snapping pics for our socials to help boost our fundraising efforts) before the barricades go up. First step, especially since it's right in front of the box office, is the Workshop Area so I can show them the tepee where we'll be performing. Once Fred and George have made a plan for setting up the recording equipment, we carry on past the catering area to the stalls beyond, then set out across the huge empty-for-now slope down to Main Stage.

When we get to the mosh pit, I signal my chauffeur (Ren) to a halt and pull out a set of Access All Areas passes.

'Yes, I am the best,' I call over the squealing and shouting, 'and you may, if you wish, grovel at my feet.'

Benjo casts himself down in front of the wheelchair. 'I am going to be backstage with my favourite band. I will never, ever complain about how bossy and awful you are again because this is going to make my entire *life*.'

'You are not allowed to use your passes to pester the artists,' I tell him sternly. 'Seriously, people, I'm responsible for you. Don't let me down.'

Benjo nods so fervently I worry he might hurt his neck. 'Please can we go there now, pleasepleasepleeeeease?'

Backstage at the festival is like backstage everywhere: disappointing and just about strung together – a mess of coiled cabling, generators, portacabin dressing rooms, catering huts, a few picnic tables, and a little tent for press (literally a tent with flimsy folding tables and plug-points).

While the others explore (I notice Maddie and Fred engaging in the time-honoured tradition of walking side by side, hands brushing, by way of silently agreeing to progress to hand-holding), Ren wheels me slowly back up the main walkway. I pretend I don't see the pity and curiosity on people's faces as they clock the wheelchair and wonder why I'm in it. Do any of them even imagine Ren's my boyfriend rather than just some poor helper roped in to deal with me?

I peek over my shoulder at him, but he's just smiling around, completely relaxed and happy. He isn't thinking a single one of the things I am – it hasn't even occurred to him that there's any cause for shame.

He glances down at me, then draws the chair to a stop. 'Too rough?' he asks, wincing. 'I could slow down.'

'It's fine,' I say, clearing my throat when my voice comes out hoarse. 'All good.'

One Day More . . .*

*insert 'Les Mis' soundtrack here

Festival Thursday is always frantic. Ms Meade and Aunt Jinnie work their way through last-minute ticket sales, while the twins and Maddie direct the pedestrian traffic (a mix of stallholders, caterers, workshop performers looking to scout the venues, and artists who've somehow missed the huge sign out front directing them to their welcome tent), Orla and Roks deal with customer service issues, and Ren gets the box office signage printed and laminated. I direct operations from my sun-lounger in the middle of the box office.

I was horrified when Aunt Jinnie produced it mid-morning and told me that if I didn't start lying down I'd be useless before the festival started. She's right, but it feels decadent and weird.

'Hey,' says Orla, when I get up to whinge at Aunt Jinnie that everyone is going to think I am lazy, 'could you maybe give us a little credit? No one on the *planet* thinks you're lazy. And I don't know why you think you need to be standing to give orders. I'd be surprised if you couldn't do it while sleeping.' It's the mix of exasperation and fondness that does it. And the fact that Orla takes my elbow on one side, while Maddie takes the other, and they literally tow me back to the chair.

'Sit,' they say as one.

The Day of Reckoning

(aka the festival opens)

The morning starts badly. I'm so tired that I end up slumped on the edge of the bed, hairbrush in hand, with no idea how I'm going to raise my arm high enough to sort out the mess on my head. Maddie takes one look and holds out her hand.

'Really, Ven? Like I haven't brushed your hair before.' She kneels behind me on the bed and sets to. 'Could you not just have asked instead of sitting there in misery?'

'Too tired to speak,' I whisper.

'I'll let it pass until you're caffeinated,' my best friend says, leaning forward to hug me.

Thankfully things do look up after I've guzzled an entire pot of tea. This is just as well because, as I'd warned everyone, there's literally not a minute to breathe.

The atmosphere is electric. It's like the moment before a show, standing behind the curtain, waiting for it to rise.

One minute we're scrambling through last box office

preparations, the next we're off to the stewards' briefing, held in the workshop tepee where we'll be performing on Sunday. The others settle beside the rest of the stewards and the junior members of the various departments, while the leaders and Festival Family get up on stage to run through all the Dos and Don'ts, and the basics of the different roles at the festival.

The Singers give a cheer when I join the Festival Family on stage. I give them the finger in return. But fondly. Then I catch Ren's eyes and the look of pride on his face makes heat rise in my cheeks ... until Copper Kev (the ex-police officer who runs our security) brings up a chair, pointing at it meaningfully, and I have to stop smiling at Ren to pout at Kev instead. He just laughs and ruffles my hair. I heave a put-upon sigh as I slouch into the seat. Then Kev moves to stand behind me, hands on my shoulders, and suddenly it's OK.

I feel the familiar buzz rising through me and know everyone else is feeling the same.

Uncle Geoff attempts a rousing speech, then Dad drags him away to deal with a crisis (quite possibly an invented one) so Aunt Sarah, Aunt Jinnie and Mum can do it properly. I stare out across the tent filled with people in their festival T-shirts, all beaming and brimming with excitement, and feel the familiar sense of wonder at this huge thing we're here to accomplish.

And suddenly it's time to *go, go, go*.

Aunt Jinnie throws me the box office keys and I unlock the front doors and people come flooding in.

It goes brilliantly until the Box Office Weekend

misadventure – where I dislocated my thumb and Stef had to finish writing the customer names onto the envelopes – catches up to us.

Armband Nog is an unusual rendering of Arnold Higgs by anyone's standards. Other highlights include Nodel Foggins (Nigel Havering) and Joanne Hog (Susan Hag).

It's madness until a little after six o'clock but, once I'm sure the worst is over, I let Ren and Maddie coax me away to find some food. None of us have had a proper break – me because I can't be spared, and them because they valiantly said they wouldn't rest without me. I expect they were intending this to guilt me into taking more than five minutes at a time. Sometimes I wonder if they know me at all.

In the end, we each order from different stalls, then share the food out between us. Kangaroo burger, artisanal sausages and quesadillas are followed by gooey chocolate brownies and cinnamon-dusted churros alongside fresh smoothies while we sit at the top of the slope down to Main Stage, listening to the final song of one of Mum's 'about to be the big new thing' picks – a girl with a breathy, folksy style whose album I'm downloading before the song finishes. We stay long enough to catch the opening number of the evening's headliner (a big-name band I couldn't care less about but who Benjo has been mumbling about for weeks), then we head back to our final box office stint of the day.

Since I took over running the box office and started getting paid, like the rest of the family I only ever manage to watch snatches of even my favourite acts. But the headliners are just about audible from the grass outside the box office, and of course in previous years I'd catch songs here and there as I zoomed around the site, delivering lost journalists to the press tent or VIP guests to their musician pals. It's weird working at a festival without really getting to *go* to it, but there's so much to absorb just being there that I've never minded – I don't need to see a whole set to enjoy the music for as long as the frantic pace of work allows.

When the final rush of the day is done, Ren stays on at the festival with Benjo and the boys, supervised by Ms Meade, but Maddie pretends she's tired and comes back with me to the hotel. It's the first time I've ever left Aunt Jinnie to close and lock up by herself, but I refuse to let myself dwell on the necessity of it.

I'm just relaxing into the knowledge that in ten minutes I'll be in the shower and bed within twenty – *bed, glorious bed, where I can be horizontal for an entire seven hours* – when we pull into the hotel car park to find both disabled bays taken.

I stare through the windscreen in disbelief. 'I told them. I told them I needed one of the spots.' I am too tired to go in and argue with the hotel then come back out and re-park the car, assuming they can get one of the idiots to move.

'Let me check if they've got badges,' Maddie says, whisking herself out of the car and trotting off to peer in one windscreen, then the next. She turns back, shaking her head, lips pursed into a flat line.

I bow forwards to rest my head against the steering wheel.

'Hey! What're you doing with my car?'

I peel myself off the wheel to see a man rushing towards Maddie, who has her phone out, taking pictures of the number plates. Her shoulders come up defensively and she takes a step back, then her eyes flick in my direction and she straightens, standing tall.

'I'm taking photos of your car – photos that clearly show you're parked in a disabled bay without a blue badge,' she says. 'So, you can get your blue badge out or you can move your car right the hell now and maybe I won't report you.'

The man's face darkens and he takes a step forwards.

Smashing my finger down on the button to open the window, I beep the horn then lean out. 'You OK, Mads?'

She gives me a thumbs up. 'I think a spot's just about to come free,' she tells me.

The man looks between us, hisses something under his breath, then beeps his car open and slams himself inside.

I back up to give him extra room, then zoom into the spot. Maddie gets the driver's side door open before I've even clicked off my seatbelt.

'Did you see that?' she crows. 'I kicked butt! I ruled!'

I stumble out, swaying. 'You really did.'

She beams at me. 'I just channelled you. And it was *awesome*. I am *so* trying that on Pip next time she's being impossible. You better be proud of me,' she says, pointing a finger in my face. 'I totally and completely had your back.'

I totter forwards and hug her. 'I love you,' I tell her hoarsely.

'Too bloody right,' says my wonderful best friend. 'Now let's get you inside before you drop.'

Although every cell in my body aches, I feel warm all the way through.

One Day Down, Two To Go . . .

In the first year of the festival, so legend goes (I was too young to remember), the family tried calling today Super Saturday, but experience has taught us that it's the day when Things We Can't Control Go Wrong. This year it's a group of people pretending to be stewards and directing people the wrong way around the roundabout in order to jam up the roads for miles around – *ha ha, soooooo funny.*

I'd hoped we could fit in one last proper rehearsal before the performance tomorrow – *TOMORROW!* – but we're too flat-out. I tell myself it's just as well: we don't want to strain our voices when we're so tired as it'll only add to our nerves. Still, excitement and stress bubble in my stomach every time I think about the clock ticking down . . . and whether I'll have anything left to give right when I need to be at my perkiest.

If the others are nervous, they don't show it, rushing between helping out and haring off to listen to their favourite acts.

It's mid-afternoon before we surface into the lull that comes when all the visitor families are in and none of the people who're just coming for the evening headliners have arrived yet. I turn to Ren and Maddie with a huge yawn. 'Who's for a nice, long break?'

I slop so eagerly out of the door that Maddie has to hurry to catch up with me for once. She winds both her arms around my left one, hooking her chin into my shoulder ... for all of two steps before my lumbering gait makes it way too uncomfortable for either of us. Then she contents herself with taking my hand and swinging it instead.

'Happy,' she says. 'We feel like us again.'

We finish the walk in silence, settling into our usual spot at the top of the slope to Main Stage.

'So, tell me about Fred,' I say as I collapse back onto the grass.

Maddie grins. 'We're going to go see the Zulu singers together on our next break.'

Ren and I exchange a look.

'That is the world's best euphemism,' I tell her.

Maddie shoves me then yelps, but I just laugh.

'I'm not damaged, Mads.'

She rolls her eyes. 'Better not be since tomorrow's the show. Speaking of, we're going back to the hotel as soon as Jinnie takes over in the box office this evening. I'm going to bring dinner upstairs and you are going to lie in bed and eat it and then sleep.'

'Are you seriously more interested in making me rest than chasing opportunities to snog Fred?'

'We'll have plenty of time to snog the life out of each other after the festival,' says Maddie serenely. 'Everyone has limits. And you really need to stop throwing yourself off the cliff beyond yours. You don't want to be too tired for tomorrow.'

I curl my nails into my palm to hold back the nasty retort that springs to my lips. I'm the one who heard the words 'So you don't screw the performance up, like you did with PopSync.' Maddie's just trying to help and she probably didn't even realise I'd take it like that.

'I don't like being sensible,' I grit out. 'It's boring.'

'Yes,' Ren drawls, 'behind-the-scenes experience at a major music festival plus a performance at said festival plus running the box office at said festival ... all totally boring. Honestly, I can't think why I'm not permanently asleep in your company.'

I laugh, turning my attention to the band on the stage below. I suppose going to bed early is a pretty minor compromise in the scheme of things, but I wish I could stay to see the others at the silent disco. Everyone wears headsets and you can switch between various songs so people end up dancing to different beats. It's very, very weird watching it in all silence, and I want to be there, giving it a go with the others, laughing and stumbling on the uneven ground of the tepee floor. I want to be there when they scarf down dinner from one of the stalls, then find a spot to watch the Saturday evening headliners as day falls into night.

But tomorrow matters more. Those are the memories I can't afford to miss out on, so I can't take any chances. No way am I having a repeat of the PopSync disaster. It's all going to be different this time. It has to be.

The Big Day

– no pressure or anything

Hours till the performance: 7

Festival Sunday starts with a rush, all of us frantically taking advance bookings for next year at the special 'Only at the festival' rate. When it's over, we head to the trees by the side of the box office to rehearse under Ms Meade's watchful eye. We run all the hard bits of our set list – the starts, pauses, key changes and any held or modifying chords where people tend to miss their cues or don't give it full punch. A quiet start is fine with songs that build, but mostly you want to come in strong from the beginning.

The only song we run in full is the mash-up. We haven't had nearly as much time as I'd like to rehearse it, but the whole group was adamant that it will be our finale. No one outside The Singers has heard it yet, so today's performance is it. And we're ready. I don't even need Ms Meade's thumbs up to know. I grin at everyone and tell them to go and have fun for a few hours.

Then it's just me and Ren, curled up against a tree.

Ren sighs, the movement of his chest raising and lowering my head. 'What the hell am I doing going on stage, Ven? No one wants to look up and see *me*. Talk about a face for radio.'

'Is this rhetorical or do I need to do some ego boosting?' I ask, wriggling around so my head is on his shoulder and I can kiss his cheek. I blink when I realise this is the first time he's ever let me sit on the scarred side. 'I don't want to take my stick up on stage either, for the record, so if you shouldn't be up there, neither should I.' I make him work it through. Sometimes he needs comfort and sometimes, like we all do, he needs a loving little kick in the arse.

'I guess if people survived looking at Pip's smarmy mug when you and PopSync did the TV shows, the two of us won't finish them off.'

'You're a bit slow sometimes, but it's good that, if I lead you halfway there, you can do a bit of thinking for yourself,' I tell him.

He promptly rolls us – carefully – over to tickle me. Yes, it's *entirely* an excuse to start snogging.

We continue snogging for quite some time.

It is lovely.

Half an hour later, I'm busy updating the box office database when I see Ren come through the outer doors and stand looking about as if confused. This makes no sense because I sent him off only ten minutes ago to deliver a lost press person to Main Stage.

Then he turns and I realise it's not Ren, but Tai. He spots me and his shoulders go up defensively, but he scuffs his way over.

'You made it!' I smile brightly – perhaps too brightly, but at least I'm trying.

He shrugs. 'Yeah. Turns out I'm not a total loss.'

'We are not sorry for ourselves at *all*, are we?' I say before I can stop myself.

Tai laughs. 'I guess I asked for that.'

I turn to the corkboard behind the counter and unpin a ticket envelope, pushing it across to him.

'Are you sure I can't pay?'

I shake my head. 'Not a chance. Like I said, buy Ren dinner or something. This is a gift – my contribution to helping you surprise your brother.'

'Oh, it'll surprise him all right, me getting my act together enough to remember the day *and* not get lost on the way. He'll be looking for flying pigs next.'

'And we're back to the self-pity party,' I drawl.

But this time Tai clenches his jaw instead of smiling, looking away. 'I'm not the one who deserves it.'

'Neither's Ren,' I snap. 'There's a lot of stuff he deserves, but pity's not part of it. You want to do something nice for him? Stop thinking that it is. Yes, he's got some scars, but they're all you seem to see when you look at him. So maybe knock it off and start noticing all the stuff you're missing.' I blow my breath out, trying to get a rein on my temper.

Tai looks away to the doors. 'Do I just show this' – he waves his envelope – 'over there?'

'You give in the ticket and they give you a wristband, then you're free to go where you like,' I say coolly.

'Thanks,' he mumbles. 'I'll see you later, I guess.'

With perfect timing, Ren comes marching through the doors. I watch his expression change as he spots Tai: surprise, concern, and then love.

I'm not well disposed to Tai, but I guess I'll just have to get over it.

Ren gives his brother a tentative hug then glances over at me, delight on every inch of his face.

'Go,' I mouth. 'Have some fun.'

Ren looks around, but the box office is quiet.

'Go!' I mouth again, making a shooing gesture.

A customer with a broken wristband interrupts me then and, when I next look up, they're walking into the festival, Tai sauntering with his hands stuffed in his pockets while Ren practically skips next to him. I get a glimpse of Tai smiling – all gentle fondness – then Ren rakes a hand through his hair, pushing it out of his eyes and uncovering the scars.

I see the happiness drain out of Tai's face, and the moment Ren realises what's happening.

My chest aches with the heartbreak on both their faces.

Then Tai takes a breath, squares his shoulders and puts a grin back on his face. It's forced and stiff, but all the tension dissolves from Ren's body instantly.

Just as they pass out of sight, I see Ren throw his head back and laugh.

Plenty of Time For Everything To Go Wrong

Hours till the performance: 3

When I reach the Goan Fish Curry van where Ren messaged me to meet him and Tai for lunch, all I'm thinking about is the fact that I wish I'd asked Maddie to bring me in the wheelchair. I've been feeling progressively dodgier all day, but I didn't want to risk a blow-up if Tai's less than impressed that I'm using a wheelchair now, not just a stick. I can't ruin this for Ren – it's too important.

When I spot him, I tone down the limp, even though it sends shards of agony into my hip at every step. 'Hey!' I call.

But then he spins round and his face is a mask of worry. 'Have you seen him?'

'Tai?' I ask, brain too full of pain to process how stupid the question is.

'No, Santa Claus.' He laces his fingers behind his head as he paces in an anxious circle, nearly colliding with a red and yellow jester on a unicycle coming one way, then a gaggle of people in university sweatshirts, silver face-paint and alien antennae going the other.

I catch Ren's arm and drag him into the relative safety of a gap between two marquee guy-ropes. 'Did something happen?'

'Yeah,' says Ren. 'Yeah, something happened. You made plans with Tai and didn't bother mentioning it to me.'

'He wanted it to be a surprise.' I don't add that I figured Tai had avoided committing himself in case he wasn't in a fit state on the day. 'I thought you'd be happy. You were over the moon when he arrived.'

'*Obviously* I was pleased that my brother came all this way to see our performance, but I was so caught up in the surprise I didn't realise . . .' He trails off, jaw working. 'I know you meant well, but why couldn't you pause to think? Just for a moment.'

I raise my hands helplessly, staggering when my stick leaves the ground and I realise I don't have a handle on my balance at all.

'It's a festival, Ven. And what do you have at a festival?'

'Music?' I offer. 'Families? Ice cream—'

'And alcohol. Lots and lots of alcohol. Not to mention pot and God knows what else. Why couldn't you have warned me, so I had time to figure out how to make it work?'

'I'm sorry,' I say, reaching out for him. 'Tai said not to tell you and I was trying to make nice with him and I honestly didn't think—' I swallow hard, blinking back the threat of tears. 'I'm sorry,' I whisper helplessly. 'I'll get the gang to look for him, then we can make sure someone stays with him and—'

'It's too late, Ven.' He turns away again, kicking out at a clump of grass. 'I should have just gone to the loo with him and messaged you. God, why didn't I just go with him?'

'We need to focus on finding him. That's all we can do now, so let's calm down—'

'Or I could just go home so you don't have to worry about your loser brother embarrassing you any more.'

We both wheel round. Tai is standing close enough to reach out and grab my arm as I stumble sideways. It wrenches something in my shoulder, but I do my best to keep the pain off my face.

'I'm not drunk and I'm not high, but I can leave if you're just going to spend the whole afternoon convinced that every loo break is me going off to get wrecked,' Tai says stiffly. 'I didn't come here to spoil your day.'

'I couldn't find you,' Ren says hollowly. 'You weren't in the queue, so I messaged you, but you didn't reply . . .'

Tai's jaw clenches. 'I went to find a quiet spot to make a call, and I figured you could survive ten minutes without me.'

'It was half an hour, Tai!'

'So it was half an hour!' Tai shouts back, then his anger seems to deflate. 'I'm sorry I lost track of time.' He flicks a glance at me. 'If you must know, I was calling my sponsor to make sure I *didn't* dive into the nearest beer tent or follow my nose to the closest dealer. I was trying to be responsible, but I . . . I needed some help with that because I'm too pathetic to do it by myself.' He ducks his head then, hands stuffed down into his pockets.

'You guys need to talk so I'm going to give you some privacy, OK? I'm glad you're all right, Tai.' I turn away, then take a deep breath and pause. 'For the record, I think calling your sponsor is the opposite of pathetic.'

Then I hobble off, managing to get myself out of sight before my hip gives way and I tumble onto the grass. For a while I sit there, head bowed over my knees, thinking self-pitying thoughts. Then angry ones. Then miserable ones. And then I realise that to crown the whole thing off I'm about to have a weeing issue and there is no way I can walk from here to the loos.

Is this going to be a regular thing every time I have a romantic crisis?

'Loo!' I gasp at Roks when she comes hurtling up with the wheelchair. 'Loo, loo, loo, *LOO!*'

She takes one look at my face as I tumble into the seat, then sets off at a run while I beep-beep the horn to scare people out of our way.

'Emergency! Coming through!' Roks shouts every time we reach a crowd.

And still people step directly into our path, or fail to stand back, and I am going to wee myself because the jolting is *really* not helping, and then I'm going to die of mortification.

Roks swerves us around a cluster of children with bubble wands, then photo-bombs a hen-do posing in matching sashes and tiaras in front of the paint-a-patch plywood wall along the side of the art tent. The act playing on Main Stage provides a suitably dramatic soundtrack as we rush onwards.

The loo block is in sight.

'Coming through!' Roks bellows and whisks me straight past the queue. She grabs the door of the disabled cubicle from the woman about to enter. 'Emergency,' she says, flashing her AAA festival pass in the woman's startled face. Then she wheels me inside and the loo is right there, only a metre away.

'Out!' I squeak.

'I could stand in the corner with my back turned and—'

'Out!'

Bliss unfounded, I get my knickers down and my bum on the seat just in time so that I do *not* wee myself.

It is a while before I come down from the sheer relief and release.

Once I do, I discover that my belly is distended and everything hurts and I still want to go even though I've gone and gone and gone and gone some more.

I try to hold on to the fact that I didn't feel the weird tug that happened before Orla's party, so maybe it won't be as bad this time, but there's definitely a pinkish tint to my wee. On the plus side, it was hours between it first starting and everything getting really bad last time, so probably there's enough time to get through the performance even if afterwards it all goes to hell.

Please, just let me get through the performance, I pray to whoever might be listening.

I'll volunteer to go to hospital afterwards if I can just get through the performance. It can't slip through my fingers again. It just can't.

I've accepted. I've adjusted. I've started building a new life, with new friends, and new goals, and it can't be ripped away all over again.

I gulp down the sob that tries to escape.

'Ven?' calls Roks from the other side of the door. 'Do you need a doctor?'

'No,' I croak back. 'Just give me a minute.'

'It's fine so long as you're OK. Take your time. We don't have anywhere to be.'

'You wanted to see that act,' I say. 'You're going to miss it all for my stupid—'

'It doesn't matter.'

'You were looking forward to it!' I think about getting up then, but I wee a little more instead.

Even when I'm done, I still need to go. How long am I going to have to keep sitting here?

Maybe it'll be better if I just get up and make myself not think about it.

When I tug the door open, Roks gives me a worried look.

'I think I should get your mum.'

'I'm fine,' I say, but I'm so exhausted and sore it comes out far less certain than I'd intended.

She hovers over me while I hobble to the sink and wash up. I'm just levering myself into the wheelchair when I freeze.

'Get the cubicle!' I gasp, and Roks springs into action, catching the door as the current occupant exits.

My wee is no pinker this time, which is something, but I still have to sit there until I wee again. And then again. And then for a while longer, but gradually the urge recedes and I get up without immediately needing to sit back down.

This time, after I wash my hands, I manage to settle in the wheelchair without having to get straight back up again.

'OK?' Roks asks as she starts pushing me towards the door. 'If we need to go back, it's not a problem.'

'I am going to owe you all the babysitting in the world,' I grouse.

'Hey,' says Roks sharply. 'I thought this *wasn't* a tit-for-tat friendship.'

'Urgh,' I groan, burying my head in my hands. 'I think I'm dying of shame. How long does that usually take?'

'Do you need to lie down or see a doctor or go back to the hotel or—'

'I'm missing the performance over my dead body.'

'Yeah, I figured,' says Roks. 'But let's see if we can come up with a way to avoid that, OK?'

The Show Must Go On . . .

Hours till the performance: 1

In the end, everything seems to settle down, though my hip is not thanking me for the jostling it took as Roks rushed me over the bumpy ground to the loos. How delightful that even sitting in a wheelchair while someone else does all the work is a problem for my stupid body. But at least a dose of morphine improves the situation and the main thing is that we don't have to turn back again. Roks insists on tattling to Mum and Ms Meade the minute we get back to the box office, but, though they fret over me for a while, it does seem like it was just some sort of blip.

The relief is almost enough to offset the sting of how I left things with Ren. Thankfully, I'm so far past exhausted I've almost started to go numb. The crash at the end of the festival isn't going to be pretty, but that's a problem for later.

I'm considering taking a break to lie down – just getting my head down would help and I'll take anything I can get at this point – when Ren comes slouching through the doors, peers at me from under his hair, then sidles over to the counter.

'Hey,' he says quietly.

When I look round, I can just make out Tai scuffing back and forth beyond the security point, talking on his phone. One hand is in his hair, but his movements are slow and loose and, as I watch, I catch a smile on his face. Still, I consider apologising to Ren again. Or demanding an apology, but I'm too tired. I want to be cross, but I also want us to be OK. Most of all, I just want today not to end up ruined.

'So,' Ren says, shooting a look at Maddie, who is watching us from the opposite counter with her arms crossed, 'Maddie has pointed out that I'm a huge hypocrite and I was wondering if we could pretend that my less than stellar behaviour earlier didn't happen. Or can we at least talk about the fact that I'm very sorry for it, and I know I say that a lot, but this time really was different because I was honestly terrified for Tai and . . .' He deflates. 'And I, er . . . we, er . . . Maddie and I, that is . . . We have a surprise for you.'

'You what?'

Ren grimaces. 'It seemed like a good idea at the time, but . . . Look, could you just try to go with it? For Maddie, if not for me? We've been working on this for ages and . . .'

It takes a moment, but then the penny drops. The 'secret' that I thought was Ren and Maddie going out – the one they refused to tell me about even after the whole mortifying misunderstanding came out.

Maddie and Ren must exchange some signal, because suddenly she's standing at the end of the counter with the wheelchair. 'Your chariot awaits!'

'*Now?* We've got the performance in ten minutes, Mads. We need to be heading over, not getting sidetracked.'

'Exactly.'

With a fresh groan, I settle myself in the chair. 'What've you done?'

She gives me a Cheshire Cat grin. 'I have been Very Clever Indeed.'

She zooms me off through the no-exit door, Ren loping beside us and Tai following behind. I think about checking to see what Tai's face is doing at seeing me in the wheelchair, but I just don't want to know.

We seem to be heading for the tent where we'll be doing the workshop. As we round the corner, I spot a pair of cameramen and a woman whose entire being screams 'reporter'. Maddie waves at them, and they wave back, then she wheels me into the workshop tepee.

'Fred and George are doing amazing work with our online publicity for the fundraising, but there are only so many people who're going to stumble across our accounts, so I thought "How could it hurt to have coverage from a proper news station too?"

And Ms Meade said it would also be great for our coursework portfolios, so I told Ren, and he had the idea to get Aunt Jinnie to talk to one of the reporters covering the festival and ... *voila*! Press coverage!' Her face falls when I just blink at her. 'Look, I know it's not anything like you'd manage to arrange. But I just thought it would be nice – an extra record of your achievement. I want you to know how proud I am of you.'

She's trying to give me another shot at the day of the PopSync disaster – or as close as she can get. And I love her for it. But I really wish I felt a tiny bit more certain that my second chance isn't going to go the way of the first.

Still, the only way I'm quitting now is if I'm dead or unconscious, so I reach up and tug on her shirt. 'Thank you,' I whisper.

I'd forgotten that Tai was lurking and nearly jump when he follows Ren into the tent.

'Are you sure you're happy?' Maddie is saying worriedly. 'Because you don't look happy—'

I twist round to grab her hand. 'You *know* my face just looks like this when I'm shattered. Don't start taking it personally now.'

Maddie gives me a dubious look. A moment later Ren joins her with the same look on his face.

'Why don't we get the ramp for the stage, then you can just stay in the wheelchair?' Ren says.

'No,' I tell him. 'I am going to take a grand total of six steps from here to the stage, then I'm bloody well going to perform on my own two feet like everyone else. I've been sitting in the lounger and the wheelchair all festival so I can do this, and no one is going to "but, Ven" me about it, OK?' I cross my arms over my chest and pout – but in an entirely mature and grown-up way. 'I just want to look normal for a few minutes.'

'Why will you look more normal standing up?' a voice asks.

For a moment I am so stunned with fury and hurt I can't even think.

'Don't you *dare* say that to her,' Ren hisses from beside me. 'There is not one single thing wrong with the way she looks or with the wheelchair or—'

Tai's eyes go wide as Ren literally shoves him back a pace.

'I didn't mean it like that,' Tai says, voice low and desperate – and hurt.

It stops Ren in his tracks.

'I just meant that sitting and standing are both totally normal. That's . . . I didn't mean . . .'

There is a stunningly awkward silence. Ren's face blanches and his hand comes up as if to grab Tai's arm to stop him bolting, but we can all see that he's going to be too late. But then Tai freezes. He takes a deep breath and looks straight into his brother's eyes in a way I've not ever seen him manage before.

'You're *all* going to look like you're talented and determined enough to perform at a national festival, even though you're still just kids. That's all anyone is going to see,' he says. 'They won't even notice the rest because it's not important.'

There are tears in my eyes as I watch them look at each other. Earlier I thought I'd ruined my relationship with Ren trying to give Tai a second chance, but now ... I'm not sure I'm ready to like him yet, but I think maybe he really is trying in a way that he wasn't before.

It's a near thing, but no one quite gets around to crying because suddenly the rest of The Singers are bursting in, and Ms Meade is settling herself in a corner with her notepad out, ready to write up her coursework assessment notes on our performance. Between checking Fred and George have their equipment set up, Roks's repurposed banner from the mall is firmly attached to the back wall of the tepee, Ren has all our first-notes ready on his phone, Maddie has distributed fundraising flyers with our social media details to every seat, and Orla is happy that we're all looking unified and presentable in black jeans, black shoes, and black hoodies with The Singers logo (courtesy of Roks) printed across the back in silver, time slips away.

I've barely time for a flare of nerves when the tent starts flooding with audience members. Since all events within the festival are free to enjoy, it's always hard to predict which workshops and acts in the smaller tents will be heaving, and which will have an audience of two. I've had more than one nightmare of no one turning up and having to chivvy The Singers through performing to an empty tent. Instead, the seats all fill in minutes and soon people are plonking themselves down on the floor along the back too.

'Showtime,' I say, my voice coming out hoarse with a mix of tension and excitement. If we can pull this off surely we'll not only ace our coursework but it'll be something to be proud of forever.

Tai reaches out and clasps Ren's shoulder, then heads off to take his seat while Ren wheels me to the side of the tent to join the others. As soon as Ren is looking away, I let my face twist into a mask of exhaustion. What I wouldn't give to suspend time so I could lie down, right where I am, for a few minutes. But sitting quietly until it's time for the performance will have to do because Benjo's flicking on the mic and kicking off the workshop intro.

The acoustics are different from those in the music room, but the sound-system has been well-teched so we don't have to shout to be heard or worry about how we're holding the microphones to avoid crackles and hisses. The key thing is the atmosphere – the audience is happy and attentive, no one scrolling on their phones, though several people are snapping pics. It's both exhilarating and terrifying that the performance is just minutes away.

Fred and George's talk goes even better than in rehearsals and, as they bring their section to a close, I look round to see Maddie beaming at Fred like a loon. I make a mental note to tease her mercilessly later.

Next Ren explains about the festival's chosen charities and how to donate if anyone wants to. As he speaks, Roks reaches out and, hidden between us, squeezes my hand.

Maddie's up next to teach the audience 'Up Above My Head' as a warm-up. Like me, Maddie has a nice but non-distinctive voice, good for blending with the rest of the group – when she sings loud enough to be heard by humans. Thankfully, as we've rehearsed her confidence has increased and now, though she starts a little quiet, she's audible and gets stronger as the audience starts joining in more and more enthusiastically.

There's a little cheer when she finishes and one small boy continues singing the looping warm-up until, with a ripple of laughter, his parents persuade him to drop his voice to a hushed whisper as Roks, Ren and Orla start to divide the crowd into groups to learn the song they've chosen – a medley of 'When The Saints', 'She'll Be Coming Round the Mountain' and 'This Train Is Bound for Glory'. Since most people already know at least one of the three base songs, we're hoping it'll make for more fun and less stress.

Finally, there's a stumble-through, then an almost passable second go. I sit quietly, trying to breathe deeply and evenly, willing the pain and exhaustion to recede just enough to get me through the next thirty minutes.

Then suddenly it's performance time and, though I know I should probably just stay in the wheelchair, I lever myself stubbornly to my feet.

I've spent a lot of time over the last month thinking about how I would get up on stage today: whether I wanted to try to manage without my stick, whether I wanted Roks or Ren to give me a hand, then I got into a whole internal crisis about what the different options represented . . . and then I told myself not to be so stupid. The whole point is to make the decision that works for me.

Occasionally leaning on people who're happy to help doesn't make me helpless, and it doesn't have to be all or nothing. There are people who love me and sometimes they want to be a bridge between what I want and what I can do – I just need to learn to let them without feeling like I'm giving in. For the past eighteen months, I've been determined to be an island as a way of feeling I'm still in control when really it's a sign of weakness rather than strength.

Which is why I put my arm through Ren's now, and we walk over to the stage and up the two steps together, then take our place at the central mic. He looks down at me, his eyes asking if I need help, but he lets me decide, hand under my elbow as I try to lock my shaking legs beneath me.

'The following songs are part of our A-level music portfolio,' Ren is explaining to the audience, as the rest of The Singers move into performance formation around us. 'They're all covers but we've done our own arrangements.'

At the side of the tent, next to where Fred has set up his tripod to film the event, I see Maddie's reporters hoisting their massive professional cameras onto their shoulders. True to their earlier promise, they keep their focus on the near side of the stage, leaving Roks and Orla in the background. I'm probably being paranoid, but after Orla's reaction to seeing her father's friend at the market it seems better not to risk them being shown clearly enough for anyone to recognise them.

Looking around, I see a little girl unfurl from her father's lap and bounce to her feet, flourishing a rainbow-coloured wind spinner. Next to her an elderly woman adjusts the wildflower garland in her wife's hair. Everyone laughs at whatever Ren is saying, though I can't hear a word over the buzz of pre-performance panic.

I can do this. I'm fine. Just twenty-five minutes and it'll all be over.

Nerves are zinging through me, making my skin prickle and my heart lurch. A cold sweat breaks out across the back of my neck.

I'm OK. It's not going to happen again. I'm OK.

The stage is rolling beneath my feet and as I open my mouth, leaning closer to the mic, I have to blink because everything's going pixelated, like someone's turning down the definition on the world.

I'm fine, I'm fine, I'm fine. Just keep it together. Less than twenty-five minutes then it's all over.

I swallow hard, trying to breathe slow and calm.

Don't panic, you're fine, it's all fine.

But it's not fine at all.

The despair hits a moment before the world goes black, then I fall and fall and fall.

Déjà Vu All Over Again . . .

I open my eyes to find Ren bending over me.

'It's OK,' he whispers.

Why is he whispering? Why am I on the floor?

It feels like wood. Where on earth am I?

And then my hearing turns on properly again and I realise people are singing.

Lots and lots of people are singing.

'You're OK,' Ren whispers again, brushing my hair back. 'Just take your time. Benjo's getting the audience to sing through the workshop song again. It's all OK.'

I turn my head, looking along a wooden plank . . . to a whole crowd of people standing just to my right. Benjo has moved to the far side of the stage to give me privacy as he leads the audience through their newly learnt song, while Roks, Orla,

Fred, George and Maddie are crouched around Ren, looking down at me . . .

Because I had to go and faint on stage. Again.

It's even worse than with PopSync. At least that time we got started before I ruined everything.

Horror floods through me. I'm too appalled even to cry.

'Don't panic,' says Roks, leaning forwards. 'We've got this. Just keep breathing nice and steady.'

I stare at her, wide-eyed, every inch of me trembling.

'Do you want to try sitting up?' Ren asks softly.

I nod and a moment later he and Maddie gently pull me up so I'm no longer sprawled across the stage. The others sit back on their heels and it's only now that I realise why they were clustered around me. It wasn't to heft me off the stage at the first opportunity. It was to screen me from the audience.

'I'm sorry,' I whisper. 'I'm so sorry—'

'Shh,' says Maddie. 'None of that. Now, you were only out for about five seconds so tell me the truth – were you just having one of your moments or is there something seriously wrong and we need to get you to a doctor?'

'I think . . . I think I just needed to get my head down.'

I'm already starting to feel better. I mean, I still feel completely grim, but not like I'm about to pass out again.

'Do you want to try to make this work or do you want out?' Maddie asks.

I blink at her. *How is this going to work?*

'It's up to you,' Ren whispers, squeezing my hand.

‘I don’t think I can stand,’ I say hopelessly. ‘Maybe ... maybe if someone got one of the tall stools from the box office ... No, there’s no time ...’

Maddie turns away, tapping frantically at her phone. ‘On it.’

Ren smiles, shaking his head. ‘Or we could just keep things simple.’

The audience breaks into applause: the song is over. It’s now or never, no third chance.

I take a deep breath and ready myself to get up, but Ren reaches out and presses me down. ‘Stay,’ he says.

Then he bounds up to collect the microphone from Benjo.

‘Thanks for bearing with us, folks. We hope you had fun practising your new song while our fearless leader recovered. We’re ready to go now, so please take your seats.’

Then he plops down next to me and offers me the mic as Benjo settles next to him. In a moment, the others have manoeuvred themselves into performance formation around us sitting on the edge of the stage. And there’s no fuss, no drama, as if this is all perfectly normal.

I look out over the audience and it’s weird to be only slightly higher than their heads, but it’s not such a huge crowd that they can’t see us. The camera crew give me a thumbs up. Ms Meade raises her hands above her head in silent, proud applause.

It’s not what we planned. Not what I wanted. And, yes, I’ve managed to thoroughly humiliate myself in public once again.

But this time I’m not going to be carried off stage, performance over, ruined. So what if we're sitting on the stage? We're here to sing, not stand.

I take the mic from Ren, letting my fingers glide over his as I smile into his eyes. And I see him know all the things I want to say without my having to speak a word.

I take a deep breath, then turn to the front.

'Hi, folks. Sorry for the slight change of plans, but thanks for . . . Thanks.'

In the audience, Tai gives me a thumbs up.

'So, back to our scheduled programming. This year we're doing arrangements of existing songs as part of our coursework, so we hope you like our portfolio selection. To introduce our first song, please say hi again to arrangers Orla and Roksana.'

I pass the microphone, then steady myself against Ren's shoulder.

I've got this.

This time, I really do.

When I look out at the crowd, I don't worry that they think I'm ugly or pathetic or useless. OK, yes, they just saw me fall on my face. But they also saw all my friends rally round to help. They saw me get back up. And now they're looking at me hold hands with the most gorgeous boy in the whole place. A boy who is treating me with dignity and respect and a tenderness that makes my eyes sting. If I were sitting in the audience, looking up at myself, I'd see someone with everything going for her. Someone centre-stage on one of the best days of her life.

Adrenaline and determination and pride flood through me,

rising up through my body until I feel the shaking fade away, all my pain dulling into the background. The world sharpens as if suddenly I can breathe deeper.

I can do this. I'm ready.

I raise my head. All I want to do now is sing. Which is just as well because Orla is counting us in and . . .

My voice comes out clear and true. I don't even have to think about the notes, don't have to feel for the rhythm. The song sings itself out of me. All that's left is the magic of the music.

We've never sung like this before. Not even close.

The tent goes hushed with it, as if everyone knows that something special is happening. For once it's effortless. Not a note or breath out of place.

It feels as if it goes on forever. And yet, in a blink, the song's done, over.

A moment later the audience breaks into thunderous applause. I feel a laugh wrench out of me, high and surprised. When I look around, the others seem just as stunned but overjoyed.

As Fred and Maddie introduce their arrangement, there's a stir among the crowd, then Dad comes marching towards the stage with one of the tall box office stools. I can't believe he managed to get away from whatever he was doing to fetch the stool so quickly after Maddie's message reached him. It's almost as if he was heading over here already.

'Ready to go up?' Ren asks, offering his hand, and the look in his eyes . . .

A moment later, I'm settled on the stool. Dad squeezes my

shoulder then slips back into the audience while the others gather around me, then we launch into our second song.

I tense, waiting for it all to go wrong, but the magic is still with us.

We had a nice audience for the workshop, but as we perform the tent fills and fills and fills. I try not to think about the reporters filming from the back. I have to hope that they'll have the decency not to include my swan-dive in their news item, but I suppose it's not the end of the world if they do.

As we start the third song, I look over to give Dad a thumbs up – and there they all are. I don't know how they've managed it, but Mum, Dad and Aunt Jinnie are all here. Even My Awful Cousin Stef and Aunt Sarah and Uncle Geoff. They are *never* all on break at once during the festival. And yet they're here. Who the hell is running things?

Dad puts his arm around Mum's shoulders, both of them looking so proud they might cry. Aunt Jinnie leans into Mum's other side, her face full of love as she smiles up at me.

I didn't realise how much today meant to them, but I don't think this is about seeing me up on stage again. It's about seeing me happy. Seeing me get to live the type of life I want, even if there are compromises and changes and limitations.

I look to my left, past Roks to Orla, then to my right, past Benjo to Fred and George.

And then I look at Ren.

When the song ends and we turn to smile out at the crowd and take a bow, his hand finds mine again and it feels like something that's been missing fits back into place inside me.

The performance has been going past in a blur, like I'm standing outside myself. Next up we do a pair of songs from our mall set list, then Benjo and George's arrangement, then 'Be Like Him', and finally, in a sudden rush of nerves – *breathe, Ven, breathe* – it's time for the mash-up.

Ren introduces it, which is just as well because I'm frozen in sudden fear.

'Ven and I' – he turns to smile at me – 'really hope you like our song because it's pretty special to us.'

Deep breath. *Just sing to Ren. Let him sing to you.*

The backing track comes on. There's seven seconds of intro. They stretch into a century.

Just focus on the words.

I lock eyes with Ren and suddenly the panic is energy is anticipation is song and even though it's just a performance, not a competition, it feels like I've won.

Because suddenly I'm barely aware of the seat beneath me. It's like I'm not in my body any more.

I'm no longer making music, I *am* music.

Everything else is gone – the pain, the shame, the audience . . . everything except me and Ren and it's as if the notes are painting pictures in the air. That day when his hand hovered over mine in class because I was in pain and he didn't know how to comfort me. That day in The Tea Party when he cut all the cakes in half so he wouldn't accidentally take my favourite. That day when we finally knew what the mash-up was really about. And later, in his bedroom, his skin against mine, my breath becoming his, losing ourselves in each other. No embarrassment or fear, just joy.

All of me, I say to him.

And he says it back.

And for a moment that feels like forever that's all there is.

Happiness

The sun is slowly sinking behind the hills, dusk settling over the Festival Village like a blanket. Around me the others loll on the grass, sipping drinks and listening to the music from Main Stage as the stars come out. With the performance out of the way and everything winding down, I am done with pushing through and focusing on the present and not letting the pain defeat me. I've made it to the finish line and now I can stop.

I can feel the crash hovering, waiting to swallow me whole. The clock is about to strike midnight on Cinderella's ball and soon all the magic will be gone, everything returning to normal . . .

And yet I did it. Even though I passed out on stage in front of the cameras all over again, this time it worked out – *sloop, gloop, splat*, wheelchair and all. So what that I needed a little help? So what that I had to use a few aids to get through? I still did my part, singing music I helped arrange with a group I've transformed from a disaster into a success. And of course that's thanks to all of us, not just me, but I was the one who got things started.

Now, wrapped in Ren's arms, with Maddie and Tai and the rest of The Singers around me, I think to myself that right here, right now, life is really pretty great. Singing makes me happy. The festival makes me happy. My friends and Ren make me happy. And happiness makes everything else seem possible.

My mind goes back to that day in the car park after my disastrous visit to the self-help group and how much I hated myself. How I felt ruined by what was happening. Only now I see that it was just the pain and misery talking. Life's still a million miles away from being easy, but it's doable again. There is enough good stuff to make all the awful bits more than worth it and, really, can anyone say more than that?

'Want to know The Singers' current fundraising tally for the domestic violence charities?' George asks suddenly.

There's a tired murmur of interest as everyone pulls out their phones. I rest my head on Ren's shoulder and watch as he scrolls though The Singer's social media, enlarging a few photos and clicking on a couple of the video clips.

'This all looks amazing,' I tell Fred. 'The editing is so slick.'

'I had no idea we'd come across so professional,' Maddie says, leaning over Ren's other shoulder to watch. 'Go us!'

'We get over that two-hundred-pound-donations mark yet?' Orla yawns. 'With all your work, and Maddie and Ren's reporters, we must have done. I know it's not much to put towards the festival's overall pot, but still it's money they wouldn't have had otherwise.'

'It's nice to know all this work isn't just about us and our coursework – it's actually going to do some good in the world,' Roks says softly, her smile weary but warm.

George taps away on his phone, though I can see from the way he's biting his lip that he's just pretending.

I reach over and poke his knee. 'Tally. Now.'

'We passed two hundred,' George reports.

There's a little cheer that almost drowns out him saying, 'And five hundred.'

Which gets a bigger cheer, which almost drowns out him saying, 'And eight and a half thousand.'

'What?' say Roks, as everyone goes quiet in shock.

'Looks like we'll hit nine in the next twenty minutes if it keeps going up at the same rate. If you ask me nicely, I'll tell you again over breakfast.'

'Wow,' whispers Orla. 'That's . . .' She sniffs, pulling the cuff of her hoodie over her hand to wipe suddenly at her cheeks. Roks shuffles over and soon they're huddled together, both a little bright-eyed but smiling all the same.

As I turn away, I realise that Ren is watching me. The moment our eyes meet it's as if we're suddenly alone, in our own little bubble, even in the midst of all our friends. He tucks my hair behind my ear with a touch that raises goosebumps across my skin as we lean into each other and a kiss that isn't just a kiss.

Then we sit there together, enjoying the sunset and the music and the end of one of the best days of our lives.

Well, I *want* to just sit there and 'be in the moment', but of course I'm me so after a few minutes of chilling I start thinking about how far we've come – and the fact that if we've come this far, this fast, then the future's looking pretty bright.

I suspect the Festival Family has just grown and The Singers will be a permanent feature from now on, but it's more than that. Today could so easily have been a repeat of the PopSync disaster, but this time we saved the performance *and* nothing bad is going to come from it: my fainting on stage wasn't a sign that singing is going to be taken away from me, just that I pushed my limits a little too much. Although I've obviously got further to go, I'm learning not just how to cope but how to thrive. Even if today isn't the beginning of figuring out my big new dream, for the first time I really believe that, whatever life has in store, it really will be just as good as if I were still dancing, if not better.

And of *course* I want to know what's next so I can start planning and organising and MAKING IT HAPPEN RIGHT NOW ... but perhaps, for a few hours, I can be content just to know that it will and, when it does, it'll be great.

P.S.

I know you've been waiting all this time to find out what's wrong with me. And I know you've been impatiently grinding your teeth while I dodged the reveal and refused to tell you.

But here's the thing: you didn't know me before.

If I'd told you, what would you have spent the rest of our time together thinking about? If you had to describe me to someone, what's the first thing you would have said? Even if it wasn't the first or even second, my diagnosis would have been right up there at the top of the list.

But now you know me. And whether you like me or not, I hope you'll have enough respect not to define me on the basis of something that is a big part of my life but isn't a big part of *me*.

I'm not what's wrong with my body.

I am what I do with myself.

I'm the life I make happen.

If you could remember that, I'd really appreciate it.

You know everything you need to and that's all there is to it, so if you're expecting more, I've got one final thing to say . . .

Get over it.

Acknowledgements

A big thanks to my family for adjusting and helping me adjust to changing circumstances – and generally being wonderful and supportive. A particular shout-out to the under-eighteen crew: George, Sophie, James and Aidan. And to my wonderful Auntie Liana (with love for Uncle Benito), Auntie Mira and Uncle Bym, Giudi and Julian, Rich and Josie, Erin, Alice, Ella, Lori, Jim and Kieran, with a shout out to Auntie Ann and all in Wales. A big hug to Simon and love to my Ros – you would have liked this one. Thank you to my wonderful Aunty Pat, who reads and edits everything a million times, and sends cake to boot. And to my amazing Godmother Dany, who gave me a home to adventure from and always supports me – and *will* finish her book because I want to read it. Thank you always to my parents, who have a lot to put up with.

There wouldn't be an acknowledgement section to read if not for Agent Extraordinaire Dr Kristina Pérez. Thank you for believing in my writing and for being the most wonderful editor.

My books are so much better for your clever, insightful input and advice. I am so grateful to work with you.

I owe so much to my wonderful friends, without whom I'd have far less fun and definitely not have managed to slog through the writing and editing of this book. Big thanks to my amazing author friends who help me navigate the wonderful but mad world of publishing: massive thanks to Holly and Louisa for amazing critique, and to Karen (hugs for Naomi and Will!), Christi and Jack, Anna (hugs for Ally!), Gina, Kate and Liz, and all the other wonderful writers who make my life (and everyone else's) so much better. Huge hugs and thanks to my non-author friends who help me keep track of the world outside the bubble, particularly Emma, Lizzie, Andy, Fauzia and Stuart, my godbrother Malcolm, Tony (with love for Aoife), James, Riki and Fran, Chris (with love for Carmel), Katie (with love for Peter), Ian and Kitty, Katie and everyone I'm too blotto from editing to remember if I forget to come back to this! A special shout-out for the wonderful young adults and not-quite-teens in my life: Katja and Alexia, Micah, Toby and Amber, Isabella Lily, William and Naomi, and Lilith. Big thanks to my blogger friends, especially Luna for reading bits of this and telling me she would one day say 'I told you so' when I despaired of this ever being published. Extra thanks to Natasha for amazing advice to help cut through the panic of knowing the right answer to certain questions is only clear in hindsight.

Big thanks to my wonderful editors at Faber – Alice and Ama for all the big-picture heavy-lifting, Lucy Rogers for the fantastic final line-edit, and the fabulous Melissa Hyder for not only catching all my stupid missteps and finding lovely ways to add nuance, but also sorting out the hyphens – *shudders*! Thank you to Leah and Natasha for all the work bringing this through the process from pitch to production, and to Beth and Sarah for all the work on marketing and publicity, and to everyone else in sales, art, production, comms, rights and more, including Emma, Camilla, Simi, Hannah, Louise, Krystyna, Sarah, Kim, Kate, Benedetta, Clare, Sara, Mallory, Viki, Bridget, Amelie, Sam and all the reps around the country! Huge thanks to Jeff Ostberg for my stunning cover – complete perfection. And thank you to Claire Wilson at RCW for our horizontal meeting at YA Shot; it helped inspire a certain scene, and was just a moment of true kindness that I will always be so grateful for.

Thank you to Harriet and everyone at Viking for helping me balance everything during The Year of Non-Stop Work.

Thank you to my lovely friends and colleagues at BSU, particularly the team marching into 2022–2023 with me: CJ, Lucy, Rachel, Karen, Anna, Louisa, Gina and Annalie, and to Sarah, Alison, Richard and more ... And to my fabulous students – I can't wait to read your published books. It is such an honour and pleasure working with you all and being part of your journeys as you've been a part of mine.

Thank you to Paul and Catriona for helping me figure out all the financial stuff, to Simon, Sue and Katharine for fun and amazing presents, and to Viv and all who helped keep the house from falling/burning down mid-edit. Shout-out to friends and family in Italy, particularly everyone in Sarnano – Maura,

Luca and Roberta, Gabriella and Fabio, *et al.* Thank you to Melvin Lobo, Gavin Wright, Vikram Khullar, Alan Hakim, Rita Mirakian, Nick Gall, Helen Walton, Qasim Aziz and Prof. Matthias.

And thank you to those who've bought, read and reviewed this book. I wouldn't have the career I love without you and your support.